Spy Hunt

Release 1.20

First in the Mick Grundy Series

by

Alexander Francis

Spy Hunt

Cover design by Alexander Francis

Graphic images from Wikipedia and modified personal photographs

ISBN: **978-1-942420-09-5** print edition

ISBN: **978-1-942420-08-8** e-book

Table of Contents

Other Mick Grundy Thrillers

The shaking returned, and the shadow man stood there with his hands describing small arcs in the night air. The shadows from the fence played across his face as he fought his body's urge to faint. In the distance, a peacock's cry hung in the night air. There was a subtle motion from the other side of the fence, and a woman's silhouette appeared framed by yellow light cast from tall poles standing guard in the parking lot.

"What are we supposed to do now?" Ahmed asked not too quietly, continuing to play nervously with the safety on his rifle.

"Plainly, we are about to die. We have executed a plan doomed to fail from its inception. Mick Grundy will kill us, and we have only ourselves to blame. We came looking for him only to find his shadow, and now we have run out of options."

Read Excerpts from other novels by Alexander Francis
At afnovels.com

Are We A Band Yet?....Beware the Exit....The Green Scarf Revenge of Jesus....Geminknot....Anthology of Childhood Schemers and Dreamers.....Memory Gap

Chapter 1

Assassin

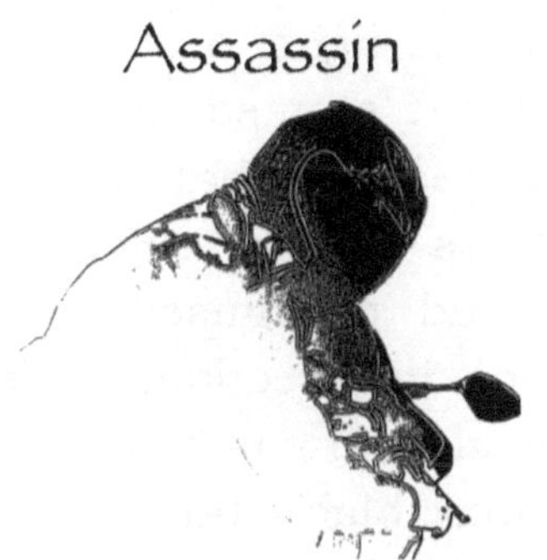

San Francisco, July 12

The limo rolled serenely along the boulevard, reflected lights playing along its black polished hood and moving along in slow curves across the fenders toward the trunk, its license stating clearly that the occupant is in the foreign diplomatic corps. A leisurely speed across the city at 10:00 p.m. indicated that the occupant was in no hurry to reach his destination. Limousines of this luxury class have a uniformed chauffeur, and this one was safely enclosed in glass, his rear access window up, music playing softly in the background. The privacy glass was dark, as were the side windows, but the driver had a pretty good idea what was going on in the rear seat. He had been directed to stop and pick up a cute girl who seemed to understand what was expected, and she got in the open rear door without hesitation. Effortlessly, they floated along the smooth streets until a traffic light switched to red, and the limo eased to a stop. Across the intersection a motorcycle with incredibly bright headlights was also waiting for the light. The limo driver pulled his sun visor low while waiting for the light to change. Suddenly, the motorcycle headlight seemed to move up more into his eyes, and he realized that the bike was coming toward him across the red light. "Another speed crazy kid," he said to himself as the bike came briskly across the intersection. Reflexly, he turned his head to that side to catch a glimpse of the bike and rider. Both were black, but he noticed something in the outstretched left hand of the rider just before the explosions started.

The force of the impact and noise was terrific, causing the rear privacy window to explode, sending a shower of glass over the entire driver's compartment. As the driver's hearing returned, he heard a continuous penetrating scream from the back compartment of the vehicle as smoke started pouring from the rear, enveloping him in a choking cloud. Before he regained his senses, his hands continued to spasmodically grip the steering wheel, and slowly he became aware of someone trying to open his door. With sudden fear, he leaned away from the window, and his hands came up, shielding his face.

"Come on, man, open the door. We're trying to help you," someone said through the glass. The driver's brain began clearing, and he opened the door hesitantly. A piercing scream continued almost without pause from the rear compartment. As he got out, he stopped to inspect the rear door and noticed its window had nearly been blown out, with only devilish jagged edges remaining, giving the impression of some ancient reptile or shark with an open maw. Thick smoke drifted slowly up and curled partly around the roof before dissipating. Someone in the crowd managed to reach in past the shattered rear glass and unlock the rear door, prying it open to the sound of falling glass. The shrieking was becoming intermittent as the screamer tired. She was on the far side of the rear seat, and the driver, in a moment of clarity, found the control panel and unlocked the rear doors. The crowd quickly opened the other door, assisting the girl out into the partial light, her hands over her face, blood seeping between her fingers. The driver tried to peer over the shoulders of the other men who were leaning into the rear of the car but couldn't see anything in the dark. "He's done for; that's for sure," one said. The distant sound of sirens grew louder.

Lieutenant Simon Grover pulled up abruptly at the intersection at 11:00 p.m. He pushed himself out of his car while pulling his pants over his expanding midsection and walked past the yellow tape toward the limo. There was a policeman on each side of the vehicle directing traffic around the car. Patrolman Jonny Sparks walked toward him with quick, anxious steps. "Thanks for coming, Lieutenant. We thought you should see this in person," he said.

"Great, I just love being out late at night all the time," Lieutenant Grover mumbled. "So what is so wonderful that I have to see it. Another hit is all I see," he complained even louder.

"No, this one is different," Jonny said and quickly continued. "No gun that I have ever seen could make such a wound. The glass on this limo is bulletproof, and the driver over there said that the shot was fired from a moving motorcycle passing from the opposite direction."

That unique piece of information got Simon's attention, and he stopped short of the car to take it all in. "You mean that the shooter went past shooting and hit what he wanted even though the glass was dark and bulletproof?" he asked incredulously. "Didn't you say there was another occupant? Where is she?"

"We already transported her to the ER because she was bleeding and hysterical. She's only a hooker and knows nothing. Larry went with her, and we'll pick him up later."

The body was still in the car, and Simon leaned in with Jonny's flashlight in one hand. Its passenger was partially upright, but his pants and underwear were down around his knees. The lower part of the face was missing with the upper teeth exposed like some kind of upside down white picket fence. Blood and tissue fragments mixed with glass shards were throughout the car.

The Lieutenant pulled back and stood up. "Damn," he said.

"What kind of gun would do that, Lieutenant?" Jonny asked.

Simon was busy inspecting the rear window. He noticed the window was constructed of half-inch glass, and likely was marketed as being bulletproof.

Guess not, he thought. Some sort of mental alarm went off, and he suddenly was aware of the sound of a motorcycle starting up not too far away. He craned his neck and slowly turned his head to locate the source. The sound was from a powerful four cylinder job; he could still hear it idling. He decided that it was just up the street in the direction that the hit man would have been going. "Jonny, jump in a cruiser and head up the street that way and see if you can pull over that motorcycle. Hurry, but be very careful."

Instantly, Jonny tuned into the sound and started sprinting for the first patrol car aimed in the general direction. As soon as Jonny started to move away, Simon could hear the motorcycle rev up as it pulled into the street. It had only been a half block away but was black and missed by everyone on the scene. Jonny's patrol car opened up when he saw the bike leaving and off they went out of sight. In the distance, Simon could hear the shriek of the bike pulling high RPM's as the sound faded out.

Just then, an ominous black SUV pulled up and two suited men emerged. "Who's in charge here?" one asked loudly. Simon silently raised his hand, and they headed in his direction. They both held up badges. Homeland Security.

"I expected you here sooner," Simon said sarcastically. Simon had his badge pinned to his jacket, and one of the men pulled out a small flashlight and inspected it closely.

"Lieutenant, what do you have here?" the larger of the two asked.

"Pretty much what you see, my friend. Dead guy killed by a hit man on a moving motorcycle. Don't know any more just yet, but I have one of our men chasing a motorcycle right now." Simon delivered this information in an expressionless monotone.

They drifted over to the car and circled it slowly. "Over here, Bro," the larger man said from the passenger side of the car. They walked around the car to see his light passing over exit holes in the sheet metal on the rear quarter panel. The rear tire was flat, and there was a fist-sized hole in it. "I count about twenty holes here," he said while looking up at his partner and Simon.

Simon was lost in thought. This was like a military shootout. It would take a twenty millimeter cannon to do this, and you certainly could not hold it in one hand. "Well, gents," Simon said. "You are the experts, any ideas?"

They didn't answer. The big one turned to face him and said, "Here it is. We are taking the driver with us. You get to send the corpse for autopsy, and you impound the car. One problem is that our deceased friend here is Muslim and attached to the Lebanese Delegation, and they will turn out in force to get the body back so you only have hours to process him, not days. We'll be in touch tomorrow." At that he turned, and they strolled across to the driver who was sitting on the curb holding his head in his hands.

Chapter 2

The Shadow

San Francisco General Hospital

His timing was perfect as he caught the door just before the latch closed and walked into the hospital corridor following the janitor's cart from the emergency waiting area. Dressed in black leathers and wearing a black stocking cap, he was more a threatening shadow than a man. One glance at the clock in the corridor confirmed the time as 3:46. At this time of early morning, few people were about other than staff and nurses. He walked purposely and quietly toward the holding rooms where she was being kept. A nurse was approaching him from the other end of the hall. Seemingly unconcerned, he engaged in a stare down with her until she wordlessly passed by. No doubt she had encountered motorcycle types in the past and discovered that it was wise not to have a confrontation with one of them. He guessed that she would report seeing him when she reached her destination, but by that time, he would have his mission accomplished. After making the last turn, he pulled back the curtains enclosing her bed.

Sally Rodgers was about 110 pounds and twenty years old. She had been injured by metal fragments and glass in the explosions but was kept from receiving a fatal wound because her customer's body position had shielded her from the blast. The emergency staff picked out most of the metal and glass imbedded in her scalp and right arm and sutured her wounds. Her face was spared because it was down at the time of explosion. She had a large gauze headwrapping around her head, exposing her face, and her arm was wrapped from elbow to shoulder. Slowly, she opened her eyes and looked at him.

He smiled at her, slowly taking her good hand in his, and holding it very softly. "I came by to see how you are," he said in a low scratchy voice. His gentle manner put her at ease, and she gave him a weak smile in return.

"I've been better. At least I'm alive, and my face is OK," she said.

He was struck by her unexpected beauty and her deep green eyes. "I think you picked the wrong fellow to be with," he said with a small warm smile.

She found him strangely appealing with his scars and irregular voice. She was used to men, and they rarely treated her with personal kindness. "What do you want? Are you with the police?" she asked in a small voice.

"No, I just came to see you and see if you need anything. Anything at all," he said.

She thought for a moment, then said, "I don't know what to tell Leroy. He's sort of my agent, but he gets upset easily. I am afraid of what he will do now that I can't work." She looked up at him and suddenly trusted this ruggedly handsome stranger, trusted him completely and didn't know why.

His purpose for being here was to have a look at the survivor from the back seat and ascertain if she knew anything about the shooter or the victim, but he could easily see that she was only connected by chance encounter. She seemed so helpless in the big hospital bed, and he suddenly wanted to do something to make things right for her. "What is Leroy's last name, and where can I find him?" he asked gently.

"You don't have to talk to him to hire me, you know," she said.

"I'm not trying to hire you, dear; I just want to talk to him so he understands what happened to you was not your fault. I want to persuade him to be more understanding with you, that's all," he said with concern, in spite of his raspy voice. She searched his face with her eyes and was silent. "Sally, would you be all right if Leroy wasn't in your life any more?" he asked.

"Well, he helped me at first, but now all he does is push me around and take my money. I would be happy if I never saw him again," she said with a little lip pout and looked away to hide her sudden tears. She covered her face with her shoulder and said in a muffled way, "I'm afraid of him."

"You haven't told me where to find him for our talk, Sally."

"Usually you can find him around a tattoo parlor near Eleventh and Harrison. Just ask any of the girls down there, and they will point him out. I don't think you will have any trouble. He's probably around there now," she said with a sigh.

He released her hand and gave her a small caress on the shoulder. "I've got to go now," he said, "but I'll see you again, perhaps soon, and see how things are going. Don't worry about Leroy, because I hear he is leaving town, and I don't think you will ever see him again."

"I can't pay you anything, Mister, but maybe I can think of something to do for you to thank you for being kind to me," she said looking up at him.

"You are sweet, but all I want is to do something for you. Someday you can buy me a cup of coffee, and we can talk some more," he said.

He slid away from her, and they kept eye contact as he drew the drapes closed. She listened but couldn't hear any footsteps. "I didn't get your name, Mister," she called, but there was no answer. He had gone.

Corner of Eleventh and Harrison
0430 Hours

The man in black leathers was standing in the doorway of a closed shop, blending into the shadows. He could only be seen when he was temporarily lit by a passing car, but otherwise, he was invisible and watching the street closely. In this early morning time before dawn, the street and sidewalk were deserted but for the occasional streetwalker who seemed determined to go until the morning light drove her inside. Finally, his target surfaced and was walking slowly toward his position.

Leroy had an exaggerated walk of importance and carried his head high and defiant. He had a nearby exchange with one of his ladies where he refused her requests to go home. "Please, Leroy, I'm tired. There ain't been anything going down for hours," she said plaintively.

"Hell no, bitch. Your ass stays till dawn," and he continued walking toward his pursuer.

"Hey, you," the man called out to Leroy as he passed. Leroy stopped to look toward the strange voice as the man stepped out of the shadows.

"What the hell you want, dude?" Leroy said, stepping back a little. "Don't go hittin me up for change now cause you ain't gettin any," Leroy said.

"I don't want money from you, Leroy," the man said as he moved out of the shadows and onto the sidewalk. He looked from side to side and saw no one in sight and advanced slowly toward Leroy.

Leroy saw that the man from the shadows was large but walked lightly. He was wearing non-reflective black leather, and his face remained in shadow. "Say man, that be close enough. What you want anyway?" Leroy complained. A very slight stress was in his voice. He reached into his pocket and took out his stiletto switchblade but kept it folded for now.

"No call for knives, Leroy," the man said calmly as he stopped within arm's length. "You have a lady in your stable named Sally?" he asked.

Leroy allowed himself a smile. "Oh, yeah man, she's one fine lady. Want to buy some time?"

"No, Leroy, I don't think you are going to see her again, because you are leaving town tonight," the man said. His voice was raspy and deep and made Leroy feel a chill at the back of his neck.

Leroy still couldn't get a clear look at the man's face. He clicked open his switchblade which remained by his side. "You mess with me, you dead, man," Leroy snarled, taking a small step back.

The shadow man remained still, breathing steadily. "You are going to leave town tonight and never come back, Leroy. That way, you don't have to get hurt, and you can start your business in some other city. Everything will work out fine for you. Give me the blade," demanded the man in leather. He made no threatening gesture which Leroy took as a sign of weakness. After an uncomfortable pause, Leroy decided to attack first and swung the blade in an arc toward the man's left neck. The response was a blur of controlled motion. A big fist hit Leroy's right arm in mid-bicep, causing a loud snap of the bone, just as an arm intersected Leroy's forearm with violent velocity, causing the opened blade to be swept back and into Leroy's neck, severing his right and left carotid artery as well as his trachea. Leroy fell to the sidewalk face first in an expanding pool of blood. "Should have taken the bus, Leroy," the shadow said as he walked away into the night.

Chapter 3

Sifting the Evidence

San Francisco Hall of Justice

Lieutenant Simon Grover glanced at the clock on his way to his desk. 9:15. He sighed. It turned out that, once again, he didn't get any sleep. The hardest parts were getting the court order for the autopsy to cover any sure-to-come argument against it and persuading Dr. Trendall Soffwith to come in the middle of the night and personally supervise the post on the shooting victim. Grover succeeded with both, but it took a lot out of him. He sat down with a cup of coffee and put his legs up on his desk. Ah, a moment of rest. His phone rang before he could take a sip. He knew that it wouldn't do any good to ignore it, because whoever it was would find him eventually, so he leaned forward and picked it up. "Grover."

"Lieutenant, this is Jonny. I've got some info for you. Can I come up?"

"Please," Simon said and leaned back to enjoy his coffee. The phone rang again. This time it was the Desk Sergeant informing him that the Feds were on the way up. Simon gulped the rest of his coffee and started picking up his desk. The same hulking pair came gliding up to his desk with their familiar sulking attitude. Crap.

"Morning, Lieutenant," the larger one said. He appeared to be in charge, and this time Simon got up to look at the temporary visitor permit pinned to his coat.

"Well, Agent Smith, come to pilfer our data again? Why don't you two do some actual police work instead of having us do it for you?" Simon said with sarcasm.

Smith looked angry at that comment and answered harshly, "Look, Detective, we have also been up all night. We spent three hours on the limo driver, because it seemed likely that he spotted for our assassin."

"Did he?" Simon questioned.

"We don't think so, but we are going to hold him for a while anyhow." They looked at each other in brief silence, and just before Smith could ask Simon what he had come up with, Patrolman Jonny Sparks appeared clutching an armful of papers.

He glanced at Simon to get his approval for butting in. "It's OK, Sparks. These are the Feds from last night. What do you have?"

"Well, first, I tried to chase down that bike last night, but I have never seen anyone do what he did or be as fast. Couldn't even get a good glimpse of him before he was totally out of sight. I called in for some help, but he got away too quickly." He carefully put the papers on the desk in a clear spot. "I brought up some preliminary paperwork from the crime lab which includes spectral analysis of samples taken from the victim and the limo. Also, the photos of the car and crime scene are online, which you can view on your monitor," Sparks reported and quickly backed away from the desk.

"Can you boil it down for us, Sparks?" Simon asked. Jonny Sparks was a real go-getter and was working hard for advancement. He had the attention of most of the detectives in the Homicide Division, but Simon also knew Jonny's father from way back and still owed him a bunch of favors.

Jonny cleared his throat and glanced quickly at each man before continuing, "The CT scan shows metal fragments in the brain and chest cavity as well as the left arm. The cause of death is going to likely be either acute exsanguination or brain hemorrhage or even cardiac injury. Doesn't matter since they all were simultaneous. The chemical analysis of the surrounding wound tissue, the window glass, even the headliner, shows RX51-PETN and Zirconium. The metal fragments are copper."

Agent Smith leaned forward and said, "Can we see the photos of the car?" Jonny got a nod from Simon and quickly clicked at the keyboard. The monitor showed the crime scene photos in miniature. "I want to see the interior behind the victim," Smith said. Jonny brought up that series which filled the screen. "Zoom in on this area," Smith requested as he pointed to the upholstery at the top of the right rear seat. Jonny enlarged the area and panned slowly across. "There," Smith said. They looked at a very small circular puncture among several more jaggy ones which was partially covered by blood and tissue. "Now show me the right rear in the area of the tire," Smith said. Jonny put it up, and they all looked at the large piece of rubber torn away from the tire.

"What's it come together for you, Smith?" Simon asked.

"Better let Roberts here answer. He was in the Green Berets and got a lot of training pertinent to this case."

Roberts nodded and spoke up, "There is some ordinance made for the U.S. military by a Norwegian company. They make specialized ammo for the 50 caliber machine guns and especially for the snipers using the new Barrett 50 caliber. The bullet is a very destructive weapon and can be used against humans, what we call soft targets, or for almost any vehicle including most tanks. There is an incendiary at the tip followed by a high explosive. The so-called penetrator is surrounded by Zirconium and is made of tungsten carbide."

"Cool," said Simon. "The problem is that the shooter apparently used a weapon in his left hand, and we believe fired two shots in quick succession. No one could fire a 50 caliber like that."

"We will check it out," said Roberts, "but it fits. The chemical pattern is there, and the tire was probably taken out by the penetrator on its way through the car. It's, therefore, evident that the shooter is using a very high tech weapon, and one that we haven't seen before."

"Not only that, he is either lucky or a gifted marksman," Agent Smith added.

"Also, he is able to ride a motorcycle like a fiend," piped up Sparks.

"Who was the dead guy? I mean who was he really?" Simon asked Smith.

The two agents looked at each other, as if needing permission to speak. With some hesitation, Smith said, "He is, or was, Jamal Mucatric el Camani. His parents were part of the Syrian hierarchy, but Jamal has been living in Lebanon for several years now. Jamal Mucatric el Camani was listed as part of the Lebanese Embassy delegation but had no apparent duties. We have cause for concern that he was in the United States to purchase illegal weapons such as SAM's, especially those stolen from our military depots. Try as we may, we couldn't catch him in the act or even identify his contacts. We both were assigned to his case full-time, and frankly, we are very happy that he got what was coming to him. The bad part is that we will never catch his contacts or find out if he was successful."

Simon looked out the window, thinking it over, then turned to the agents and said, "You sure that we want to find his killer?"

"Well, the killer isn't one of the good guys, because he removed a link in the chain. We sure as hell didn't do it; so, yes, we need to find out who did this and why," Smith said.

"How would be good too!" Jonny injected. They all looked at him like he was a child, and he shrunk away for a glass of water.

When he was gone, Simon and the agents continued to discuss the case. Simon spoke first, "The person we are looking for is someone with a motive to kill this fellow, which may be one of many motives. He is superbly trained and equipped. He was able to track his prey on his own and kill on the first try. He watched us at the crime scene until he was sure his victim was dead and then easily got away."

"That sums it up, Detective," Roberts agreed.

Simon thought for a moment, then said, "Frankly, gentlemen, sounds like one of ours."

"We thought so too. We strongly feel that it isn't someone currently in the service. It could be a rogue former agent, but it's more likely he is a foreign operative," Smith said.

"Anyway, you guys can sift for information in Washington?" Simon asked.

Smith answered, "We are supposed to be sharing information since 9/11, but frankly, the CIA doesn't share unless they want to, even under considerable political pressure. The type of individual you are looking for would need both a military and CIA background."

After small talk, the agents left with a promise to do what they could, but warned that they would likely be assigned to a new case shortly. After they left, Jonny returned, still very interested in the case.

"What happened to the hooker, Jonny?" Simon inquired.

"Nothing. Larry went with her to the ER, and we picked him up about 3:00 a.m. She might still be there."

"That sounds a bit sloppy. Go call the hospital and find out," Simon ordered a bit sharply. The kid shouldn't even be in here, he thought, but until they assign me another junior detective, I need the help. The phone rang again. The Captain's secretary was calling, and Simon was to report at once. Sighing, he pushed himself to his feet and headed down the long hall. He wasn't afraid of the Captain, but a short, fat, bald guy given to yelling is never pleasant to deal with. Once shown into the Captain's office, he started to pull up a chair.

"I didn't tell you to sit down, Lieutenant Grover. This isn't a social call. I have had calls from the State Department and the Lebanese Embassy this morning about a stiff we are holding. Both groups are pushing hard to get him into the soil and want the body released. What the hell is this all about?" As usual, the Captain was just one decibel under screaming.

"Captain, I stayed up all night getting this case started. We finished with the body this morning so they can have it," Simon said.

"Well, that answer isn't good enough, Lieutenant. Give me the rest of it," the Captain shouted.

Simon sat down in spite of the previous order and cleared his throat. He laid out his present knowledge of the case, and in clear, short sentences declared what was known and facts he hoped to clarify. After Simon's summation, the Captain rocked back and thought it over.

"This killer, Simon, did it occur to you that the CIA might have been behind the killing because of facts we can't discover?"

"How could that be the case? I'm afraid I don't get it," Simon said while scratching his head.

"They could have felt that the agents you met were about to close in on him, and it would uncover something that they didn't want out. The law prevents the CIA from hitting him inside the country but wouldn't stop them from hiring it done," he said.

Simon immediately shot back, "Granted, that is possible, but would mean that a hit man is out there, and he could have other targets and other assignments that put the public at risk. My opinion is that we should still try to get to the bottom of it. Frankly, we need some expert's opinion, and his help to go over the facts with us and hopefully suggest where we go for more information. The Homeland Security boys aren't that interested now that their suspect is dead."

The Captain stared at Simon while he was thinking through the case. "I know someone who might help. Damn him, he better help. It happens that my asshole brother-in-law is a one star in Army Intelligence. Too bad he doesn't have any, but nevertheless, he owes me for putting up with him and his brood every other summer at my place. We expect him and his family to come in tonight, and I'll get him down here to get his input in the morning. Don't expect too much, though. Until then, do what you can."

As Detective Simon approached his desk with a fresh cup of coffee in his hand, he saw Patrolman Jonny Sparks waiting for him. "Jonny, join me in a cup?" he said as he dropped into his chair.

"The hooker is gone from the hospital. No valid address," he blurted.

"Jonny, that's bad police work for a budding want-to-be detective," Simon said as he blew on the hot coffee.

"You are right, Lieutenant," Jonny said. "I feel bad about it, but I called Hal Reicher in Vice to see if they have a listing of any Sally Rodgers, and he said he would check it out and get back to me."

"Pull up a chair, Jonny, and let me give you a list of things to check," Simon said. "The body has been fingerprinted, photographed, and autopsied, and we have extensive chemical testing of it. We have the DNA. We know who he was. We don't know where he has been, especially in this city, and who he has been in contact with. We need to know if anyone was watching him other than our two agents. By the way, it would be nice to know if anyone was watching the agents. Once they release the driver of the limo, we need to get him in here for our own grilling. Take any one of these issues and run it down. Me, I've got to get some quick shuteye so we'll talk again this afternoon."

Jonny responded, "Will do, Lieutenant. By the way, I didn't get any sleep last night either."

Simon looked over his shoulder at Jonny on his way out and said, "Yes, but you are young, and I've already made Detective."

Chapter 4

Saving Sally

The Castro District

M ick was walking with purpose along Market Street at the edge of the Castro District. A call to the hospital earlier confirmed what he expected but didn't want to hear. Sally had checked out. He turned into Gold's Gym and nodded to Pete at the desk who gave him a short wave. For a short period after his return from Germany and a long hospital stay, he badly needed physical conditioning. He signed on as an instructor for a few months until some of the members started complaining about his rough methods. Nevertheless, he was always welcome back when he was in town, and his locker was still his locker. He quickly changed and went straight to the speed bag to warm up. The sound of his rapid hits drew the attention of a couple of professional fighters who also used the gym for some of their training.

Bubba watched for a while and then tapped George, his trainer, on the shoulder. "Hey man, that guy is good. Think he'd want to spar with me or Sonny some time?"

The trainer knew Mick and had seen him in action. "Bubba, listen to me carefully. Never get into it with that one. Never. You are a tough kid, and I know you don't feel that you have any limits, but he is different from anything you have seen."

"I'm ranked, man, in the PKA. Don't you put me down like that," Bubba sneered.

"No, Bubba, I'm not. I know you could beat the stink out of me, but that one is ex-Special Forces and some other stuff. He wouldn't fight like you expect, and it's possible he would kill you without intending to. Stay away from him," George warned in a hushed voice.

Bubba continued to look at Mick working out but eventually and reluctantly went back to his own exercises. After a half hour on the bag, Mick found George and pulled him aside. "What was that about, George?"

The voice had the usual effect on George and beads of sweat quickly appeared on his forehead. "Hi, Mick. That fellow is called Bubba, and he does some pro fighting. Thinks he's good. He wanted to spar with you, but I talked him out of it. That OK?" he said.

While toweling off his head and upper body, Mick was staring at Bubba who was across the room. He turned to George and asked, "Know anyone in here who might use hookers?"

George was surprised by his question and said, "Man, you don't need a hooker. All the women in here have always followed you with their eyes. You could probably take your pick."

"George, I am trying to find a certain one, and not for that reason. Do you know anyone or not?"

George looked around the room. "I'm not sure I want to tell you this, but that fellow, Bubba, is the best bet."

Mick threw down the towel and headed across toward Bubba. Bubba stood up as Mick came up and looked him up and down. Mick just stood there wordlessly. "I've thought about it, and I think you are much heavier than my weight class. I don't want to spar with you, man," Bubba said.

Ignoring his response, Mick asked, "I'm looking for a hooker named Sally Rodgers. Know her?"

"I might," he said. "Mostly, I don't know last names, but there is a Sally who lives with a couple girls I do know well. She is short, blonde, and pretty cute. I haven't used her, but I see her around sometimes. Her pimp is a nasty dude called Leroy."

"Thanks, Bubba. I think she may be the one. Where does she live?" He moved closer to Bubba during the conversation, and Bubba knew for certain that George was right. He didn't want anything to do with tangling with this one. There was a presence about him, and he radiated danger like a coiled animal ready to strike. The voice that gave most people chills had the same effect on Bubba. Bubba wanted to give him his information and get away from him as fast as possible.

"She lives on Cumberland, which is in the Castro, and I think about five or six blocks from here. I don't remember the street number, but it is the only boarding house on the block near the dead end. She is in apartment six." Mick nodded and turned away. "Nice to meet you!" Bubba called out. Mick never responded.

Cumberland Street

Mick found the apartment building, and it was dingy as described by the gym rat, Bubba. He walked in, found the stairs and started climbing to apartment six on the second floor. The hall and stairs reeked of urine, and there was a single light bulb on a long cord hanging from the brown ceiling. Mick knocked on a smeared brown door. After a pause, it opened a small crack, and he could see a trace of blonde hair and an eye at the crack peering back at him. He didn't say a word, waiting for her response and standing very still, trying not to look threatening. The chain unlatched with a rattle, and the door slowly swung open, revealing a small, timid blonde girl wearing a head and arm wrap. She stood back as if to ask him in but continued to watch his face as if she expected some mistreatment.

As he came in, she said, "I heard what happened to Leroy. I assumed that it was you." He walked in and looked about. Three working women lived here, but as far as he could see there was nothing in sight fit to own. "Come to collect?" she asked in a small voice.

"Why did you leave the hospital so soon?" Mick asked.

Sally looked away from his stare, and said, "I didn't want to see the cops again. I gave them a false address so I had to get out early."

"Would you like to do something else for a living?"

"I didn't even finish high school. I have no other skills."

"Would you try if I could find you something?"

"I would, and I would be so grateful to you if you could help me forget that I ever lived this life. Now that I am rid of Leroy forever, I would like the chance to get out and not look back."

Mick pulled up a chair and sat backwards with his arms across the back and looked at her. "You need time to heal first," he said. He reached into his jacket pocket and pulled out a roll of money. He pulled off a small stack and put the rest back. "Take this, please. No strings except one. You have to stay clean. No drugs, no hooking. You OK with that?"

She nodded, then took and quickly counted the money. "Two grand!" she exclaimed. "You mean that you want nothing in return?" she asked.

He didn't answer but instead pulled a small piece of paper from his wallet. He reached into his pocket and pulled out a key. "Here is the key to a safe house you can stay at until you get on your feet. The address is on the paper." He handed both across to her, and she held them in front of her like they were crystal and could break. Tears streamed down her cheeks, but she made no sound. "Don't tell anyone where you are going. It's the only way you will be safe. I will be around to check on you soon, and I promise you that I'll find you a good job."

"I don't even know your name," she said.

"I have reasons for not telling you right now, but don't worry, because everything is on the up and up, and I will never take advantage of you or expect anything in return. I just want to help you," he said. She wanted to hug and kiss him but resisted, because it might make him feel dirty knowing what he did about her. "Time is up for me here, Sally. I've got to go. I want you to leave right now for the other place. Take nothing with you. You will find that the room is all set up for you, and you can buy new clothes on the way over."

Mick stood up and gave her a hug, kissing her on the part of her forehead that was exposed under the wrap. He left her standing in the middle of the room holding the paper with the address and the key to the future.

Chapter 5

The Search for Sally

San Francisco Hall of Justice

Detective Grover walked toward his desk under the clock which said 4:02 p.m., not exactly rested but at least fed, and reluctantly sat down and started going through the new papers laid there for him. Last night's case...he still had to write up last night's case as well as several new ones to dig through. Another long, late night ahead. The phone rang. "Grover," he said.

"Simon, Hal Reicher here. I heard from your boy that you wanted to find some hooker you lost last night?"

"Hi, Hal. Got anything on this Sally?" he said.

"We have busted her a couple of times in the past," he said. "Cute little thing. Frankly, I always felt sorry for her. Her pimp is a black dude who calls himself Leroy Brown but is really Franklin Collins. I heard that he got killed on the street last night. You boys in homicide would know about that though. We never get real names or addresses on those girls. They know enough not to carry real ID so I can't help you find her, but I would suggest going down to Eleventh

Street and asking the other hookers. You likely won't get much cooperation, I'm afraid."

"Killed you said?" Simon repeated as he quickly sorted the papers on his desk. He found it and scanned the highlights. Leroy Brown, throat cut and left on sidewalk at approximately 4:45 a.m. He studied it while Hal waited.

"If there is nothing else, Simon, I've got work," Hal finally said.

"Oh, yeah. Say, thanks for looking into this for us. We'll send someone down there with a little cash to trade for info. You guys watch out for her, and don't bust her, please."

"I'll bet that will be Carol, right? We know her, don't worry. Bye now," and he hung up.

Simon leaned back and picked up the phone. "Find Carol Buckley and send her this way, if you will. Yes, it's a homicide case," he said into the phone.

After ten minutes, Carol came up and stopped at his desk. He looked up at her and then looked her up and down. "Sergeant Buckley, how good of you to come. As always, you are remarkably radiant. If you aren't positively swamped right now, you can come with me and bribe some hookers."

"Right now, Lieutenant?"

"I'll buy you supper if that helps," he answered.

She rolled her eyes and said, "I have a date already for tonight, and this is a hell of a way to ask a girl out."

"Lucky for you, my fine prize, I am happily married so you can consider this work," he said, grinning.

"Let's get it over with then. I'll call him from the car, and you can explain why I'll be late tonight."

"Agreed."

"We have to stop by the purser and get some bribe cash. Two hundred should do it,"

On the street, Carol quickly sought out the prostitutes one at a time under Simon's watchful gaze from the car. He finally saw one gal in a minidress take some cash and then start pointing down the street while she talked. Carol was nodding and then she touched the girl on the shoulder and headed for the car.

When she got in, she said, "Got it. Head over to Cumberland in the Castro District. Only cost fifty. They all know about Leroy getting it and are very jumpy right now. He had about fifteen girls, but some have already been snatched up by other pimps."

Simon knew the way and drove quickly while they chatted. Carol was OK, he thought. She was good-looking, could pin a suspect to the ground as quickly as a male officer, and she was an expert with a handgun. She was only the second black female ever to make Detective in the homicide division. Simon always enjoyed her company and was thankful to have her with him tonight. He never liked dealing with the hookers. He just couldn't get any cooperation. Probably they sensed that he didn't like them.

They pulled up slowly in front of the brown-stained boarding house. "This is a rat hole, Carol. You don't have to come in with me," he said.

She quickly said, "No way, Simon. Someone has to see that the hookers don't start your motor. Remember, you are a married man!" she teased.

He looked a little sour, but said, "You go up first. I'll be right behind you." They went up the dark, smelly stairs and knocked at apartment six.

A light-skinned black woman opened the door. She was wearing only a bra and panties and had a long cigarette dangling from her lips. "Crap, it's the cops. Look, honey, we didn't kill him, but we like having him dead, if that is what you want to know."

"Where is Sally?" Carol barked.

"She ain't here. You can come in and see for yousef," and then she stood back from the doorway. They walked in and looked around.

"I see that Leroy pays pretty good," Simon said to the walls.

"I ain't seen Sally since last evening. I know that she didn't kill Leroy, but Lord knows she had plenty of reason."

"She got shot up last night and was in the hospital, left without being discharged. If she isn't here, where would she go?" Carol asked.

"Shot up! Oh, God, we gots so much misery anyway and now some dude shoots her too. Why, why would anybody shoot that little girl?" she said and started shedding real tears.

Simon looked at her and said, "Her customer was the target. She got sprayed in the gunfire. We suspect that the shooter didn't know she was even there. That's why we want to talk to her. She isn't in any trouble."

Clariesa looked around and opened a couple of drawers. "Her stuff is still here. I got no idea where she would go. It's not like we make a lot of friends in this business, you know."

"Clariesa, have you seen anyone strange around here or around her lately?" Carol asked politely.

"Gal, all the people we deal with are strange, but as far as I remember it's just been business as usual. We don't bring the johns here. Too dirty for even them. Most of them have cars."

"If she comes in, could you get her to call us?" Simon asked, while extending a card to her.

"Maybe, for a little money, I might remember. Otherwise, no," she said, hands on hips.

Carol took a twenty out and gave it to her. "More there if she calls us," she said. Clariesa nodded and took the money.

As promised, Simon took Carol to dinner. Unfortunately, it was fast food. They sat in a booth across from each other and talked. "I have an idea," Simon said. "If you will go with me to one other place, then I promise to deliver you safely back into the arms of your lover with apologies in triplicate."

Carol sighed, "Where now, big spender? To Walmart?"

"No, we need to go by San Francisco General and see if anyone saw anything concerning this Sally while she was there. The reason for doing it now is to catch the night shift who probably were also working last night," he said, while chewing.

"Eat up then, Lieutenant The Donald, and let's get this over with."

They quickly ate and hurried over to the hospital, stopping by the security office, catching an on-duty guard watching the monitors. They both displayed badges for him, and Simon said, "You had an admission from the ER last night, and we understand that she went to room 410. She left without consent sometime before morning. The one duty nurse seems to know nothing about it. Were there any reports from early this morning which came by this desk?"

"Maybe, Detective," he said as he looked through the stack. "Here is one from 4:00 a.m. which reports an unauthorized male in the hall leading to that unit. Nurse Barbara Jones saw a large man in dark clothing, possibly leathers, heading that way. She didn't converse with him. We all have learned not to do that, and we instruct the nurses not to risk a confrontation. There were no other sightings or complaints. Hold on, let me see if our cameras picked him up." He swiveled back to the monitors and pushed some buttons on the keyboard. In a moment, they could see a dark, almost shadow of a man going down the hall and turning into a room.

"Which room would that be," Simon asked. "Well, the camera is at the end of the hall. That is the left side, and I count four doors. Room 410, Detective."

As they watched, about ten minutes elapsed, and the shadow emerged alone from the room and headed down the same hall. Too dark for facial features. All that could be seen was that he was dressed in dark clothing and was large. They sped the tape up until Sally could be seen to emerge soon after. She hurried down the hall and had her head wrap and arm wrap still in place. "Well, he didn't seem to hurt her in the room," Simon said to Carol. "We'll never know what he said to her to make her leave in such a hurry."

As they drove back to The Hall of Justice, they talked the case over. "Does this mean that she was involved in the hit, Lieutenant?" Carol asked.

Simon cleared his throat, "Call me Simon, please. We have eaten together, we are close friends, and I won't tell your lover anything." He smiled at her, and she made a pucker like a kiss. "I don't know what it means, Carol. If she were an accomplice, he sure put her at risk firing a weapon like that into the car. It is a miracle that she's alive. It doesn't make sense."

"What if she were an accidental victim, and he felt bad about hurting her because he didn't know she was there?" Carol ventured.

Simon leaned back in the booth and gave some thought to what she said. "You mean a hardened, possibly military-trained, killer feeling for some unknown hooker that got injured? Get real. There must be some other explanation. Also, who killed Leroy and why? Perhaps this fellow on tape has nothing to do with the shooting, and he came to rescue Sally from Leroy."

"If that was the case, she should have left with him. Or if he was going to kill Leroy, she could have just stayed in the hospital and gotten treatment," Carol rebutted. They drove back toward headquarters in silence, lost in thought.

Finally, Simon observed, "It appears that she is still alive but hiding somewhere. Find her, find him."

Carol agreed, "Yes, you have to find her."

Chapter 6

An Old Friend

Sunset District

Mick rode smoothly on his motorcycle down Wawona Street with Pine Lake Park on his left. He was looking for 23rd Street and soon found it, turning quickly and deftly picking up a little speed. Bob Thrasher was an old friend from his Army days, and they kept in contact occasionally. He always closed his letters with an invitation to stay with him at any time for any length of time. Since Mick had given Sally the safe house, he needed another base, and a place where no questions would be asked. He had called ahead, and Bob said he was looking forward to a little reunion and would leave the garage door open. The safe house was on Rockridge, just opposite the Golden Gate Heights Park, less than a mile from where he was at the moment. Sally would be safe there, unless she went out frequently or told anyone where she was. He found Bob's address and slowly rolled into the open garage and switched off the bike. As he was pulling his helmet off, the garage door started down, and the interior door opened.

"Mick, you old cuss. God, it's great to see you again!" Bob said as he came closer with two open beers in his hand.

"Hi, yourself. And thanks again for letting me stay with you. We have a lot of catching up to do," Mick said. He swung his leg off the bike, and Bob pushed a beer into his hand.

"Damn, man, you look good. Keeping fit, I see. Not like me," he said as he was looking down at his own waist. Bob and Mick had been in basic training together before Mick was selected for Special Forces training. They parted ways for a while, but eventually Bob was stationed at Hohenfels in Germany, and Mick ended up in Stuttgart at a Special Forces base. There was occasionally enough free time that they could get together and share a love of motorcycles. Bob discovered a race track in Mannheim where they both took several days of instruction for motorcycle road racing. They bought two used 600cc bikes and prepared them at the Army base for racing. "We had some great times in Germany...you remember, Mick?" Mick nodded while taking the first sip of beer. "Say, do you remember the Motodrom, Mick?"

"You mean to remind me of my spectacular crashes there, don't you?" Mick answered with a smile, because he did remember it well.

"Yeah, man, they were spectacular. We were always amazed that you didn't get killed out there. You were so aggressive; it was bound to happen." Bob remembered while shaking his head at the memory and grinning as the images came back to him. Bob stood back and looked at Mick's bike. It was a dull black, but a closer look showed the carbon fiber at the surface. Bob peered at the motor, partially visible under the fairing, and then inspected the brakes and rotors. "Wow, this is some bike. Never seen anything like it. What kind of bike is it?"

Mick hesitated. He didn't want to tell even an old friend everything. His training required that his life remain very private, and there were a lot of things he could never discuss with anyone. "A German friend of mine and I pieced it together from discarded wrecks. It isn't a brand. It's just an assortment of parts." Bob kept looking at the bike and discovering more amazing detail. Mick said, "Aren't you going to ask me in, Bob?" he said to distract Bob from dissecting the motorcycle any further.

Bob stood. "Well, sure, my friend, come on in. You remember that I have been divorced for some time, don't you?"

"Right," Mick acknowledged, then remembered, "She got the kids." Bob shook his head without answering. The memory was obviously painful.

"You never got caught, did you, Mick?" Bob asked.

Mick realized Bob was talking about women. "Who would want a torn up bum who rides a motorcycle everywhere? No, I love women, but nothing lasts too long with them," he said truthfully.

They wandered to the living room, a typical bachelor room with a big TV on one wall and tasteless furniture scattered about. In the light, Mick could see that Bob was balding and overweight. The house was in a very upscale area and was probably worth a lot, but inside it was run-down and tattered.

The apathy of loneliness was all about the place. Mick took off his leather jacket and laid it across the back of the couch.

Bob got a good look at his old friend then and said, "The scars on your head and neck. That why you got out?"

Mick didn't want to go over it with Bob for several reasons, and for national security, he wasn't allowed to discuss some things with anyone. "Bomb. I was in rehab for a while, and they decided that I was done after I healed. Stayed in Germany bumming around for a few months and then briefly was in the U.S. Marshals Service," Mick summed up for Bob all he needed to know.

"Why did you leave them?" Bob innocently asked.

"Didn't. They kicked me out."

Bob knew him well enough to know when not to ask further. "What are you into now?" Bob continued.

Mick hesitated, then explained, "I do some PI work up in Tacoma and Seattle." Bob wanted to know more, but he understood that there were going to be limits on what he could ask. They settled into chairs with their beer and had a long look at each other. Mick was obviously very fit and trim. He still wore the military, short haircut, and there was a horizontal scar in the right temporal area, typical of the incisions used to control a brain hemorrhage. There were a couple of depressed facial scars, also on the right side, which could have been caused by penetrating metal bomb fragments. A long ragged scar on his neck appeared causative to the unusual voice he was afflicted with. There was something else obvious about Mick. His bearing was threatening, even to Bob. He was like a coiled spring which might fly apart at any time.

"Are you still selling software, Bob?" Mick asked while finishing his beer.

Bob responded, "Not for a long time. I run an employment agency. Not a bad job...good hours, lots of women." Bob gave a little chuckle as if there were an inside joke attached to the statement. "What are you doing in Frisco?" Bob asked.

"Working a case. Afraid I can't discuss it though. You understand."

"I didn't see any clothes or luggage on the bike. Where is that stuff?"

"Across town. I have a room, but I wanted to see you again. All right to stay a couple of days?"

"Sure, man, stay as long as you want." Bob began to realize that they had changed over the years and didn't really have anything in common any longer. He could tell that Mick was unwilling or unable to tell him much about himself or about what he was doing. It dawned on him that he was being used by Mick to hide from something or someone, and he hoped that it wouldn't follow Mick to this house. "Are you in trouble, Mick? Someone chasing you?"

Mick fixed him with a unnerving hard stare which made Bob regret being so forward. "I have been tracking someone since Germany. The person who tried to kill me and almost did. He is here, and I am looking for him, and he might be looking for me. You are safe for now, because there is no way he can track me here, but I can't stay long or I will lose his scent and he might pick up mine."

Bob was holding his breath while Mick spoke and now let it out with a whoosh. "Are you on your own with this, or are you still working for the Company?"

"How did you know about the Company, Bob?" Mick asked, his voice dark, nearly sinister.

"Harvey Longren, remember we used to call him Harv Longjohns?" He gave a little laugh. Mick didn't move. Bob cleared his throat and said, "I ran across him a couple of years ago, and we started talking about you. He said that you were pulled out of the Special Forces unit you were in together and got assigned to the CIA. After that, he didn't know anything about what became of you. He was very interested that we still communicate from time to time."

Mick asked in a low voice, "Did he say anything else?"

"He talked about some of the missions you did together. No details, you understand, just an overall picture," Bob replied. The conversation had taken a bad turn, and Bob started to detect energy building in the air.

"You know that he could be put in prison for saying anything about those missions. Some might want to go even farther. That stuff is off-limits. Period. I'm disappointed in Harvey. Very clumsy of him. Don't tell me any more, Bob."

Bob quickly said, "No, no, no. Don't worry, that is all I know. Really, he didn't say much, and after all, I was in the Army too." They looked at each other for a while, then Bob tried again, "So what did you do in Germany when you were bumming around?

Mick looked like he was carefully choosing his words, "Mostly, I fell in with a bunch of young Germans who were into motorcycles in a big way. We raced, we built some bikes, we occasionally stole some parts, and we drove the roads of Germany at fantastic speeds at all times of day and night. We drank and sought out girls in our spare time. Finally, I got enough of it and went home."

"Did you or your guys ever enter real races?" Bob inquired.

"We did, and some of us were pretty good. I never could get a sponsor so my racing career never happened, but I learned how to go fast on a motorcycle."

Bob motioned to the garage, "Is that where this bike came from?"

"Mostly. The Army sent it home for me gratis. I've worked on it constantly since."

"Looks fast," Bob observed.

"Probably nothing on the highway is faster than this bike. You should never say you saw it at all if anyone asks. You understand?" Mick said.

"Sure, buddy, sure," Bob said sincerely.

Chapter 7

Meeting With The General

San Francisco Hall of Justice

On his way into work, Detective Grover went over to the area where Leroy was murdered the previous night. He had a photo of Sally from an earlier soliciting bust on his phone, and he had gone around to all the small grocery stores in a several block radius, showing the photo to employers and workers. One recognized her, but Simon felt from his expression that it was from a sexual encounter. None had seen her since her injury. Supposing that she had removed the head wrap, she still had injuries on her arm, and from the report of the emergency room physician, the wounds were significant and would prevent her from using the arm for some time. Frustrated, he drove back to the Hall.

While walking to his desk, he ran into Jonny Sparks. "I've been looking for you, Lieutenant," Jonny said.

"Good morning to you too, Jonny," he said and kept walking.

"I have been working on the assignments you gave me, and I have some information."

Simon stopped and turned toward him. "OK, let's have it."

"Well, I called most of the major hotels in San Francisco and the Bay Area, and there was no record of Jamal Mucatric el Camani at any of them, at least under that name. You know, of course, that the closest Lebanese office is the Lebanon Consulate in Los Angeles. I called there, and they appeared to have never heard of him. So, I guess I have nothing positive to tell you," Jonny said with a frown.

Simon resumed walking toward his desk. "Amateurs," he growled. He stopped abruptly and turned to Jonny, "Get a photo of the missing hooker from our files and send a bulletin to all the squads working this morning, and instruct them to go to all the small grocery stores in the city and ask about her. Tell them to be sure to mention her injured right arm."

"Yes, sir," he answered and hurried off down the hall.

Simon passed by the Captain's office on his way to the coffee machine, and when he glanced in, he saw the secretary frantically motioning to him to come in. "Oh, I get it, you miss me!" he said brightly to her as he opened the door.

"It must be your fine figure, Lieutenant," she said sarcastically. "You are late, and he has been looking for you and is psychotically mad. You can go on in, but I'm telling you goodbye now because I'll never see you alive again." She resumed her desk work and ignored him.

He heard voices through the closed door, shrugged and turned the knob. The Captain was sitting at his desk and pleasantly said, "Good morning, Lieutenant Grover," but his eyes were shouting anger. The opposite chair contained a senior officer of the U.S. Army. The Captain said, "Brigadier General Chuck Adams, I want to introduce my best man, Lieutenant Simon Grover."

The general remained seated but nodded, smiled and stuck out his hand for a handshake, then said, "Eddie has been telling me about your case, Detective. Can you sum up what I can do for you this morning?"

Simon had been in the Army some time ago but had never had a face-to-face with a General. It was intimidating, and he also could perceive a very thin veneer of pleasantness in the air. "Good morning, Sir. Thank you for taking the time to lend a hand. We had an assassination of a Lebanese diplomat early yesterday morning. The killer was incredibly skilled and used an unusual weapon that none of us have ever seen. The bullet was penetrating, incendiary as well as explosive, much like the APEX made by Nammo for the U.S. Army, but in a caliber small enough to shoot from a handheld weapon, possibly a handgun. The effect was that the first round took out a bulletproof glass in a limo, and the second blew most of the face off of the victim. They were fired in rapid, nearly simultaneous, fashion from a speeding motorcycle. We believe the killer stayed nearby and made his escape when he was sure that the victim was dead. He left on a motorcycle and appears to be an expert rider. The victim was being followed by Homeland Security who were attempting to build a case against him. There was a prostitute in the car who was injured, and there is a possibility that she knows the assailant. We are looking for her now."

"Sounds interesting. What do you need me for?" General Adams inquired.

"We want to know if the ammo came from the Army or the intelligence organizations in the U.S., or did it come from a foreign government? The assailant appears to have advanced skills. The question begs: is he one of ours?" Simon summarized.

"Well, that's news to me, son. I have never heard of such a bullet. As far as the training, the Army doesn't train on motorcycles so I assume this is only a singularly skilled individual. I certainly don't know that our side ever kills anyone within the country's limits; in fact, it is prohibited by law," the General said, smiling up at him. Simon thought that this was a big waste of his time, and he shot the Captain a look of distain.

"Chuck, you came all the way down here in your fancy suit. We are impressed by it, but we are not impressed by your ingratiating smile and your goddamn platitudes," the Captain shouted. Simon smiled. This was the Captain in action against someone else for a change. Now enraged, he continued, "If you can't go over to my computer and find out anything useful for us this morning, you can check in to the Holiday Inn for the next several days and check out of my place." His eyes bulged out when he was really mad, as they did now.

Simon could tell that Brigadier General Adams never got chewed out by a lesser man. Simon didn't dare say a word, and there was an uncomfortable silence. The General cleared his throat and leaned forward. "Anything I say to you has to be treated as privileged information and cannot be spoken of outside this room and cannot be written down. I will deny saying anything and will call you both liars if there are any repercussions. Do I make myself perfectly clear?"

They both said yes at once.

"Go out there and dismiss your secretary, Eddie," he said. When that was done he motioned for both to come closer and said, "I can't go to an unsecured computer and type anything, because I would be flagged right away. Most of the information you want to know about are things I can't discuss, and some of it is very high clearance only. Some of this is known only by the CIA, and let me tell you, they only share what they want to. I can tell you that the bullet you speak of is 45 ACP caliber and is being produced in this country, though it is possible that another country is manufacturing some. I don't know for sure, but I doubt it. The Army has Special Forces units scattered abroad, but the headquarters is here. These highly selected men are trained differently for the various theaters, and the training is rigorous, occasionally specific to a task. There are some who are selected for operating under the covert forces of the CIA, and your killer fits the type. Unfortunately, very little information about their activities is returned to us. There are occasionally deaths and injuries, and we have suspected the CIA Black Ops have been, at times, compromised by another so-called double agent. On rare occasions, it happens that persons from the same team become adversaries. I am not being specific here, but, at times, we and the CIA have problems being sure whom to trust, and the investigation and subsequent prosecution may take years. If you have been unlucky to blunder into such an operation, you may need to be alert that you are only seeing what someone wants you to see. The real truth will be buried deeply." With that he rose to his feet and said, "See you at home, Eddie. Bring the beer."

The General departed and slammed the door. Simon and the Captain looked at each other before the Captain said, "What the hell do you mean being late this morning. We are lucky he stayed this long." His eyes were bulging again.

"Police work, Captain, regular police work," Simon answered, then remarked, "I didn't get anything useful out of what he said. Did I miss something?"

The Captain sat back down and rocked back. "I think he told us a lot if you listened between the lines. He inferred that the shooter may have been, or likely was, trained by Special Forces and the CIA, and that there is a mole in the CIA that they are looking for. The killing has something to do with an ongoing operation the CIA is running. There is also an internal struggle with conflict between two agents. He as much as stated that the ammo you described is secret and available to U.S. forces. We did learn a lot but not much that helps with this case. I have one other source to tap who may be able to help." Simon raised his eyebrows, scratched his head and waited for the rest. "I had a partner when I was a flatfoot like you. He was a sharp boy and was recruited away from us by the FBI. I heard that he is still with them but runs a desk now. I'll call him today and see what he can do for us."

"Aren't contacts a good thing, Captain?" Simon said.

"You get what you earn, Simon. Remember that," he answered.

"I'm going back to work. Don't forget the beer tonight," Simon reminded the Captain over his shoulder.

"Yeah, thanks. It'll be the cheapest goddamn beer I can find," the Captain muttered.

Chapter 8

Sisters

Coffee Shop Near Golden Gate Heights Park

Mick was nursing his second cup of coffee, seated in the only booth with a long view of Rockridge Ave and the apartment building entrance where Sally was staying. He had walked over from Bob's instead of taking the motorcycle, which could be noticed. After spending two hours on countersurveillance, he felt pretty sure that no one was watching, yet. If anyone had located Sally, he was unable to spot them. This safe house was only known to him, and he had gone to elaborate lengths to cover any trail back to him. Any piece of information can be gleaned over time, but they would have to know where to start. She was safe for now unless she was spotted in the area. The police had to be looking for her by now, because they would suspect that she could have known either the shooter or the killer of Leroy.

Just as Mick was about to leave, he saw her emerge from the front entrance, her arm wrap was still on, but her blonde hair gleamed, exposed to the sunlight. He thought it was possible that her long hair would conceal her head lacerations. She began walking away from the park using a brisk, purposeful stride. He waited, watching her and for others around her. Nothing was moving. He slowly, casually got up, leaving a tip on the table, and headed in the opposite direction, unconcerned. After a block, he paused to look covertly behind him. No tail. He crossed to the opposite side and picked up the pace. Sally was still in sight, and he kept a block behind her.

In the apartment, he had left a clean cell phone, accompanied by instructions to only use that phone for calls, and a warning not to call any of her former girlfriends, under any situation. Mick, seeing her now, wondered if she had followed his instructions. The apartment had been well-stocked with food for an extended stay, and a small bandage and medical kit for emergencies was in the bathroom. A quick assessment of Sally suggested that she had not changed the dressing on her arm. They kept walking for two more blocks, when abruptly, she turned to enter a doorway and disappeared. Mick crossed the street to have a look at the door from a distance, and determined that she had entered a small restaurant. He waited and watched, running over details in his mind as he leaned into a wall. Generally, standard policy in a professional hit like the one she survived is to leave no witnesses. The driver had been kept out of harm's way, but when he was released by the police, he wouldn't live too long. Sally was an obvious target, and without a doubt, she was also being sought by the killer, who probably didn't realize she had been in the car at the time. The killer couldn't be positive that she was only a recent pickup. The only way to be sure would be to take her out.

After he decided it was safe, he crossed the street and looked through the glass window. Sally was sitting with another girl, closely inspecting a menu, obviously not cooperating with his instructions. She was a cheap little street hooker, innocent in every other way, but unfortunately for her, she was being pursued by a resourceful and highly skilled killer, and Mick wanted to be there when she was found. He went into the restaurant and explained to the manager that he wanted to sit with his friends, motioning toward the girls. The manager was an effeminate young man who looked him up and down haughtily, instantly understanding that Mick could not be refused without consequences. Mick was led back toward the booth in the corner, and when the girls looked up at him, Sally appeared startled and put her good hand up to cover her open mouth.

"Good morning, Sally," he said, "may I sit down?" She consented with her eyes but kept her hand over her mouth, her shocked expression following him while he slid into the bench across from her. Mick realized that Sally didn't have a name to use for introduction to her guest. He turned toward the second woman at his shoulder, about to speak but stopped with his mouth open. She was remarkably beautiful, and she was calmly looking right into his eyes. He recovered a bit and said, "Hi, my name is Sam Jones, but everybody calls me Sammy. It is a pleasure to meet you," and he stuck out his hand toward her.

Ignoring him, the second woman turned to Sally, "Who is this guy to you?"

Sally put her hand down, looking at Mick with renewed appreciation. "He is a new friend, and he has been helping me out since my accident."

"Say, I did find a position for you when you recover, and I think you'll like it. How would you like to be the manager of Extreme Body Fitness? I know the owner, and he is looking forward to talking with you," Mick smiled at her, and she caught on.

"Sammy, this is my sister, Sara. I haven't seen her for some time and decided to meet her for lunch. I'm glad you showed up when you did, because I was about to tell her about you." Sara was looking back and forth between the two faces, sensing a fabrication.

Mick tried to steal a glance at Sara from time to time. The deep green eyes were the same as her sister's, but her face was more perfect, set off nicely by her brown hair. She wore no jewelry or rings, and she dressed in restrained elegance. Sally's face looked worn and lined by comparison, and her skin color was sallow, certainly not healthy and radiant like Sara's. Her new clothes didn't look like the choice of a streetwalker but more like her sister's. Her instincts and her upbringing were still in her and capable of returning.

"Sally," Sara asked, "Didn't you say that you had an apartment close by here?"

"Yes," she responded. "It's only four blocks down the street."

Sara paused to think, looking at Mick closely, studying his face. "Give up the lying both of you. I can't be taken in so easily. Exactly what is your interest in my sister, Sammy?" She emphasized his name with sarcasm.

Mick thoughtfully perused Sara's eyes before answering. "How much do you know about your sister's current life?"

"Everything," she answered without blinking. Sally put her hand over her mouth again, while leaning forward, hiding her face. Sara studied her sister dispassionately for a moment and then turned her attention back to Mick, "I'm waiting for an answer." Her eyes went back and forth between his, as if anticipating a forthcoming lie.

He answered truthfully, "Right now, I'm trying to hide her from some really bad people. I accidentally saw her come out of the apartment building earlier, and I followed her to be sure they, or he, hadn't found her yet. She will only be safe in the apartment as long as she stays there, out of sight, until the situation is resolved. I am serious about the job offer, but that's for later."

Sara's eyes never left his face, taking in his intense blue eyes, his military bearing as well as the scars. She could tell that he was hard as nails and probably very dangerous. "Really...who are you?" she asked.

"At the moment, I must remain her nameless protector, or you could call me Sammy, if you like."

"I don't like any of this. What did she do that she has to hide like this?" Sara asked.

Mick glanced at Sally, who now had her head upright, and then spoke as if talking to Sally instead of answering Sara, "She did absolutely nothing but be in the wrong place at the wrong time."

They ordered a light lunch, the conversation remaining sparse and terse. Mick finally couldn't resist asking, "Has it been a long time between visits for you two?"

"Don't you go putting any blame on me for her lifestyle. She had a good home, but she liked the high life too much and went off the map from me and our parents. We tried repeatedly to find her and finally hired a PI who eventually sent us her arrest sheets. We got the picture and left her alone. Sally just called me yesterday for the first time in years with the news that she was getting out and was going to change her life. I am here to help her do that, but it would appear that you may be the only person who could actually change her, and if that happens, I will be grateful," Sara said. Her eyes were moist after her little speech, and Mick realized that she had a soft side, especially about her sister. "Are you going back to the apartment with us after lunch?" she inquired, hoping that he wasn't.

"No," he answered.

"How can she get hold of you?"

"She can't." He paused for a moment thinking, then said, "Your arm will give you away. People notice a pretty girl with a bandaged arm. They remember. You have to stay out of sight until it heals. It's also possible that someone could use me to track you down, so I have to keep my distance, but I intend to keep an eye on you, because I want to be sure you are safe." He noticed that Sally had resumed crying, trying to cover her face with her good hand. "No, Sally, don't do anything that will call attention to yourself right now. You can cry all you need to back in the apartment." He turned back to Sara and leaned closer. "The people we are hiding from will look at her relatives closely and track their movement. It may have already started. You are not at risk, but you can put Sally's life at risk without realizing it. Her pursuers are relentless and have resources which are limitless. I don't think you should go back with her or meet her again until this is over."

The two women were finally realizing how serious this had become, and he could see fear taking possession of their eyes and faces. "I need you both to stay right here until I come back. There is a dress shop down the street, and I want to get a scarf which Sally can use to hide her arm bandages for the return trip. One more thing I need to know. Where have you been since you arrived at the apartment, and how did you get there?" Mick asked.

She looked at the ceiling and rolled her eyes, remembering the details. "I hired a cab with the money you gave me. He waited outside the dress shop for me, then took me straight to the front door. Later the first day, I needed to go to the drug store down the street for some personal things you didn't have in the apartment. I walked there and back. Other than that, I have been in the apartment," she said.

"Do your remember the cab company and the driver you used?" he asked.

"It was United Cab, and the driver was a middle-aged black man. I don't remember his name, but he whistled a lot as he drove."

"That helps. Who have you called on the phone I left for you?"

"Only Sara," she said.

"Be right back," Mick said and got up.

While he was gone, Sara looked at her sister with pity welling up in her heart. The anger she felt previously had evaporated when they met, and she was able to see just how low Sally had become. "Can you really trust this guy?" Sara asked.

"There is something about him that makes me trust him completely. I don't know why. He has already done a lot for me, and he asks nothing in return. I have never seen anyone like him. I hope I'm not wrong, but because of him, I finally have a chance at life again." The tears came back, and she struggled to act normal as Mick had instructed.

Sara didn't admit it, but she instantly felt trust for this stranger also. He looked like the most dangerous person she had ever seen, but her female intuition told her that he could be counted on, and she trusted him. He silently reappeared and handed Sally a silk scarf. She unwrapped it and draped it over her shoulder so that it would cover her arm.

"Sara, I want your phone number, just in case of an emergency," Mick said with a low voice. She wrote it and her address down for him, and he carefully put the paper away. "You two can't talk on the phone again. They will track all of Sara's calls soon, and they will find you. I'll get Sara a clean phone, and then you two can talk. I can't call or give you my number for the same reason. The less traffic the better. This whole thing could take a week to resolve, but I really don't know for sure," he said, looking between them.

Mick put his hand on Sally's shoulder and said, "Do not open the door to your apartment for anyone, and I mean anyone. That includes the cops." He studied her reaction, then observed, "We need your hair to go brown. I'll leave some stuff for you as soon as I can. I want Sara to leave first. When she is clear, Sally, it will be your turn. Go straight back to the apartment and stay there. I will keep an eye on you while you are in the open, but don't look about for me. I'll be there, you can be sure."

Sara got up to leave. She paused to look at Mick for the last time. "I would like to see you again when this is finished," she murmured.

"I would like that too, Sara."

Corner of Cesar Chavez and Mississippi

Mick parked his motorcycle across from where the cabs exited, and settled in to watch, hidden in a small alley. He could clearly see the drivers as they stopped to make the turn, and he began a list of all possible cab numbers. One fellow driving Cab 256 appeared to be whistling as he left. Mick walked unhurriedly back to his bike and pulled on his helmet. A quick turn and rapid acceleration caught up to the cab quickly, and he hung back, mixing with traffic. The cabbie slowly weaved his way through the traffic toward downtown, took 4th street and made the turn onto Mason. Mick, guessing that the cab was headed to the Fairmont Hotel for the supper crowd, accelerated and passed the cab without looking at the driver. He found a small alley off California Ave. and parked behind a garbage dumpster, then walked slowly toward the line of cabs assembling in front of the famous hotel. Right on target, Cab 256 pulled up at the end of the line near the corner of the block, the driver still whistling. Without alerting the driver, Mick opened the door and got in. The surprised cabbie turned and looked over the seat at him. Mick didn't look at all like the typical tourist, and he didn't act like one.

"Drive over to the Embarcadero. I'll tell you where to stop." The driver's card clipped to the sun visor read Amos Murphy and showed his smiling face. The cab remained stationary as the driver cautiously studied Mick's face from his rear-view mirror. Two twenties floated over the seat, and Amos shrugged and drove off. The other cabbies gave him a dirty look as he passed. It was supposed to be first come first out, and they tried to live by a pretext of fairness.

Mick remained silent, and he and the driver watched each other's eyes. As they neared the dock area, Mick said, "Pull over to your right, driver." The cab came to a stop in a parking lot containing scattered cars because of the time of day. A good place for a robbery.

"Say, Mister, if this is a stickup, I keep all the money in a strong box up here," Amos said to the rear-view mirror.

"I want to put some more money in your strong box, Amos," the strange voice in the rear said, "All I want concerns a gal you picked up yesterday. The small blonde with a bandaged arm. You took her to Rockridge, remember?"

After some hesitation, Amos said, "Sure, she had her head wrapped also. She was dressed like a hooker."

"That's the one," the voice said. "What will it cost to make you forget her completely, even to the cops?" the voice rasped.

"Why should I do that?" Amos said and started to turn around. A big hand placed on his shoulder instructed him to stay facing forward.

"Let's make this simple. I'll give you a wad of cash to forget you ever saw her and forget this conversation, or I'll kill you now or later. You choose," the voice said.

Amos started to sweat. "Who's after her, man, that makes it this important?"

"I'm sure the cops would like to know where she is, but I assure you that other than being a hooker she has done nothing wrong. There is a man hunting for her, though, who will kill her if he finds her, and the cops may unintentionally help him. If you take my money and then talk, you will never sleep soundly the rest of your life. I never forget those who double-cross me."

The voice of the man in the rear seat was chilling, and it made Amos remember some creature from a Hollywood movie he had seen once. "Like, man, I have no choice here. Just give me the cash, and I'll never say a word, I promise." He made another attempt to turn around and was prevented. A roll of cash came across the seat in a small arc. He felt the back door of the cab shut and the cab rocked a bit. He picked up the cash. "A thousand bucks!" he exclaimed. He quickly looked around, but the man was out of sight.

Chapter 9

The FBI

San Francisco Hall of Justice

Lieutenant Grover glanced at the wall clock which displayed 5:15. He muttered to himself, "Christ, I have never been able to leave this job on time. Not once in fifteen years." After lunch he realized that another possible place Sally might go would be to a pharmacy because her injury would eventually need a dressing change. He typed in a directive that the squads should also check with pharmacies about the little blonde with the arm bandage. So far, there were no reports of seeing her anywhere, so he considered grabbing some food and coming back later. He cast around for someone to go with, preferably a woman. The Captain's secretary, Jane, was always fun, but she was already gone.

He looked up and saw a very sharp woman headed his way, one who appeared confident about where she was going. She walked purposely to his desk and announced, "Detective Grover, I believe."

Simon stood without thinking, somewhat taken aback. "Yes, I'm that fellow," he mumbled, taken by surprise by her authoritative manner.

"Special Agent April Chauncy, FBI," she stated, smiling blandly. "I was instructed to contact you and provide you with information about an ongoing case of yours," she said, pulling out the side chair and arranging it to face him from the side. He must have looked perplexed, because she added, "The shooting of the Lebanese official night before last?"

"Yes, of course! The Captain mentioned that he had a contact in the FBI"

"I am here to tell you what we were able to gather about the case. We are not involved, but we like to keep informed...you understand." No, Simon didn't really understand. Did that mean that the FBI was aware of what actually happened, he wondered.

"Sure, sure. Please, anything is better than the nothing I have now," Simon said.

Special Agent Chauncy smiled, reaching for her small briefcase, efficiently and noisily snapping it open while watching his face. "Your Captain was interested in anyone similarly trained as your shooter who might be involved, and I have something along those lines that we are willing to give you." Simon sat up attentively as she sorted her papers. "There are limits to even the FBI's ability to gather intelligence from the covert agencies. They are officially directed to share information, but they simply don't or only do it selectively. Some things we can gather without their cooperation, so we infer information out of pieces that we assemble. We are willing to assist you, though, because any missions in progress in San Francisco are being conducted illegally, outside of the FBI, which is the sole agency in charge of operations inside the United States. They are breaking the law, and we don't like it, so we are willing to be involved and be helpful to you." She smiled again. He noticed that she was very attractive but more like a painting or a manikin. The real woman was deeply hidden inside her official self.

Special Agent Chauncy continued, "There are only a few persons who have had all the necessary training and experience. One that stands out is a former soldier named Mick Grundy. He had Special Forces training and was stationed in Germany at the base responsible for operations in Eastern Europe. He has a brilliant service record and speaks fluent German, French, Italian, Slovak and can pass for any of those nationalities. He can also get by on his passable Russian. We have no record of his missions while he was assigned to CIA Black Ops for two years, but we do know that he was injured in a bomb blast while on an assignment for them and required treatment at an Army hospital in Germany. As a result, he acquired extensive facial and neck scars as well as a damaged larynx. He remained in Germany on personal time for fourteen months. During that time he passed as a native and was heavily involved with the motorcycle crowd. We are not sure that he was ever completely dismissed from an active CIA status, and his life after discharge from the Army could be a lengthy cover for a new or an ongoing operation. Grundy's record is rife with incidents that demonstrate that he quickly resorts to killing if he determines that it is required to carry out his mission. Most of his colleagues in Special Forces were wary of him...scared would be a better term. He eventually returned to the United States and was quickly recruited into the U.S. Marshals Service, which promptly asked him to resign after several episodes of excessive force being used on suspects. One unfortunate incident resulted in five gunshot wounds to the chest of a suspect being pursued. Since then he has applied for and received a license as a private investigator in Washington State and usually operates in the area around Tacoma and Seattle. He has never been charged with a crime, but there are suspicions about his connection to several missing or deceased persons."

She finished and was putting the paperwork back into the briefcase when Simon spoke up, "Is he a bad guy or a good guy? After hearing this, I can't make up my mind."

Agent Chauncy snapped the briefcase locks closed and adjusted her coat. "He is exceedingly dangerous and superbly trained. We don't know the answer to your question."

"So is this the guy we should be looking for?" Simon asked her.

"There are a few others which also fit your suspect, but they are all active in covert operations and their files are locked. If this Mick Grundy isn't involved, he may have insight into what is going on. I suggest that you try to find him, but...good luck with that," Agent Chauncy said as she was getting up. She smiled a warm but obligatory smile and left the way she came. Simon looked longingly at her hips as long as she was in sight.

Chapter 10

Beer Hall Encounter

Five Years Prior
Paulaner Am Nockherberg, Munich, Germany

Mick led the way through the noisy crowd. The outside area was reserved for the Lampion Fest crowd, and the noise level was at least tolerable. The tables were decorated with football-sized glowing globes of several colors, and most of the seated patrons were older. Inside the *Biergarten* was the noisy, younger set who were cheering the German Soccer team in a title match against the French. There were occasional deafening eruptions of cheering or booing. Mick and his companions chose the end of a long table and gave polite nods to the strangers seated at the other end.

Mick sat on the left of Tom Speizer and across from Harvey Longren. They had been allowed a short leave following several weeks of rigorous training at the Special Forces base near Stuttgart and decided to party in Munich. Mick had grown to really like the German people, who loved to work and play hard. It was sometimes obvious that his fellow soldiers didn't always share this sentiment and would, at the wrong moment, give voice to their feelings. Since Mick could speak German so fluently and had worked hard to develop German mannerisms, he usually felt more like a tour guide than a buddy. The usual rivalries occasionally flared among his fellows, which was understandable given that they were all selected for their competitive nature. They understood that when they returned to base, training time was over, and they would be available for missions. Even though they dressed in civilian clothes, their short hair and muscularity set them apart, especially when seen together.

"Hey, Longjohns," Mick called out over the live band. "Want anything special or do you want me to order for you as usual?" Harvey smiled and nodded back. Mick knew he probably didn't hear a word and shrugged. "Brats and beer then?" Harvey smiled and nodded.

Tom, though, could hear and laughed out loud. "Not for me, Mick, thanks. I think I can manage for myself tonight."

The cheers got louder. It was obvious that Germany was doing well tonight. Some of the outside crowd cheered also and clicked their steins of beer together before taking half a stein of beer down in one swallow. A pert waitress came by carrying six large mugs of beer intended for the other end of their table. She expertly swung the tray down without spilling a drop and was rewarded by a small round of clapping from her customers. She smiled at Mick and his friends at the other end and came toward them, past Harvey. As she passed, Harvey grabbed her buttocks, and she quickly spun around, giving him a hard slap to his face. Tom sputtered into laugher, as did Harvey.

Mick stood and went around to stand in front of her. He apologized to her, saying, *"Es tut mir leid, Fräulein. Mein Freund hat zu viel zu trinken."* He gave a small bow with his hand over his waist. She gave a short curtsy and lifted her head high and left.

Harvey stood, demanding, "What did you say to her, Mick?" He was confrontational and angry.

"I just apologized for your behavior. This isn't the Middle Ages, you know. Most of these girls are college students just earning a few bucks. They are not used to getting grabbed like that." Mick lowered his head in a sign that he would not back down if it came to blows.

Harvey broke out in a laugh. "We're not going to fight over a tramp waitress, Mick. Also, I know you would kick my ass. Forget about it." They sat down and waited for her to return. She didn't.

Mick finally spoke up, "Well, I don't think she is going to serve us tonight. We could go inside if you can stand the noise."

Harvey angrily blurted, "I hate soccer! Don't understand it. Why can't these stinking Germans play real football?" Mick had no reply for such a dumb comment.

"Hey, I saw another joint down the street when we came in. Let's go down there and drink," Tom suggested.

Harvey agreed, but Mick hesitated. He had locked eyes with their little waitress from across the room, and she had given him a return smile. "You guys go on down there, and I'll catch up," Mick said. They both looked irritated about splitting up, and Harvey was still a little angry from before. Harvey playfully slapped Tom on the back, a signal that they were leaving as they headed for the exit. Mick stood still, watching the waitress make her rounds carrying heavy mugs of thick beer. As fit as he was, he wasn't sure he could do what she was doing. She noticed that he continued to look at her, and she put down her tray and wiped her hands on her apron.

She came up smiling and said, *"Sind sie ein amerikanische?"*

He smiled back and said, "Sure, I'm an American. Speak English?"

"Some," she said. "English was not my strongest subject."

"You sound delightful to me. Nearly like you are from Chicago," Mick teased. He grinned at her, and she gave a little chuckle.

She said, "I thought you were a German, but I could see that your friends are American soldiers, and you look much the same."

"Only on the outside," he said.

"If you will sit again, *bitte*, I will bring you a beer," she said.

Mick asked, *"Willst du mir deinen Namen sagen?"*

Again, she rewarded him with a big and perfect smile. "Anna," she said over her shoulder as she was walking away.

As Mick waited for her to return, he noticed that the group at the end of the table seemed to be discussing him. *"Wird er sie fragen, für ein Datum?"*

the older fellow asked. They were all smiling at him for encouragement. He smiled at them and shrugged. They were watching closely when she returned with a large stein of beer. She leaned provocatively close to him when she put it on the table.

"*Bitte*," he said. "Is there any way I can see you again, Anna?" he asked. The other end of the table strained to hear their conversation over the ambient noise.

"I finish my work at umm....*elf Uhr dreißig,*" she said pertly and left. Halfway down the aisle she turned her head and gave him another charming smile. There was gentle applause from the other end and much head nodding. It was only another hour before she was finished. He could wait, and so could his friends, but he wasn't really worried about them. Tom knew enough German to get by, and he could look after Harvey. Mick started to think about Harvey. Very hard guy to like. Once he felt that Harvey cheated him on the firing range by shooting at Mick's target instead of his, lowering Mick's score with a deliberate miss. It was a little thing, but it showed at lot about Harvey's character. Mick never said anything about it and took the loss of the competition in stride. Harvey, who smiled at every joke and seemed everyone's friend, wouldn't hesitate to lie. There were small lies and big lies, and he seemed to never get caught. Mick knew that someday he might be in a situation that was life or death, and he hoped that Harvey wasn't around at the critical moment. Tom, on the other hand, was solid and dependable. He was from a small Midwestern cattle farm and, although not worldly, would always be there for a buddy in need.

Chapter 11

Making Lieutenant

United States Special Forces Base
Stuttgart, Germany
Two Days Prior To Leave

Prior to their leaving the base, Mick was called in to the Major's office. Also in the room was his superior officer, First Lieutenant Speigle. "Sergeant Grundy," the Major announced.

"Yes, sir." Mick snapped to rigid attention, came to a stiff salute and held it.

"At ease, Sergeant. I want to personally congratulate you on your training here. We feel that you are among the most superior soldiers we have trained in years. Your file is in front of me, and I see that you really have no family left back in the States. Is that so?"

"Yes, sir, that is correct," Mick answered. He was adopted as a child of five, and his older, adoptive parents passed away a few years ago. He had enlisted, having few choices of any kind, and applied himself as if the Army was his family.

"Sergeant, for the reasons that you are a singularly fit and well-trained soldier and the fact that you no longer have any kin, I am recommending you for missions which may be considered higher risk. Do you understand?"

"Yes, sir. Thank you, sir," Mick said and resumed his salute.

"At ease, son," the Major said. "We are also recommending that you be given the rank of lieutenant effective immediately. However, this is contingent on your performance during the pending missions and on you going to OCS when they are complete. Dismissed."

Chapter 12

Parking Lot Assailants

Munich, Germany

At precisely eleven thirty, Anna was walking toward him. She had changed her waitress smock for more fashionable clothing, and the effect was to reveal her striking figure. She had also taken her hair out of braids, and it hung past her shoulder, part of it resting on her chest. He studied her carefully to comprehend that she was the same girl he was waiting for.

"Forgive me for looking you over, Anna, but you are simply stunning. I can almost understand why Harvey grabbed you!" he said playfully.

"Now, my nice *Amerikaner*, don't you become naughty also, and by the way, what is your name?"

"Mick Grundy."

"Pleased to meet you, Mick," she said and stuck out her small hand. "I am Anna Michner. Would you like to accompany me somewhere?"

Mick took her hand and turned it over and looked at the palm. "What are you doing, Mick?" She laughed, pulling it away from him.

"It's just that I was trying to figure out what makes you so strong. I was looking for muscles, but all I see is a beautiful, graceful feminine hand," he said with a boyish grin. She gave him a playful swat on his head and touched him on his shoulder.

"You feel like a rock. Such muscles!" she said admiringly and patted him again. They continued to walk toward the exit and the street. Mick gave a quick glance at his watch. Nearly midnight.

"Anna, would you go down the street with me to tell my friends that they can leave without me tonight?" he asked.

"*Ja*. Then you can go with me to a party across town, yes?" she responded.

"They said that they were going to a little bar just up the street. I remember that *Hacker-Pschorr Bräu* was across from where we left the taxi. They are probably still there," Mick said, pointing up the dark street.

She agreed to go with him, and they strolled the two blocks arm in arm, chatting. They alternated freely between German and English, some sentences containing both languages. As they entered the bar, loud English speaking voices were arising from the back, mixed with riotous laughter. Mick rolled his eyes in embarrassment, and they headed toward the noise. His comrades were in a booth and were obnoxiously intoxicated. The waiter was standing beside the table waving the tab which had obviously not been paid and cursing in German at them.

Mick came up behind the waiter and asked, *"Wie viel ist die Rechnung?"*

The waiter looked surprised and handed Mick the tab and said, "135 Euro." Mick opened his wallet and paid the waiter, including a generous tip. *"Danke,"* the waiter said huffily and walked away quickly.

Mick leaned over Tom, tapping him on the shoulder, "Come with me, you guys. They are mad enough to call the cops, so you have to get out of here right now."

He pulled Tom to his feet and then did the same with Harvey. Over his shoulder, he could see the waitstaff watching them closely. Mick put his arm under each man's arm, and the three staggered toward the door with Anna in tow. As they exited, Mick turned to the headwaiter and remarked, *"Ich entschuldige mich für meine Freunde. Hoffe, dass sie nicht zu viel Mühe."* The headwaiter responded with a scowl and waved them out with the back of his hand. No translation was necessary. Once they made it to the street, Mick looked in vain for a cab with not one in sight. He heard Anna speaking on her cell phone and turned to look.

"I called a taxi. It should be here soon," she said. Within seconds, a taxi stopped, and the driver rolled down his window.

Mick opened the back door, loaded his buddies inside and again reached into his wallet and, after extracting thirty Euros, handed the cash to the driver. *"Hotel Stadt Rosenheim, Orleansplat."* The driver nodded and they lurched away. "Those two are eating up all my cash!" Mick complained to the disappearing taxi.

"You won't need any more cash tonight. We are going to a party near LMU," she said and showed him her wonderful smile while folding her arm into his.

"Now can you call us a cab?" he asked.

"Nein, wir verwenden werden mein Auto." she said and took his arm, leading the way to her car. She was parked in an employee lot which was about two blocks away, but the night was warm and pleasant and so was the walk.

The car was in a nearly empty lot and was parked in a dark corner. Mick gave a casual glance at the car and caught a slight movement. He became instantly alert and focused. Anna must have sensed the change, and she stopped talking as they came closer to the car. Two men emerged from the shadows and lingered beside the car. As they got closer, Mick put his arm in front of Anna to guide her behind him. One of them stepped forward and snarled, *"Wir haben gewartet. Wir möchten eine Fahrt in Ihrem Auto mit Ihnen."* He was carrying a short pipe or club and slapping it into his open palm. Mick reached behind him, pushing Anna further away, then advanced toward the man. The other started around the car toward him. Almost casually, Mick grabbed the wrist holding the weapon, his other hand plowing into the man's abdomen with open fingers and grasped the lower rib cage, pulling violently back. "Snap." The man dropped to the pavement in agony, screaming, *"Er brach meine Rippen."*

Before the other man could react, Mick used the hood of the car to support his upper body, and used his foot to strike him in the neck. This one, too collapsed to the pavement, grasping his neck. Mick grabbed their collars and dragged them roughly away from the car. He remarked with a laugh, "I thought this only happened in America!"

Anna put her hand to her mouth and said, "My lucky stars that you were here tonight. Will they die now?" she asked innocently.

"No, but next time, they will," he answered.

Chapter 12

Chapter 13

Meinen Bruder, Kurt

Munich, Germany

She drove faster than he expected, taking the turns very hard, causing the tires to squeal. He held on to the grab handle by the door and checked his safety belt. "Have you considered fighter pilot training, Anna?"

It was a mistake to ask, because she drove even harder, laughing at him as he held on. "Is the soldier frightened?" she scolded and gave him a long look.

He gently pushed her face back forward, and they both laughed. With a loud shriek from the tires, she made a sudden sliding stop and shut the car down. "It's just up there." She pointed at a large high-rise apartment complex, then turned to him with a serious expression. "Mick, you can easily pass for a German, and I think at this party, you should not be identified as an American soldier." She could see his puzzlement and continued, "There are some students here whom you would call Marxist and who feel that American Forces should all leave Germany. We are here to party, and I wouldn't like to see a fight tonight. Would you mind?"

"Anna, we have known each other for less than one hour, but I feel that I have always known you. I have never had that experience before. Believe me, anything I can do to stay around you tonight, I will do."

Anna didn't answer him, but he could see the glitter in her eyes reflected from the street lights. She leaned forward and gave him a kiss so lightly that he wasn't sure her lips touched his, but, for a brief instance, he felt the warmth of her face close to his. She sat back up, and they had a moment when no conversation was necessary.

The small apartment was filled with energetic college students of both sexes. The music was loud and was that uniquely German techno-style. The beats came as thumps which you could feel as waves hitting you from all around. Someone had set up a lamp in the corner which flashed colored strobe beams around the room as beer flowed as only Germans know how to drink it. In a lull between musical numbers, Anna grasped his hand and pulled him into a small hall. She tapped a young blond fellow on the shoulder, and when he turned, she brushed her cheek against his, both smiling as they gave each other a quick embrace. She turned to Mick while her arm was still around the fellow's waist and said, *"Ich will Sie in meinen Bruder, Kurt einführen."*

The fellow was her brother, Kurt. Mick stuck out his hand, and they shook vigorously. There was something about Kurt that Mick instantly liked. His smile and Anna's smile were just alike, and he could see the affection they had for each other. Mick noticed that Anna gave him a quick chin up motion of her head which said, "Remember, you are not an American!" He returned the movement to let her know that he understood.

"Sind Sie ein Student hier in München?" Kurt asked.

"Ja, konzentriere ich mich auf das Erlernen der Englischen Sprache," Mick replied.

"Great, I love to practice my English, could we speak only in English, Mick?"

"I would like that, Kurt. Could you let me know if I make mistakes?" Mick asked.

Kurt liked that answer and agreed to catch him. Anna rolled with laughter, and Kurt gave her a questioning look, then shrugged. "Female humor," he said to Mick. Mick nodded agreement and gave him a knowing look.

"What are you studying, Kurt?" Mick asked.

"I am in Engineering. That is when I can pull myself away from the racetrack," Kurt said with a faraway look.

Mick didn't understand. "Are you a gambler, then?"

Kurt and his sister laughed. "No, I race motorcycles. Road racing. I hope to get a sponsor and someday race in the World Superbike series."

"I don't know of a racetrack near Munich for motorcycles," Mick replied.

"There isn't a good one. I like to go to Sachsenring when I can. It's a long way, but the speed there is very high." His sister rolled her eyes to suggest that the motorcycle endeavor was beyond her grasp. Mick gave her a little smile.

"I have been on the race track near Mannheim. The Motodrom. Ever heard of it?" Mick asked.

Kurt looked surprised and said, "You mean on a motorcycle?" As he spoke he took another look at Mick as if seeing him in a different light.

"Yes," Mick answered. "On a 600cc Japanese bike. A couple of years ago. I ride a bike most of the time for transportation, because I don't own a car right now."

Kurt smiled. "You are much larger than me. That's a lot of weight to ask a 600cc bike to drag around."

"You are right, Kurt. I have to get a bigger one someday when things calm down for me." Mick could tell that they were instantly friends There was a lot to talk about racing with Kurt, but he could see that Anna was not interested in motorbikes. He shook Kurt's hand again and returned to Anna. "Your feet have a little left for a dance with me?" he asked gently in her ear, over the music which had resumed.

As a reply, she placed both hands loosely over his shoulders, and they moved laterally into the larger room. There was barely enough room to stand, but they danced and looked into each other's face from arm's length. Mick was mesmerized by Anna, a feeling which grew stronger by the minute. It was like looking at someone whom you know well and have always known. He felt that he knew everything about her: what she liked and disliked, her moods both happy and grumpy. Her face in the low light was a constantly changing pattern of shadow and highlight, and her long hair gradually moved over her shoulders, framing her face like a nun's habit. Mick placed his hands respectfully on her waist, feeling her move and spin under his gentle touch.

She leaned toward him and yelled into his ear, "You dance well for someone so muscular!"

He answered her, but in a lower voice, close to her ear, "And you move like you haven't been on your feet for hours." The tone of his voice moved her even closer to him. The dance would have been divine if only the music fit his mood better. He motioned to the door, and she readily agreed. They went into the hall outside the suite of rooms and found three other couples who had gone out for smokes. She pulled him to the end of the hall where there was a small glassed-in balcony, and they sat down in privacy.

"You must tell me everything about yourself, Mick," she said with sincerity. They were sitting on a short couch, and she placed her forearm and hand on his right leg. He was sure that contact with her was burning a hole in his jeans. It was like radiant energy, and he could focus on nothing else.

He forced his mind from her hand and sighed before speaking. "My story is not so glamorous, in fact, somewhat depressing. Are you sure you want to hear it?"

Anna said, "I feel that you will be asking me about myself. It's only fair, you know."

She was right, of course. He looked down, organizing his thoughts, but avoided the sight of her arm on his thigh. "I was an orphan in Chicago from birth. I never knew either one of my natural parents. I was just over five years old when an older couple from the suburbs agreed to adopt me. Previously, I believe, I was in several different foster homes. My adoptive parents tried to make me part of their life. Both of them were college teachers of various languages, and both were originally native German, fluent in several languages. They constantly coached me on my language skills and that is why I can pass for German. I practically am one. When I was about ten, we went abroad for an extended vacation and toured Germany. By the time we got back, my English was rusty." He paused, remembering.

"Are you still close with them?" Anna interrupted.

"They were both killed in a car wreck when I was seventeen. They never changed their will so all their money and property was left to relatives in Germany. I was back on the street again. I survived...avoided the authorities until I was eighteen and truly on my own. There were no options for me, so I joined the Army and made it my home."

"Where are you stationed in Germany, Mick?"

"Stuttgart."

She thought for a moment and then said, "Isn't that the Special Forces base?"

Mick gave a long pause. "There are many Special Forces bases in Germany. We are not allowed to discuss the subject with anyone." He didn't look at her after he spoke. After she withdrew her hand, he looked into her eyes. "I'm sorry. I trust you, but I cannot discuss anything to do with my unit."

Anna took a deep breath, as if gathering her resolve. "My father's mother is still alive and lives in Stuttgart. I have been there many times. Perhaps someday we can meet when you have leave."

Mick could sense a difference in attitude from Anna when she realized that his first duty was to the Army, essentially he was married to the U.S. Army. A serious relationship with her would be distracting, especially now that he was to be sent on both sensitive and dangerous missions. Mick had already experienced a lifetime of hurt, and he didn't want to do the same to some woman whom he knew he could grow to love. The moment of clarity saddened him, and he saw before him something that he couldn't have...the devoted love of a woman. He had never experienced love before, and now, the possibility seemed to slip away right in front of him.

"Anna, your turn. Tell me all about yourself." He tried to look upbeat and interested, but reality had closed in on both of them.

Anna considered his face before answering. "Nothing so exciting as your life, I'm afraid. I went to school and studied, and I am still here studying. My parents own a small clothing shop not far from here. I am endeavoring to get a degree in merchandising, and after that, I don't know." She continued to study him, adding, "I have never met someone such as you, Mick. I don't know how to act with you, but I know I have enjoyed your company very much. You are such a gentleman, even given your martial arts skills I saw with my own eyes." She was trying not to fall for him, because she could see that his life was not his own right now, but he was proving to be irresistible.

"Anna, I have been around girls before, but I have to be honest; I have never been so strongly drawn to anyone." He glanced at his watch. "Three hours and I don't want to part from you. It's amazing."

"Mick, when are you returning to your base?"

"I have two more days. After that, things will change for me, and I have no idea where I will be or when I can get away again."

"From what you have said and the way I feel, I think that we are really going through the same thing in our heads," she said. "I have decided to take the next two days off from work and school to spend with you. We need to understand if we have any future together or if it is a dream after all."

No longer able to resist her, Mick took her in his arms and kissed her with passion, and she responded the same. As they broke away, she said, "Let me take you back to your hotel so you can get some sleep, and I will ring you tomorrow. I plan to show you *München*, and I think we will have a good time together during your last days of freedom."

They could hear footsteps getting closer and looked up to see Kurt coming toward them. *"Da bist du ja. Ich dachte, Sie verlassen wurden,"* he said. Then he put his hand to his forehead and gave a quick slap. "Oops, we were speaking English, weren't we?"

Mick smiled back at him, *"Sie kam gerade noch rechtzeitig, Kurt. Wir sind bereit, zu gehen."*

Kurt laughed, "Well, perhaps we can get together sometime and talk just motorcycles. Even ride together, Mick."

"I would very much like that. I'm sure that I will learn a lot from you," He turned to Anna and said, "I can catch a cab back, and it will save you a lot of driving, but may I have your phone number first?"

She wrote it down for him and then called for a cab.

Chapter 13

Chapter 14

Meeting The Parents

Munich, Germany
0832 Hours

As soon as Mick wakened, he looked at his watch. Too early to call her. Tom and Harvey were still out and were exhaling enough alcohol to start a fire. They would be in bed until noon, he guessed. He quickly showered and put on fresh clothes. There was supposed to be a small free breakfast area in the hotel, and he left the room to search for it. After two cups of coffee and a bit of newspaper reading, he looked again at his watch, 9:45. He searched for his cell phone and dialed her number.

She answered on the second ring, *"Guten Morgen, Mick. Ich wusste, dass Sie früh rufen würden."* He could picture her smiling, and her soft voice caressed him like a comfortable old shirt.

"Good morning to you, Anna. How did you know that it was me?"

Anna responded, "Because, if you thought about me last night as much as I thought about you, I knew that you couldn't wait any longer." Again, he could picture her smile.

"You are so right, Anna. I am anxious to see you again. What do you have planned today?"

"If you are interested, the Villa Struck is not far from where I am and is most entertaining. There is a museum cafe there which is delightful for lunch. Does that sound like a start?" Quickly adding, "Should I come to get you, Mick?"

"I have my bike. If you are willing to ride on the back, I will come get you, but you have to tell me where to find you."

"That sounds like fun. I will bring my brother's old helmet to wear. You can pick me up on the corner in front of the Munich City Apartments, *Goethestraße* 23. Can you find it, O.K.?"

"I'll leave right away and see you soon!"

She was waiting just where she said, wearing jeans and a stylish short green leather jacket. When he pulled up, she hopped on like she had ridden before and reached around his waist to hold on with both hands. Their helmets collided when they talked, but he managed to hear her directions, and very carefully and smoothly made their way through traffic to the Villa. Once there, he could see that she was right. The Villa was a great starting place with lots of room for walking together and talking, with few other visitors. Perfect weather, sunlight and blue sky made for a memorable day. Arm in arm, they toured the expansive old home, eventually discovering the small cafe. The cafe's ceiling was glass, making the space bright and cheerful, corresponding to their moods. Sitting across from each other, they engaged in small talk as budding lovers do, a kind of necessary conversation, but much of what was being passed over the table was not in words. Mick traced her face and hair with his eyes, becoming more attracted to her each minute they spent together. She had a way of pronouncing "J" sounds by over-puckering her lips, which he found endearing, and waving her hands in graceful feminine arcs while speaking. When she looked at him, she flicked her blue eyes between his eyes and his mouth.

He remembered that her family had a clothing shop which explained her simple but elegant tastes with fashion. "Anna, for just wearing jeans and a leather jacket, you look wonderful. Actually, I don't think there is anything you could wear that wouldn't make you look like a Hollywood star."

"Mick, you don't have to flatter me. I'm already falling for you anyway." She sat across from him with her chin propped on her fist, holding him in her steady gaze. "How can a guy as tough as you seem to be also be gentle and considerate?"

"It must be you that's doing it, Anna. No one has ever said that about me before today. I feel more like a big moose around you, and I am trying not to let you see me as I am. It's like you are made of crystal or are a dream and will go away as quickly as you appeared. I'm afraid of closing my eyes, because you might be gone."

Anna reached across the table and patted him on the back of his hand. "No, Mick, I'm not leaving until I lose the attraction I have for you. By the way, you are not a moose. You move more like one of those big cats in the zoo." She paused and pursed her lips, "Let's see how my parents react to you and you to them. They are good judges of character, and, also, you need to see who I come from. Okay?"

"Will I be an American or a German today?"

"My parents have been around long enough to know that the American Army has kept communism at bay, and we are again one country thanks to you. They respect the Americans. We all know that our German Army is a paper tiger, and we need the Americans to stay. Be an American. With Kurt, however, it's different. He has a lot of radical friends. I think he will come around in time, but you should become closer to him before you tell him the truth."

Anna's parents' shop was west of Munich a short distance. They rolled toward it, somewhat slowly while Anna was pointing out the sights of the city. He loved the feeling of her arms about his waist. Mick gulped with apprehension when they eventually pulled up on the curb outside of her parents' shop. Gucci, the sign said.

As he pulled off his helmet, he said, "Little shop? This explains the clothes you wear and also shows how little I know about such things." He looked down at his pants and the worn sleeves of his leather jacket which he had purchased used. "I'm ashamed to go in there, Anna."

"Nonsense," she said. "The look you have is what all the trendy seek to look like. You are simply the real thing." She smiled encouragingly and took his arm and led the way in. The door bell chimed in an old-world way, but inside, the store was upscale with brass and glass everywhere, using ornate, black woodwork to set it off. A distinguished gentleman in an impeccably tailored suit came toward them smiling, his arm extended toward Anna.

"Anna, Anna, mein schönes Mädchen, ein unerwartetes Freude, Sie heute sehen. Gibt es keine Klassen an der Universität heute?" he said and gave her a quick kiss on the cheek.

Anna ignored her father's question about not attending school today. She looked at Mick, winked and said, "I came to introduce a new friend, *Vater*, meet Mick." They both looked at Mick for comment.

"Michelangelo, sir, ma si può chiamare me Mick. Hai un negozio meraviglioso riempito con il migliore dei mondi abbigliamento. Italiana, naturalmente," Mick said with a flourish of his arm, taking in the whole shop.

Anna's father was taken aback and looked confused. Anna broke out in laughter which doubled her over. She clung to Mick to keep from falling on the floor. Mick smiled and said, "Pleasure to meet you, sir," and stuck out his hand in greeting.

"Mick, you certainly fooled me with that. Excellent Italian. I have them in here all the time, and you were acting and speaking like a carbon copy," Herr Michner said.

Anna was wiping away tears from her laughter and said, "I had no idea you could also speak Italian, Mick." Any other surprises in store for us?

"No more surprises, Anna," Mick said, patting her hand which rested on his shoulder.

"You are American?" Herr Michner asked.

"Yes, sir."

Herr Michner looked him over carefully. "Soldier?"

"Yes, sir."

Herr Michner put his hand to his chin and asked, "*Spezialtruppen*, excuse, Special Forces?"

"Yes, sir."

"What rank do you hold?" Herr Michner asked.

"Second Lieutenant, sir."

Anna pulled at his sleeve. "You never told me you were an officer."

Herr Michner locked arms with Mick, and as they were walking toward the rear of the store said, "You are welcome here, son. I am glad to make your acquaintance. Do you also speak any German?"

"As well as you or I, *Vater*," Anna said from behind them.

"Excellent," Herr Michner said. "By the way, I would prefer you to call me Alfred, *bitte*."

"Thank you, sir."

"Where is your family from, Mick?" Not too many Americans are multilingual," Alfred asked.

"Sir, I never knew my real parents, but my adoptive parents were German. We lived near Chicago. They are gone now, so I only have the Army."

Alfred looked at Anna and asked, "How long have you kept him a secret from us, Anna?"

Anna laughed. "Only since last night, *Vater*."

Mick looked at his watch and said, "Eighteen hours and thirty seven minutes, sir, and we were apart most of that time."

"Oh my goodness, *meine Kinder*. So fast," Alfred said. He looked back and forth at their faces and shrugged. "I wish I were so young again."

"*Vater*, Mick saved my life last night!" Anna said.

"Are you serious?" Alfred said and looked at both of them in turn.

"It was nothing, sir," Mick said.

"He took two thugs out, *Vater*. Two seconds and they both were on the ground. It was amazing." Anna waved her arms over her head while speaking. "He never said a word to them. They would have hurt me or killed me except for him."

"It was an honor, sir, but it was just a small event, really," Mick said.

"Would you please stay here and dine with us and Frau Michner, Mick?" Alfred asked.

"I would very much like that, sir."

"*Und, bitte,* please call me Alfred."

"Yes, sir."

At dinner, Mick was made to feel at home by Anna's parents, and they seemed to like him very much. Anna's mother, Frau Michner, was more formal and spoke English with difficulty, so he only spoke German with her. Their house was just a short drive from the store and was very well-appointed inside. To his surprise, Anna and her mother made supper, and he was left alone with Alfred. Anna was right about her father. Alfred Michner did seem to like Americans and was not troubled by Mick being in the U.S. Army.

"Are you to be staying in Germany for a while, Mick?"

"No idea, sir. I would like to, but, as you know, we just follow orders."

"What are you going to do when you resign from your military service?"

"I don't know much, sir, except about the Army. The thought of being out frightens me."

Alfred thought about that for awhile and said, "Seems to me you could do anything you want to do. I think you will not have a problem." Alfred settled back in his chair. "By the way, we have a son named Kurt. He is currently infatuated with the radicals at University. You may not want to discuss with him that you are an American and especially not an officer. He may yet turn out all right but is very much not like you, I'm afraid."

"I did meet him, last night, sir, and I like him, and I think he feels the same way toward me. On advice from Anna, I pretended to be a German student. We have a common interest, sir. Motorcycles."

"Yes, I saw you both on it. I am fearful for Anna on a motorcycle, I must tell you," Alfred said with concern.

"I swear to you, sir, she is safer with me on my bike than driving. I survived being a passenger in her car last night. I promise that she would never be at risk on that motorcycle, sir."

Alfred had a good laugh. "I know what you mean, Mick, and you are right. I won't worry about her when she is with you."

The dinner went well, and the conversation ranged from politics to the absurd. There was lots of laughing and lots of sincerity. Mick felt like a member of the family within the first few minutes. Alfred knew enough to stay away from subjects Mick would be prohibited from discussing. Schnapps came out of the cupboard after dessert and also lubricated the conversation.

Frau Michner asked, *"Haben Sie schon einmal verheiratet,* Mick?"

Mick answered, *"Nein.* I have never been married. I have never been in love or had a significant lady friend. My comrades are all male, and we have little free time in our lives."

Alfred asked, "Do you think that you want a serious relationship with our Anna?"

"Sir, your daughter is a gift of nature. Any man would want to be around her. I would and I do. There are things in my future unknown to me and which are out of my control, so I have to take life one day at a time right now."

Alfred said, "Mick, you must meet my mother who lives alone in Stuttgart. She has a colorful history, and at one time was an agent of the Federal Republic of Germany and worked for them in the GDR before unification. She is a heroine to the people who know what she went through and the risks she took. She is somewhat bitter about the breakup of her marriage years ago which was a part of her cover but became real. She knows the sacrifices which are made in the name of patriotism, and she may be able to give you some insight about how to manage your private life in balance with your duty to your country."

"Thank you, sir, for the suggestion. I would very much like to talk with her," Mick said. "There is one other thing you all should know. Because of my assignment, there may be a vetting process for any friends or acquaintances I have made or will make in Germany. There will be people asking questions, and you may hear about it or even be interviewed. I am sorry about that, and I hope it will not cause any distress."

Alfred spoke first, "That sounds like you are in a covert unit, Mick. You won't have any problems with us or Anna, but the red flag will go up over our son, Kurt. My mother no longer will speak to him."

"Perhaps one day I can spend some time with Kurt and let him see a different view of the world. I would like to try, at least."

Anna could not hold back the tears and put her head in her hands to hide her emotions. "I don't understand, *Vater*; we weren't raised to think like Kurt does now. He keeps some really bad company, and I fear that he may be led into something rash."

Mick looked at his watch. 11:03. He stood and said to all of them, "This has been one of the best days of my life. I can't thank all of you enough for making me so at home here, especially Anna. The time is late, and I must leave and let you get some sleep." He turned to Anna who had also stood and said, "What time would you like me to come pick you up tomorrow, Anna?"

She still had tears in her eyes or was making new ones. She took his arm and said, "Let me walk with you to your bike, Mick."

The Michners both got up and shook his hand. Alfred said, "It was a great pleasure, Mick. Why don't you come around 8:30 and have some breakfast with us? I might have some suggestions for you two for tomorrow."

Mick looked at Anna for confirmation and saw that she vigorously nodded yes. "Thank you, sir. I will look forward to it." He took Anna's arm and picked up his worn leather coat and helmet, and they went outside in the cool air.

At the bike, they looked at each other in the dim light. Anna came close and said, "Mick, I have never had anyone outside of my family that I felt so close to. You are already very dear to me. I don't want to call it anything else, because we have spent so little time together, but it feels so right to be with you." She put her arms around his neck and drew him down for a long kiss. "You will be careful on that thing, won't you?" she asked, pointing to his motorcycle.

"Anna, at this moment, I think I would do anything for you," Mick said. He pulled on his helmet and opened the visor to see her better. He swung his leg over the bike and said, *"Auf Wiedersehen bis Morgen."* He hit the starter and was gone. She stood and listened to the diminishing sound of his motor until it faded out.

When he got back to his hotel room, Mick found a note from Tom and Harvey sarcastically wishing him well. They had left earlier on their motorcycles with no word about where they went.

Chapter 14

Chapter 15

Capture Or Kill

Six Months Later
Sevastopol, Ukraine

Assembly had started sometime after midnight. The little apartment had admitted its present contingent of men one at a time, and the time was approaching early afternoon. They were all finally present. Mick was sitting on the floor next to a hard type whose muscles bulged visibly under his summer sport coat. There had been no introductions and minimal conversation with an occasional muffled whisper showing the building apprehension. The fellow beside Mick had been furtively looking him over, sizing him up, and Mick was doing the same thing. Harvey had arrived two hours earlier than Mick and Tom and was across the room leaning into the wall. Tom had his brimmed hat pulled low, and his eyes darted nervously over the several men seated on the floor. The door from the adjoining room opened as two men came in and stood near the front of the room.

"Hello to the lot of you," one man said. He was the larger of the two and was holding a sheaf of papers. The short, heavy one appeared to Mick to be someone from the area, wearing a large dark mustache typical of many Russians. The larger man continued, "The mission you were sent to carry out will be engaged shortly. For those of you who were not briefed previously and for those who need to know the latest intelligence, let me sum this up. We are after a Turkish Intelligence official who is suspected of being turned by the GRU and who was being watched by our allies in the Turkish Army. He is going by the name Ozker Kocadal at the moment. He may not be the only double agent involved, because he fled to Sevastopol apparently after being warned about gathering suspicions. Right now, he is in the Aurora Hotel on Kozhanova St. in room 336. He is being watched by the GRU around the clock, and our information is that he is to be transported to Moscow soon. As all of you know, possession of this part of the Ukraine has been disputed by the Russians, and they keep a strong military presence here. There is a Spezsnaz base near the harbor which will react quickly and in force if alerted. With our Turkish allies, and that includes Major Karamat over there," he pointed to the man next to Mick, "we plan to abduct Ozker back to Turkey. We don't want to shoot this out with the Russians, because they will win. We are simply outnumbered here, and we want this to occur without them knowing we were even here. If you have been around for awhile, you know that the Russians always retaliate somewhere or sometime. Always. If we can snatch Ozker out from under their nose, we will put him on a special delivery back to Turkey where their Army can deal with him."

David Ridell paused and studied the faces in the room, one by one. They had all been screened downstairs and their identities confirmed before being allowed in the briefing room. There are always contingency plans. You can never be sure about even a well-thought-out plan working and that was the reason for getting such a varied group together so fast. Plan A was to talk Ozker out of his room by letting him think that the GRU had finally decided to move him. Following this plan, Ozker would freely go with them past the Russian agents to a car and be quickly driven away from Sevastopol toward Yalta where a fast boat was waiting to take him to Istanbul. Ridell had been careful to insure that the entire plan was only known by him alone. But this plan had so many flaws that you could reasonably doubt its success.

Plan B was to snatch Ozker from the hotel by force and quickly flee the area before the Russians could get organized. This was a free-form plan and would have to be acted on as things developed.

Plan C was to assassinate the traitor in his room by gunfire or by bomb. Should this one be implemented, it was going to become difficult to get his team out intact. Everyone assembled had been provided false papers and were using a once-only operative name. The group of eleven men included four CIA agents, including himself and his second in command, Borisky, three Turks from their Red Beret unit and four men assigned from American Special Forces. All of them were well-trained and could speak a variety of languages.

David Ridell continued, "Fredrick, since you can pass for Russian and since Borisky is Russian, you two will go to Ozker's room just after dark and convince him to come with you for transport to Moscow." Harvey nodded agreement, because at this moment, the group knew him as Fredrick.

"The other Americans, Huey, Dewy, and Louie, will go earlier to the Aurora Hotel and identify the Russians who are watching and prevent them from intervening with the first team. Killing is a last resort, men," Ridell continued. Mick, Tom and Steve shook their heads in understanding of their part.

"The rest of you will come with me and bring the three cars around. I will go to the front of the hotel and signal you when to drive up. The van will be used to transport the target out and will be first in. The two cars will pick up the remainder of the team and run interference, if we are pursued." Ridell looked at all of them carefully to let the message sink in. Planning and assembly had been rushed since the defection of Ozker, and there was no additional time available to pull this off. Borisky had been instructed to execute Plan C if there was no other choice. The Turks were there to deal with the trip back to Istanbul, if they could get that far, but all the agents were capable of finding their own way back if things went badly, and all were heavily armed.

Mick had already been in two other covert operations, but this one was far from base, and there were a lot of unknowns. There was no support out this far, but he was trained to be able to make his own way back to base. He knew that his Russian would pass if he didn't speak too much of it. Once he got as far as Poland or Slovenia, he could easily blend in, but traveling north through the Ukraine toward Russia was the last thing he wanted to happen. If he could team up with Harvey, he would have a better chance, but he had learned not to trust Harvey very far. Tom had been trained to speak Anatolian Turkish which would be useful if they were to go south or west to get out. The best trip would be to have the whole group make it to a boat where they would head out into the Black Sea and meet up with the Turkish Navy, which would be hovering, waiting to pick them up.

Ridell and his second went back into the side room and closed the door. The men knew not to make any noise, and any conversation was brief and whispered. Mick stuck out his hand to the Turk sitting beside him, and it was taken with a smile. Judging by his handshake and broad shoulders, this Major Karamat was a tough and hardened soldier. Mick knew the Turkish Red Berets were as rigorously trained as he was and were well-respected. This was a good man to have at your side. Tom continued to sit there and quietly observe the others under the brim of his low hat. He had become more suspicious after a couple of close calls on other missions, and his good-natured side had disappeared. Harvey looked cocky as usual, as if he had not a care in the world. He continued to lean against the wall, and Mick noticed that he was also covertly studying the group.

The side door opened suddenly, and David Ridell came out looking at his watch. "Our information is that there are three Russian GRU agents at the hotel, but at this moment, two have gone to supper together. This is the moment, gentlemen. Good hunting, and if this thing doesn't work, I hope you make it home in one piece."

He motioned for Huey, Dewy and Louie to move out. Mick got up with the others and headed to the door. There was no talking, but all eyes were on them until they reached the hall. They were all dressed in loose fitting, worn clothes, partly to hide the assortment of weapons they carried, and they left by the apartment building side door, blending into the street and staying separated by 200 meters while working their way toward the hotel by differing routes. Instructions were to enter the hotel side entrance, and in case they were questioned, use the supplied passes identifying them as part of the maintenance staff.

As Mick turned the corner to the hotel employee entrance, he saw Tom being stopped by a heavy man in a baggy dark suit standing in the door. GRU. He took the card from Tom and studied it carefully looking back and forth between the card and Tom's face. If he were to start to pat Tom down, Mick knew that Tom would react quickly with deadly force. Mick held his breath while advancing on the scene with ever-quickening steps. The guard handed Tom the card and made way for him to enter. He caught sight of Mick coming toward him and stepped out onto the sidewalk to face him. Mick looked him up and down quickly. Big, strong, but fat and likely slow. He pulled out his worn ID card and reached it toward the guard. *"Ночная смена, Товарищп,"* he said with a smile. Silently, the guard took the card while not looking away from Mick's eyes. After a time, he closely studied the card and turned it over a couple of times. Mick tensed, ready for action. The man handed the card back and stood aside glaring intently at him as he passed. That one would have to be the first taken out, Mick thought. There was another guard somewhere if two were out for supper. There was also the possibility that there were more guards around than spotted previously.

Once inside, he spotted Tom motioning to him from farther down the hall. He hurried there, and Tom pulled him through a side door. Tom held up a set of keys smiling. "What's that?" Mick asked.

"This is a set of passkeys."

Mick became aware of a noise and turned to the sound. There on the floor was a middle-aged lady dressed in a white smock. She was lying on the floor face up, trussed securely with a gag in her mouth. Her eyes looked wildly and pleadingly at him.

"There is a box of tools across the room against the wall," Tom said, pointing.

Mick pulled it forward with his foot. He cast around, spotting a small set of lockers. Opening one, he found a white smock similar to the one covering the lady on the floor. He threw it to Tom and, after opening two more lockers, found one for himself. After putting them on, Mick picked up the toolkit, and they returned to the hallway. Mick paused, looking both ways and listening. Steve should have been in by now. Something had changed. They looked at each other knowing that the plan had gone awry already. There was no choice except to proceed, and they headed toward the door leading to the lobby. Pausing at the entryway, without drawing attention to themselves, they had a quick look around. No one was in sight except the clerks behind the registration desk. Trying to act as if they belonged, they headed across a short section of the floor toward the staircase and opened the door. Once through, they stopped to listen for activity. There was a frightening stillness. They silently headed upward toward the third floor, watching and listening as they climbed. The door to the third floor was locked from the hall side. Tom reached for his passkeys and tried three before the cylinder turned. Very slowly, Tom cracked the door to listen for activity and then a little wider to look at least one way. Room 336 was in the other direction, and there could be a guard sitting in front of the room. There was no way to tell what was waiting in the hall. Tom slowly closed the door.

"We have to secure the hall, one way or the other," Tom said. He shrugged, stood upright, and opened the door fully. Tom looked both ways, let the door go and headed down the hall toward the target's room. Mick blocked the door from closing all the way and listened. There was some conversation going on, but he couldn't make out the words. Hearing sounds of scuffling, Mick pushed into the hall. Tom had a guard by the neck from the rear and was holding his wrist in the other hand. There was a large pistol hanging from the man's waist, and he was trying to reach it. Mick sprinted the distance and hit the man hard in the abdomen, and as he was sliding toward the floor, Mick plucked out the gun from his waist. Tom leaned over the man and lifted his head away from the hard floor and sharply snapped it down again. They quietly dragged the unconscious man toward the staircase.

"What now?" Tom asked.

Mick grimaced, "Something happened to Steve. He would be here by now. I have a bad feeling about this." Tom silently nodded agreement.

There was sudden muffled gunfire, a pistol from the sound. An automatic weapon returned fire and then silence. Tom and Mick continued to stand in the otherwise empty hall outside of room 336. There was another couple of handgun shots heard from a more distant location. They could hear footsteps coming from the closed door to the stairs. Both drew handguns and pointed them in the direction of the sound.

The door burst open and Borisky appeared looking a bit wild with his Beretta already in his hand. "Compromised," he shouted while running toward 336 and urgently knocking on the door. After a long moment, the door cautiously cracked open, and Borisky pushed it hard, slamming the occupant backward. Mick caught a glimpse of an older balding man looking with fright at Borisky who raised his pistol and fired three shots into the man's face.

"It's over, boys," he said in heavily-accented English. "You are on your own, I'm afraid. Try to get out quickly. I'm going to look over this room for any papers Ozker may have brought with him and then get out if I can. Hurry now." He waved them away with the gun still in his hand.

They both sprinted for the hall door. Just as the door was closing behind them, a machine pistol rattled from inside the hall, and one round went through the partially open door, ripping a jagged hole. They stepped over the unconscious guard and took the steps down, three at a time. At the ground level, they stopped and listened to the hotel main lobby. There was commotion but no gunfire. They both straightened up and put their guns back under their coats and walked calmly into the lobby. There were several suited men standing with guns drawn and two bodies on the floor. Mick and Tom strode toward the door to the service corridor. Just as they entered, someone called out, "остановитесь тут же," from somewhere behind them, and Mick pulled the door closed. Tom sprinted down the hall toward the exit door as Mick stopped and drew out his machine pistol. Simultaneously, Tom opened the exit door on the far end, and the door near Mick opened to the silhouettes of two dark-suited Russians, guns drawn. Mick opened fire, and they fell together, blocking the door. Loud yelling erupted from in the lobby, and Mick sprinted for the exit. The door was again closed, and he assumed that Tom was waiting on the other side. He slammed it open, catching sight of legs and shoes lying on the sidewalk, and pulling back just in time to miss several bullets tearing through the door from the other side. The door swung partially shut from the impact of the bullets, and Mick hesitated. Sounds from the lobby were getting louder. The door started to swing open on rebound, and Mick fired a short burst of automatic fire through the door, then pushed it fully open.

Tom was sprawled on the left where he fell after getting shot. The large guard was lying on the other side. Mick spun around and sprayed bullets down the hall toward the lobby door, then sprinted across the street away from the hotel. The sun had gone down, and in the glow of twilight, he was still visible. He jumped a stone wall and stopped, listening, trying not to breath, while crouched. There was loud shouting coming from the hotel. He surveyed the terrain for possibilities of escape. The farther he got from the hotel area without being spotted, the better his chances were going to be. Behind him was an older residential building adjacent to a small trash-filled alley. He stood up and walked steadily toward the street on the far side, trying to act like he belonged there and was not fleeing. He discarded the nearly empty machine pistol in a trash can and quickly shed the white smock, leaving it with the gun. Mentally, he went over his assets. The Beretta had four extra magazines, each holding fourteen rounds of 9mm. Two small hand grenades were strapped to his waist. An ID card identifying him as Ukrainian was in his pants pocket and sewn into his coat were several other ID cards for different areas. There was folding money stitched into his belt. Enough, he thought, with any luck.

Chapter 15

Chapter 16

Escape From The Crimea

Sevastopol, Ukraine

Screaming sirens converged on the hotel, still only a block away. Mick turned right, up a residential street, taking his time, trying to walk normally but inspecting the alleys as he passed them. A car turned onto his street somewhere behind him, and its headlights danced his silhouette on the sidewalk as the car approached. He reached into his coat and gripped the handgun tightly but continued to walk as if he were part of the community. The car behind him slowed, causing him want to turn and look, but he knew that he would be blinded by the headlights so he continued to walk without hurry. The car accelerated and came to a stop at the curb beside him. Mick spun toward the car, gun in his hand.

"No, No, Huey," the voice pleaded. "Please, quickly get in. We have to get away. Quickly, please." In his gun sights, Mick saw the face of the Turk Major. Without a word Mick jerked the car door open, and they sped away. There was no one else in the car.

"Major Karamat? Yes?" Mick asked.

The Major answered, "Yes, and you are Huey, I believe," he said. He turned a corner sharply, then looked at Mick a little longer. "What happened upstairs? Is Ozker still there?"

"Yeah, Ozker is still there, but he no longer has a face. Borisky took care of it," Mick answered. "Major, where are the others?"

"Fifteen minutes after you three left, the men we knew as Borisky and Fredrick were sent out. That left six of us to get the cars and wait until signaled. We were spread out, as a result, I couldn't see the van from where I was parked. Gunfire started from that direction. There were three in the van including Ridell and two in the second car. I was alone in this car to provide room for when you came out. After the gunfire started, the second car started toward the hotel, and I followed. Over the radio, they said that they wanted to rescue anyone who came out so we all went over there. They were about a block in front of me, and when they stopped in front of the hotel, they started firing into the lobby. I could see that gunfire was being returned, and the car burst into flames. I turned and got a few blocks away as fast as I could, just now returning to find anyone trying to escape. So far, you are the only one."

Mick asked, "Major, can you ride a motorcycle?"

Major Karamat glanced at Mick and responded, "Motorcycles are a way of life for many Turks. We all can ride one."

Mick started looking carefully at parking areas as they passed and found what he wanted. A small bar with a blinking neon sign was set back from the street, several dark riderless motorcycles waited out front. "Pull over here, Major," he said. The car stopped with a jerk, and Mick got out and walked toward the tavern, scrutinizing the bikes. He saw two which had larger displacement motors than the others, and he looked them over more carefully. "These two will do, Major. Okay with you?" The Major nodded agreement from the car.

Mick took note of the license plate numbers and went inside the bar. Once inside, he looked around the dimly lit and smelly room. He was noticed, and most of the patrons turned to look at him. Mick glared back and pulled back his coat far enough that his pistol was slightly visible. "*Полиция*," he said menacingly. Invoking the name of the police usually got people's attention. In Russian, he asked for the owners of the license plates he read out to step forward. After some hesitation, two rather burly fellows came away from the group.

"Outside," he commanded, pointing with his thumb, and followed them outside. "Give me the keys to your motorcycles," he said with authority and held out his hand. Grudgingly, they placed the keys in his hand. He pointed to the car with the Major behind the wheel and said, "Go with this officer to headquarters." The two made protest and became angry until Mick drew his pistol. The Major nodded his approval and drove away with the two men in the back seat. Mick waited in the shadows around the corner of the bar until the Major came walking back. He nodded and winked to Mick as an indication that he had taken care of the problem. Mick didn't ask what had happened and didn't want to know. They each selected a bike and rode away into the night. After several miles, they pulled over to discuss plans.

"Any ideas, Major?" Mick asked.

"We have a boat waiting in Yalta, about 125 kilometers from here. If we can get there before dawn, we can get out. It was my responsibility to plan the escape route. We are going to take the road through the mountains, because they might block the roads by the sea. I know the route well. It's in my head," he said pointing to his temporal area. Mick was encouraged by the Major's confidence. He suggested that they first find petrol for the bikes, and the Major agreed. When they stopped by some pumps, the Major had another surprise. He tossed Mick a wallet from one of the bikers they had captured. Money and ID. Could be useful, Mick thought and smiled at the Major's resourcefulness. They were able to get some *selyodka* on black bread at the petrol station before heading into the mountains east of Sevastopol, and they ate ravenously, knowing that food wouldn't be available again for some time.

The motorcycles Mick had selected were Dneprs and, fortunately, had the usual side cars removed. They were rugged, heavy, not particularly fast, and worse, the headlight was marginal for the dark mountain road they were using. The road rose higher and higher and was heavily switchbacked. Mick instructed the Major to go ahead of him in case his motorcycle skills were low, at least he wouldn't get left behind. After success with a couple of very tight corners on gravel, he felt better about the Major making it to Yalta.

The mountain air turned chilly as they climbed into the night, but fortunately there was very little vehicle traffic on the twisting narrow road. Mick's thoughts wandered back to Anna and her charms as he followed the lead motorcycle through the night. They had spent a glorious day together on his last day of leave. Thinking about her summoned her charming face in front of him as if he were back in Munich again. They had sat together in a park under the swaying trees, and the shadows played on her face in the sweet air. The more he looked at her and heard her voice, the more in love he became. They sat with shoulders touching and talked lowly for privacy but said nothing. Her eyes smiled at him, he remembered, and the blue of the sky mingled with her blue eyes in a pool that he could never stop falling into. He became aware of her breathing, and the subtle swell of her chest struck him with the magic of life itself. They crammed everything into that day that their energy and time would allow, but at this moment, all he could remember was her face.

They started downhill. That meant that Yalta was ahead, but it also meant more danger on the steep, rutted road. A cold rain started, slowly at first, but growing in intensity as the wind started to blow. Neither of them wore a helmet or goggles which forced the speed of descent to slow to a crawl. The temperature continued to plummet, and slowly they both were becoming wet down to the skin. The road relentlessly spiraled down toward the Black Sea, a black serpent slithering through the dark pine forest. At a sharp bend in a switchback, the Major finally took a spill. Their speed was so low that he had time to jump off before the bike went down. Mick stopped, and together they righted the heavy bike.

"Gonna make it, Major?" Mick asked. He could see that the Major was having shaking chills, and Mick felt close to hypothermia himself. His companion didn't answer, letting Mick understand that they both would do what would be required. There was no other choice. From their elevation, they could see the flicker of lights along the coastal area. It wouldn't be much farther.

After another thirty minutes the road flattened out, and they were able to resume some speed, but at the risk of additional chilling. The lights grew closer and structures on the fringes of Yalta came into view. Mick had spent some time studying maps of the area on the way over. After landing in Bucharest, they had travelled by car to the Romanian port of Mangalia before embarking on a small ferry to Sevastopol. The sea leg was 500 kilometers and took overnight. He realized that their present route would emerge from the mountains on the northwest side of Yalta. The harbor was nearly in the city center, and he suspected that the police or the Russian military would likely extend any dragnet all along the coast. How quickly was the question. Looking at it from the Russian side, they could not be sure how many foreign agents were involved and how many were left standing. A quick analysis would lead them to surmise that NATO forces were involved, and, of course, they would suspect CIA involvement. After thinking about what he knew and what the Major had told him, there were only two from the entire group unaccounted for. Steve never showed and may have been apprehended before the action started. Harvey should have been with Borisky but could have been taken or killed in the lobby. Borisky said that they were "compromised" and that could mean that the operation was expected by the Russians, and therefore, meant that somewhere there is a mole. Assuming that the Russians wouldn't actually kill their informant, then the missing two are the primary suspects. He remembered that the van contained three CIA personnel, but the Turk Major was not an eyewitness to what happened during the first attack. So, there are unknowns, and no way to sort it out. His mind wouldn't let it go, and he worried that if there is an informant, the Russians would not only know how many were left but exactly whom they were looking for. If he believed the Turk Major, only two people knew the location of the exit boat and that was the Major, who had arranged it, and David Ritter, who was in charge of the operation but now dead.

They turned sharply east just as the outskirts of the city were reached. The rain continued, unabated, but at least there was only the very infrequent car. Mick got a look at his watch under a brief source of light, 0345 hours. According to the Major, the boat will wait until dawn, no later. Only two hours left. The bikes turned south for a few blocks until the Major gave an arm motion to halt, and they rolled silently into an unlit alley. They both switched off the bikes and got off, dripping water from their clothing.

"Only about four blocks to go until the waterfront. I suggest that we cover the distance on foot from here," the Major said in a low voice.

Mick nodded his agreement, and he looked around to become oriented. The Major pointed down a small side street. Both had been well-trained for military operations, and as they headed out, they naturally separated by some distance, the Major leading. Mick kept the Major in sight and used the shadows as much as possible. The path they took was not straight, and any moving vehicle they saw, necessitated taking an instant change of direction. Gradually, Mick started to hear hissing waves being churned up by the wind, accompanied by the occasional diesel motor of a working boat. The Major put up his forearm in the universal signal to stop. They both stood still and listened. He waved Mick to join him, and when he came up, the Major pointed to a road block on the road that was parallel to the water and near the harbor.

There were several men and two trucks blocking the road, and even from this far away, Mick could see the rifles. Russian Army, he thought. The Major pointed across the street and headed out first. They couldn't be seen from this distance unless there were people watching from the many shadows. Radyanska Square was just ahead, and they moved farther north to cross above the square using a small alley. Moskovaka Street also had to be crossed and was wide and lit with street lamps. Huddled in the alley they studied the street closely, looking for anyone stationary who may be watching. The only thing moving was the occasional delivery truck. They decided to cross the street just as one passed so that its lights would block them from vision at least in one direction, the one from the waterfront where Russian troops were standing. The Major stood upright and confidently strolled slowly across with Mick following a few paces behind. They paused to see if they had been detected but didn't see any threats. There was a park in front of them, full of trees and shadows which would provide cover for another block.

The destination was the docks on the jetty wharf on the Black Sea side of the harbor. The manmade dock was about 500 meters in length and was cluttered with several large boats pulled out of the water for dry dock maintenance. After reaching the long dock, they had good cover among the boats and again walked shoulder to shoulder. The Major pointed out the boat waiting for them near the end of the wharf, silent and bobbing harmlessly in the water. With about 75 meters to go, a man suddenly stepped out of the shadows ahead of them. They stopped as he approached, muscles tensed and alert. Mick looked around, but the man appeared to be alone. He casually opened his coat to have access to his pistol.

"Это - ограниченная область. Вы имеете разрешение быть здесь?" the man requested.

Under his breath, Mick said, "He is asking for our permissions to be here. Let's show him the biker wallets."

Mick stepped forward with the wallet in his hand and extended it to the man as they closed the distance. *"Доброе утро, товарищ,"* he said, smiling. The man accepted the wallet, taking out his flashlight from his pocket and opening the wallet to study its contents. The Major slowly edged behind him while his attention was diverted and suddenly put his arm around the man's neck as Mick restrained his hands. The Major dragged the unconscious man deep into the shadow of a stack of crates. They both crouched in silence with guns drawn. The only sound was the lapping of water near the boats. The dawn was rapidly approaching with slightly more light than minutes before. The Major walked to the boat he had spotted and peered in. A shape emerged from the dark interior of the boat, and they shook hands. The Major summoned Mick with a wave, and he hurried over. There were three crew members hidden on a boat built for big waves in open water, fitted with a high prow and covered deck and wheelhouse. They were ushered below deck with congratulatory slaps on the back from the crew.

A rough-looking sailor came downstairs and started to speak to the Major in rapid Turkish. After he went back to the deck, the Major turned to Mick and said, "Now, actually getting out is next. They were ordered by the harbor police not to leave, so, if we cast off now, we will be pursued. There is at least a day of high speed travel before we can get protection from Turkey." He paused, looking into space thinking the problem through, then resumed, "If we don't get out now, they will search the boat eventually. The Captain says that there is fog out a little way from the harbor, and if we head straight south, then under cover of fog turn northeast to Hurzuf, we may be able to make them think we got away. Tonight, we will try again."

Mick asked, "Is there a place near Hurzuf that we can hide?"

"We have to hide in broad daylight, like we don't have to hide. Otherwise, we may not have any chance to get away," the Major said with gravity.

The engine started, and the boat came alive with noise. Suddenly, the boat lurched forward, and Mick could tell that it was faster than it looked. The boat made a high speed turn to the left, and they braced themselves against the hull. After the boat straightened out, he could hear the slapping of the waves on the hull as the boat moved more on the surface. He thought he could hear sirens in the distance, but the sound was fading fast. After about fifteen minutes, the boat made a sharp turn to the left then continued with a steady throb of the motors and the waves.

"No gunfire," the Major said with a thumbs up grimace.

Mick could see outside through the open cabin door that the sky was a uniform pale grey, and occasionally wisps of fog made it into the wheelhouse. They continued for about an hour, then the engines slowed to a gurgle as they crept forward toward Herzuf. As they bobbed toward the coast, the Captain came back down and spoke to the Major. They discussed the topic vigorously with much pointing back and forth.

After the Captain left for the deck, Mick asked, "What's happening, Major?"

He fingered his mustache and gathered his thoughts, "Herzuf is a famous resort for the Russians and the Ukrainians. There is a very high population of tourists this time of year. That is good for hiding in a crowd, but this boat is not the typical yacht and will stand out. We can't get anywhere near to the city and the beaches because of restrictions, and the fact that we will be seen by fifty thousand people. Our Captain proposes to go past Herzuf to the rocky prominence they call Ayu Dag or The Bear. There is no wharf, only rocks on the far side, but we may be able to anchor during the day there. Frankly, this does not fit my idea of hiding in plain view like we planned."

"This is us on the line here, my friend. Let's go on deck and see for ourselves," Mick suggested.

They both emerged on the small deck aft of the wheelhouse. The coast came into view as the fog diminished and the land grew closer. Mick could see the many multicolored buildings along the beach, extending up the hills behind the city. There was a mountain extending to the sea on the right which was shaped like a sleeping bear. Occasional flashes of sun reflected off of moving autos showing that the place was a lot more active than the rest of the Crimea to the west. The Captain steered a course which would keep them well off of the beach areas, headed to Ayu Dag. Mick and the Major leaned on the rail and watched as the town slid by on their port side. The crew nervously looked behind them and toward the sea which thankfully showed no activity, the fog hiding all but the nearest boats. The sea was mostly calm, and they rode along the swells on water which reflected the ever-bluing sky.

The boat made the gradual transition behind the mammoth rock of Ayu Dag and got a look at the other side. There was a rocky shore with breaking waves strung along a long graceful curve. Somewhat further down the coast as the terrain leveled out, they could see more jetties and colored umbrellas of the beach crowd. A sailing yacht bobbed midway and was moored roughly one hundred meters out from the rocky shore. Small figures could be seen moving about on its deck. The Captain decided to move in near to the moored boat, slowly moving into position about 50 meters from its shoreward side.

As the craft tediously inched into position, some young ladies on the nearby yacht were visible waving to them, and close inspection with binoculars revealed that they were topless, all eight of them. The sailboat was ketch-rigged with sails stowed and seemed to be fully eighteen meters at the waterline. Two blond men came up from below and studied the interloping boat with their own binoculars as the Turkish vessel dropped anchor, settling in for a long day in the sun. The crew passed the binoculars around and chuckled at their luck. When the Captain finally had enough, he dressed them down and pointed out at the sea where he wanted them to watch for patrolling vessels. The crew went about changing the boat's name on the sides and stern and had paint ready for the task. They also painted a decorative color stripe diagonally across the bow with red paint. All the work was done quickly and without direction as if they had done this previously.

About three in the afternoon, a cry came from the crewman on watch, and Mick looked up to see him pointing at the sea beyond the mountain. As they all looked in horror, a grey naval vessel came slowly moving into view. The warship was long and close to the water and looked like a predator hunting for prey. It was following the coast about eight hundred meters from shore, and they nervously watched as it slowly came to a stop. Mick was no expert on the Russian navy but knew that the vessel was about the size of a submarine chaser which would make it about fifty meters in length. Time seemed to stop as they eyed the warship prowling out in the Black Sea to see what it was going to do. The people on the adjacent boat were in a frenzy of activity on deck, and it had something to do with the appearance of the warship hovering off the coast. A flash of dark yellow off the side of the warship let them all know that an inflatable boat full of armed sailors would soon be coming their way.

The Major and the Captain quickly conferred, and they both kept looking at Mick as they talked. After the problem was resolved, the Major came over to him and said, "We are about to be boarded, it seems. You are the only one here who isn't Turk, and you look different. It will be hard to explain. Could you make your way from here back to your base on your own?"

Mick said, "I believe so, Major. That is my training. I have papers and some money that will help, and I also agree that we have run out of luck here."

"Perhaps you should slip away out of their view while you still have time. I am going to try to stay here and pass inspection, and we also have sets of papers with us that we hope will fool them. There is no outrunning that ship or fighting it out with them," the Major said.

Mick hurried below and gathered his things. He took off his shirt and used a borrowed knife to cut his pants off above the knees then strung his shoes together and looped them around his neck. Using the knife, he opened the lining of his coat and removed the pack of passports and ID cards, fastening them under his belt in their waterproof case. The bundle he made of his clothes also contained his weapons and when he tossed it overboard he watched it disappear into the deep green water. Mick quickly shook hands with the crew and saved his last goodbyes for the Major. They stood face to face for perhaps the last time. It had been a good friendship, and they had worked together with mutual trust as if they had always done so.

Wordlessly, they embraced and then shook hands with sincerity. Mick went to the side and started to climb over when he felt the Major's hand patting his back. When he looked up, he could see tears gleaming on that hard rough face, now brimming with emotion. Before letting go the rail, he returned the smile, then slid silently into the cold water.

Once in the water, Mick swam toward the adjacent boat which provided cover as the Russians approached from the other side. The passengers on the yacht realized that he was swimming toward them and started gathering on that side of the deck. Mick waved repeatedly at them to get back, until finally they got the idea and dispersed. He was almost beside the yacht when he heard the outboard motors of the rubber Zodiac boat come by on the way to the Turk boat. Mick went around to the seaward side of the yacht and hid in the shadows of the hull.

Mick held his position by clutching the anchor rope and staying low in the water. Above him he heard a soft female voice calling to him, "Нужны ли вам какие-либо помощь?" She was asking if he needed any help. He looked up at the port rail above him and saw that she was hanging off with her head and shoulders showing. He also noticed that she had put back on some clothing.

Mick decided to ask why her shipmates also appeared afraid of the Russians, *"Почему вы боятся русских?"*

She leaned a little closer to him and put her hand to her lips to form a small megaphone and said, "Pornography." The word was the same in any language. Mick knew that the Russians weren't after them, but that wouldn't stop the Russian marines from searching the yacht when they finished with the Turks. He decided to swim toward the shore in a long diagonal path which would hide him from the nearby

Russian inflatable boat, but this meant that he would be in plain view of the large Russian warship. He hoped that from this distance they wouldn't be able to see him and staying put was even more risky. Once again, he looked up at the young pretty blonde and saw her give him a little wave, then he pushed off trying to keep his arms below the water as he moved forward.

The water became warmer as he neared the shore, but waves were breaking on the rocks, and landing was going to be tricky. He had to time his arrival at the same time as a wave and try to do it without being seen. Emerging from the water, he would be in full view of the warship, and there were probably several pairs of binoculars scanning the area at this moment. Nearly in desperation, he finally spotted a solution. There was an opening between two large boulders, and he could see sunlight on the other side. The pair of rocks would prevent him from being seen as he emerged on land. He had only one chance to get it right. Floating and treading water for a moment, Mick tried to imagine the wave under him as it hit the shore. At last he figured out the timing and let himself be carried on the front side of the small wave. The rocks moved toward him at frightening speed, but the momentum of the wave put him right where he wanted to be, on the sand with rocks hiding him from vigilant eyes on the sea. He scrambled up the back side of the boulders, peeking over at the three boats off shore.

A few Russians could be seen on the deck of the small Turkish vessel, and the remainder on the raft were pointing guns in that direction. He heard a diesel motor start up and realized the yacht was going to try to get under way. "Fools," he called loudly. He could see the Russians on the Turk boat rushing to get back to the inflatable, and they were pointing toward the yacht. From the distant warship, a "whoop, whoop" warning was given. This was a clear signal that the yacht was to cease movement at once. At first, he thought the yacht was going to ignore the warning, but the headway slowly ceased, and the boat started drifting with the wind. All eyes were on the yacht, and it gave him time to start working his way along the rocks, trying to stay as low as possible. He discovered a small trail at the base of the mountain which led in the direction of Herzuf, and the farther he went from the boats the safer he felt.

As he walked toward Herzuf, he had time to put together a new identity for himself, and this time he would become a German tourist. He extracted the German passport which had been fabricated by the CIA and which would pass any inspection. He was fluent in German and looked German. He was confident that it would work, and he picked up his pace. A quick appraisal made him realize that he had no shirt and only cut-off pants, but, after all, aren't tourists in a summer resort expected to do the unexpected? His first task would be finding new clothes, after which he could call one of the numbers he had memorized, contacting the CIA for extraction.

His muscular body did work in his favor, and at the first of the tourist areas he found a couple of attractive Ukrainian girls who willingly offered him a ride to town. They even offered suggestions of suitable clothing stores without ever asking him how he came to be dressed like he was. He had a ready alibi but never got a chance to see how it worked. A long night was spent wandering from night club to bar until dawn.

Early the following morning, he met with a CIA operative at a coffee shop and was passed tickets for a small steamer bound for Greece. From there he easily, and in comfort, traveled overland by train toward Germany and into the welcome arms of the U.S. Army, or so he thought.

Chapter 17

Interrogation

United States Special Forces Base
Stuttgart, Germany

Sweat glistened on their foreheads as they sat in the small debriefing room. Mick faced his questioners across the wooden table as he had done for the past several hours. They had taken his watch, and no clock was visible. This was the second set of interrogators, and this time they were dressed in the uniform of the U.S. Army. One wore a Major's braid, and the other was a First Lieutenant. The scruffy previous team wore civilian clothes, and he had assumed they were from the CIA.

"Lieutenant, we are sure that you understand that your mission to the Crimea was a disaster. Is that not clear to you?" the Major asked again.

Mick responded, "Sir, the mission was successful in that the target was eliminated, but our mission appeared to be expected by the Russians." He decided he wasn't going to back off again. The leak was their problem as far as he was concerned, and he knew that he had done everything by the book and more.

"Lieutenant Grundy, you are to answer the questions only and not give an opinion unless asked.

Do I have to repeat myself all day to you?" the Major rebuked.

"Understood, sir," Mick snapped. He remained at attention, with a straight back, not touching the chair behind him and stared at the wall behind the officers. He noticed that neither one of them could hold that posture for long, and they had given up as the interrogation dragged on.

"Do you have an opinion as to where the a leak might have come from?" the Lieutenant asked more politely.

"Sir, you haven't informed me regarding who were killed, survived or captured, so I can't form an opinion without any information to go on, sir," Mick said to the wall.

Out of his peripheral vision, he could see them confer wordlessly. The Major gave his grudging consent to something, and the Lieutenant shuffled his papers. "The survivors are yourself, Sergeant Harvey Longren and the Turkish officer, Captain Yosef," the Lieutenant said.

Mick must have looked puzzled. "Captain Yosef is the man you knew as Major Karamat," the Lieutenant explained.

"What about Steve, what happened to him?" Mick asked out of turn.

"We don't have enough information yet to be sure what happened to Sergeant Sumker," the Major said. "By the way, Captain Yosef's debriefing supports your summary word for word, and he had a lot positive to say about you."

"Thank you, sir, for telling me. I'm glad to hear that he got away," Mick said.

"One more question regarding that," the Major said, then continued, "He said that the Russian marines pulled out after searching both vessels, but the warship remained guarding the area for another twenty four hours. Captain Yosef said that his men got together with the other boat to pass the time. He says that he wishes that you could have been there. Exactly what did he mean, Lieutenant?" the Major asked.

Mick didn't allow himself to smile and said, "I have no idea, sir. About the other question, I assume that the informant would have survived the mission, sir."

The officers got up without word and left the room. Mick remained at attention and continued to observe the wall. He knew that he was being watched from somewhere, and he wasn't going to give them the satisfaction of letting his guard down. After fifteen minutes or so, the door opened and the Lieutenant came in. "At ease, Lieutenant Grundy," he ordered. Mick remained motionless. The Lieutenant pulled up a chair across from him, and Mick allowed himself to look directly at the other officer.

"Let's just talk this out for a while, Mick. No cameras, no recordings, no tricks, just you and me. We have to figure out how this went bad. The way I look at it, the informant had to actually be there. The CIA man, David Ridell, was a very experienced operative and followed procedure in that each man was told only what he needed to know. He was the only one who knew in advance what the plans were.

The informant got word to the Russian GRU after you all were briefed on the mission by Ridell, and the Russians quickly assembled a team. This wasn't in time to prevent the loss of their spy, however, and they are embarrassed and angry, very angry. We expect some retaliation, but it's anyone's guess as to when and what that will be."

Mick had thought about this a lot. He looked across to the other officer and said, "You know it wasn't me. That leaves Captain Yosef and two others. If the Turk was the informant, he went to a lot of trouble to help me survive. I don't believe that he was the one, because I was around him during some very stressful times, and he is someone you can trust to the limit. I did."

The Lieutenant said, "Well, if you were going to make an ideal cover for yourself, this is how you would do it. Don't you think that if he were the one, saving you was the best way to make us think that he couldn't be an informant?"

Mick thought about it and said, "I see your point, but I was joined at the hip with him during the escape, and I'll never believe that he could be a spy." He looked at the Lieutenant and said, "That leaves two. If you don't know what happened to Steve, have you ruled out Harvey?"

"Harvey's story checks out. He has an exemplary military record, and we have no reason to suspect him any more than we have to suspect you, Mick," the Lieutenant said.

"Lieutenant, I am pretty good with languages. Better than most. Harvey can speak perfect Russian.

I mean perfect. He could fool anyone. Where did he acquire that kind of skill, do you know?" Mick asked.

The Lieutenant studied his nails for a moment, then looked up and said, "I am not authorized to discuss a fellow soldier's record with you. Remember that all of you were chosen for skills in addition to your Army training. I say again, we have no reason to suspect Sergeant Longren. By the way, he is making Second Lieutenant at this moment. Thought you should know. Also, he has voiced some suspicions about you during his debriefing, Mick." The Lieutenant stood. "I think we are finished here. I have been authorized to tell you that you have some leave coming. The Captain's office has a ten-day pass waiting for you. Enjoy."

Chapter 17

Chapter 18

Grandmother Triska

Stuttgart, Germany

Before even going to pick up his pass, Mick ducked into an officer's lounge and dialed Anna's number.

"Ya, hallo?" she said.

The sound of her voice went into him like an electric charge. It had been a month since they had spoken at all. After each of the three previous missions, he had been given a leave of absence, and he spent every possible minute of his free time with Anna. He always went to Munich to see her, and each time he took the train instead of his motorcycle, and she would pick him up at the station. They frequently dined with her mother and father, almost as if they were married. Mick's adoptive parents loved him in their fashion, but they were older, formal in the German way. Physical contact, that is the hugging and kissing part, were never part of his growing up years, so he didn't really miss it, that is until he met Anna. He started to feel that the Michners were his new family, and he was grateful that they treated him as one of them.

Anna, though, was not family. Feelings about her came from deep within him, and he couldn't get enough of being with her. He dreamed about her in his sleep and thought about her while he was awake. If he could count the times in a day he thought about her, it would likely be in the thousands. When he was with her, he kept noticing little feminine things about her, such as a displaced tuft of hair and how absolutely beautiful it was. The little downy hair on the back of her neck, when she had her hair up, was fascinating to him. He thought there would never be enough time in life to see all the beauty that she wears so well, yet he was always amazed when he discovered, time and time again, that she is innocently unaware of how beautiful she is.

"Anna, it's me," Mick said into the phone.

"*Geliebter*, you have returned safe to me again!" she bubbled. "Where are you now?" she asked.

"I'm still in Stuttgart. I haven't even packed my bag. I just got in yesterday," he said.

Anna said, "I have a surprise for you, Mick. This time I am coming to you, and I'll leave as soon as I can."

"Where are you staying tonight, Anna?" he asked. He was afraid of her answer. Afraid that she was going to say that she was going to be with him. He knew that it was coming soon, longed for the day it would happen, but he was so afraid of displeasing her or disappointing her that in some ways he dreaded it. He worried many times how it might mess things up for them. He always treated her like she was a precious treasure, one that he was afraid to set down too hard lest it break. She was the best thing that ever happened to him, and she was the only person that he had ever loved, or who had ever loved him, and he couldn't lose her.

"I am staying with my *Großmutter Triska*. I can't wait for you to meet her. I have told her all about you!"

Relief, disappointment, happiness, it all was mixed up inside him. "I also am looking forward to meeting her. Your father speaks so highly of her. Can I come get you, Anna?"

"Silly. You have a motorcycle, and I have luggage. They don't mix. *Großmutter* will come for me. You can meet us at her house. I'll call you when we are there, and you can come for dinner. Yes?"

"I'll be ready. By the way, I have ten days this time."

"Ooh, too much, Mick. I may have to quit school because of you. This may be a problem for us, but we can talk about it tonight. Yes?"

"I love you, Anna."

"Now you have made me cry, Mick. I cry happy tears, though. I also love you with all my heart, but you know that," she said. "I will try to leave soon. Wait for my call."

Mick knew from experience that the train from Munich took two hours and twenty minutes. He consulted his watch. He guessed that she would arrive about 5:00 p.m. He decided to go get a shower, get changed and perhaps a quick bite to eat. He almost forgot how tired he was.

The interrogation had started the previous evening, and they went at him all night trying to trip him up. There was a spy somewhere, they all knew it. In his heart, he knew it couldn't be the Turk Captain. It was an American who was the spy. There were too many unnecessary deaths because of that spy, and resulting events had almost swept up all of them. He suddenly changed his mind about the shower and headed to the barracks, determined to meet Harvey face to face. Mick pushed open the double door and asked the private manning the registration desk where Longren was. The private looked at his books and said that he didn't know, but Lieutenant Longren wasn't in the barracks at this time.

Mick walked into the long corridor and found a group of GI's talking. "Anyone here know Sergeant Longren?" Mick asked them.

"Sure, Lieutenant," one said.

"Who does he hang around with, anyone know?" Mick asked.

They conferred and said, "Mostly Sergeant Smith, they seem to run together lately," the man answered.

"Know where Smith is?" Mick asked.

"Probably in his bunk. We had an all night march last night, and we just came in. Try over at the end of the E wing."

Mick thanked them and headed that way. He found the Sergeant's room easily and knocked on the door. No answer. He knocked louder and finally heard some noise. A very large black fellow in his underwear pulled the door open. He looked angry but when he saw Mick's insignia he softened. "Yes, sir, you looking for me?"

Mick said, "Look, Sergeant Smith, I heard about last night, but I need you to answer a couple of questions for me, please."

"Sure, sir. Come on in and sit on the bed, if you will," he backed up and let Mick in. Mick closed the door behind him.

"I'll get to the point, Sergeant. I have known Sergeant Longren for a long time. We just got back from a mission together," Mick said.

Sergeant Smith interrupted him and said, "Yeah, I heard about that one. Pretty bad, wasn't it?"

"Yeah, it was. Say, how well do you know Longren anyway?"

"We go drinking and looking for girls at times, but I wouldn't say I know him. In fact, I don't really know anything about him other than he is a pretty friendly guy and knows all the hot spots."

"I know what you mean, Sergeant. I've been around him for years, and I can say that I don't know him either. You know that he speaks Russian?"

"Gee, I didn't know anything about that. I know that he doesn't speak German and really doesn't seem to like the Germans, other than the girls, you know."

"Ever heard him talk about the States, like where he was from?"

"We talked about U.S. cities at times. Ball clubs a lot. Say, I don't think I ever asked him about his home. I don't remember he ever talked about stuff like that."

"What you say is also my experience. Thanks for our talk, and I think I should let you get back to sleep. By the way, you should keep this conversation private, know what I mean?"

"Yes, sir, I get your meaning. It does give me something to ponder though,"

This time, Mick did make it to the showers and tried to put the questions behind him and think only of Anna whom he would at last see again and soon.

She called about 5:45 p.m., and Mick answered on the first ring. "Mick, dearest, I am with my grandmother, and she asks you to dinner here. You may come at any time. She has a small apartment on Alexanderstrasse in the 600 block. When you come, I will be waiting to show you in."

"I have my motor already started. It should take me about twenty minutes to get there, and I am very anxious to give you all the kisses I have been saving!"

Anna giggled, and they hung up. Mick quickly consulted a map, memorized the route and headed out. He cruised slowly down the Alexanderstrasse which seemed to be an endless row of apartment buildings. Ahead, he saw Anna in a white dress waving at him, and as he drew close, she pointed to an available parking space. She threw her arms around his neck before he could get his helmet off, and after he did, they embraced again with that eager intensity of love. Her tears made his face slick, and he could taste the slight saltiness of them as they kissed.

Kissing and crying made Anna's face slightly red and puffy. "Oh, what will Grandmother think?" she said as she patted her face and smiled at her sweet dilemma.

"Your grandmother will think that you are in love, and I'm sure she had the same problem in her youth," Mick answered. He held her at arm's length and said, "You are more beautiful than ever. It almost hurts my eyes to look at you!"

She smiled and playfully punched his hard shoulder. "Come on, she is waiting!" They started climbing the stairs to the fifth floor. As they approached the door, it opened and a small elderly lady beckoned them inside.

She was short but lean, erect and moved quickly and with purpose.

Bright, penetrating, youthful blue eyes made her face alive and appealing. She gave Mick an up and down appraisal and nodded her approval. She abruptly stuck out her hand in a masculine way, saying, "I'm Triska Michner; you must be Mick Grundy." The words were spoken with perfect and unaccented American English. Mick could hardly believe that she was anything but an American. She saw his face change and was amused by his stunned look as they shook hands. "English was one of my skills, Mick, useful on both sides of the Iron Curtain. I understand that you have mastered several languages also, is this true?"

"I am honored to be here, Frau Michner, and I have heard so much about you from your family. To answer your question, I do well with languages. It is about all that I do know other than what the Army has taught me."

"Mick, we are to be friends and friends go by first names. I will call you Mick, and you are to call me Triska. Would that work for you?"

"Of course, Triska. Thank you very much for considering me a friend."

"You better be a friend, Mick, if you are kissing my granddaughter that hard," Triska said, twisting her thumb toward Anna's reddened face. They all had a laugh.

Mick felt that he was being probed by a higher order of intelligence. Triska listened carefully to everything Mick said and watched him intently, obviously forming an opinion of him. She was a gracious hostess and insisted on a small glass of sweet white wine before dinner. Mick could see that the table was already set and food nearby in covered dishes. The apartment, the furniture and even Triska were all small but very efficient. They sat down for dinner, and Triska, with seductive intensity, gently probed Mick for his attitudes on about everything from politics to international energy policies. She even had a good working knowledge of fast motorcycles and tested him about his knowledge of famous racers. Spend an evening with Triska, and she would eventually find out everything you ever knew, and she would do it with disarming smiles and charm. In their conversations, Triska switched effortlessly between German, English, French, Italian and Russian and watched him carefully to gauge his comprehension and response. In return, he did the same, and when they met eyes, it was clear that there was a developing mutual respect.

"Mick, I know that you can't talk about it, but I understand that you have been on some covert missions. I want to be frank with you and tell you that I still have contacts in the *BND*, or what you may call the *Bundesnachrichtendienst*. They have good cooperation from the American Intelligence services based on German soil. We work together very closely. We have better relations with the Americans than with anyone else in intelligence. I am aware of what you have been doing, and I also know about the most recent event," Triska said with a little grin. She knew that he would be stunned to learn that his girlfriend's grandmother was still a spy. "If you are dating my precious granddaughter, that gives me the right to check you out. By the way, you pass with flying colors."

Mick noticed that Anna was beaming with her grandmother's praise of him. "You know a lot, Triska, but it's dangerous to possess this kind of information as I'm sure you do understand. I have never talked with Anna about anything I do... I wish I could tell her, but even a wife can't be told. It puts us all in danger to discuss national secrets."

"Yes, that is what we are told, Mick. There is another side of things, though, where knowledge is strength. We won't discuss this anymore in front of Anna, but I offer you my insight and also my connections should you ever need them. You may find that things get murky in your business, and sometimes it's very hard to tell who is a friend or the one you must mistrust."

Mick looked out the window at the building across the street and said, "Triska, I already have that problem."

"Mick, I have to tell you this last thing. There is a double agent working your side. We at the BND are intent on finding him using a different approach from what your people are doing, and we are working with the Americans. If I tell you not to trust anyone, you couldn't do your job. You have to trust people. Your life depends on it. Keep your eyes and ears open, though, until he is caught," she said.

"Do they know who it is, Triska?" Mick asked.

"We are not certain and neither are your people, but we are down to a very short list," Triska said.

The subject thankfully changed, and Triska entertained them with tales of when she was young and in love. Time went by too fast as Mick found Triska to be as wonderful as all the other members of Anna's family that he had met. He sat beside Anna on the couch, and they leaned against each other while talking to Triska, who sat across from them.

"Have you two consummated your relationship?" Triska asked frankly and without emotion in her voice.

Anna instantly turned red and looked toward Mick to gauge his reaction. He had no outward physical change, but inside his head was different. Without warning, Mick was faced with discussing a subject that he and Anna had not yet considered, openly at least, "Well, I suppose that is your business, Triska, especially after our previous discussions. No, not in the physical sense. Speaking for myself, I am deeply in love with Anna. I can't begin to express all the feelings I have for her, and I haven't even been able to tell her anything other than the simple 'I love you.' There is a fear that I have of doing something wrong that would cause me to lose her. Also, it isn't fair to Anna to go that far with someone who might not come back someday." He could feel Anna tightening her grip on his arm as he spoke.

"A fool could tell that Anna loves you, Mick. I don't need to ask her. One comment I have for you both. Which would be better if Mick doesn't come back, to complete the love you share or to be left wondering what it would have been like? The difference is in the memories."

Mick found himself even less sure of what he should do. He felt that Anna loved him as he did her, but he also suspected that she would never get over him if he were killed. It might be a burden to her the rest of her life. He felt guilty now about her feelings for him. It was risk in a different way than what he had already experienced in the field. Triska appeared to suggest that they should have a physical relationship, but Mick knew Anna well enough to know that an additional level of love may make losing him even more unbearable. He had been thinking about it only from his point of view. Now he could see the risks she was taking being with him.

It was clear that guys like Harvey, who only wanted female companionship for sex, may be more right than he thought. If they lived to be discharged from the Army, they could always find someone, if they had any feelings left to share, that is. Mick's problem was that he was in love and so was Anna. Emotion that powerful can't ever be taken back without pain. Love for Anna would last for the rest of his life, even if they separated, and would continue regardless of how they separated. The only difference would be variations of the same pain if they parted. He resolved that he would never ask her to go farther than they had gone. If he could somehow remain alive for the next several months, when his enlistment came up again, he would resign and offer to marry Anna.

The wall clock and his wristwatch said the same thing. Nearly midnight. He felt suddenly heavy from fatigue. Anna noticed and guessed correctly that he should be in bed. "Mick, my dear, you should get some sleep." Triska stopped talking and was watching him for a response. He got up and momentarily looked confused.

"Gee, you are right. I better get on my way. I didn't realize the time."

Triska wrapped her arms around his waist and looked up at him. "You are too good to lose, Mick. You will be careful on the way back to your bunk, please?" He nodded yes and bent down and kissed her on the forehead.

"Triska, you may be my friend, but I wish you were my grandmother, too," he said.

"Easily arranged, Mick," she said with a wink.

"I'll walk with you downstairs to your bike, Mick," Anna offered.

"No, you won't. I'm too tired to beat up muggers tonight," Mick said and then swept her up in his arms, leaving her feet dangling. They were face to face and nearly nose to nose. "Did I tell you how much I love you tonight, Anna?" he said nearly in a whisper.

"Only once," she answered.

"I love you, Anna." Then kissed her briefly and put her down. He scooped up his worn jacket and helmet, and with one last look at the four blue eyes watching him, he slowly closed the door.

"I love you, Mick," Anna said from behind the closed door, just loud enough for him to hear.

Chapter 19

The Chase Starts

U.S. Special Forces Base
Stuttgart, Germany
0817 Hours

L ieutenant. Lieutenant, wake up," the voice said. A hand was on his shoulder, shaking him. "Wake up, sir, the Captain wants to see you ASAP," the voice said. Mick rolled over and, with one eye, looked at this rude jerk.

"Go away, soldier, I'm on leave. I'm not getting up yet," Mick said and turned over.

"That won't do, sir. The Captain gave me orders to bring you right away, and he outranks you," the Corporal said. The patting on the shoulder continued.

Mick sat up rubbing his face. "Do I have time to take a shower?" Mick asked into his hands.

"No, sir, the Captain said you are to come at once."

Mick threw on his dress pants, shoes and shirt and grabbed a tie to put on as they walked. "What does the Captain want, Corporal?"

"I'm sorry, sir, he didn't tell me. He does have a civilian in the office with him, if that helps."

In silence, they walked across the manicured lawn to the Command buildings, taking the stairs two at a time. Mick was fully awake by this time, and his mind was spinning with questions. The Sergeant On Duty saluted Mick and opened the door for him. "Lieutenant Grundy, sir," he announced. As Mick came in, he surveyed the room. The Captain was in his usual position behind his desk. A civilian, dressed in a dark suit, stood when Mick entered. The man was youthful, but his age was hard to determine. The suit hid the man's physique, but Mick could see that he was very fit. An American, Mick guessed to himself.

"Lieutenant Grundy, this is Ron Zeskie from the CIA. I think you should hear what he has to say." Mick extended his hand, and they shook briefly. I was right, Mick thought, the man is very fit.

Zeskie spoke directly to Mick. "I have read your file and the results of your debriefing. I want to say that you conducted yourself in an outstanding way in your recent mission. You are a merit to the Armed Forces of the United States."

Bullshit, Mick thought. Why is he really here?

"Since you returned from your mission, we have intercepted several attempts by hackers to read your military file. Someone is interested in you, Lieutenant, and we haven't been able to discern who or why as yet. The probes aren't from a friendly. They would come right out and ask. It would seem obvious that the effort is related to your recent mission, and it proves that someone knows which men we sent and the names of those who got away. You went off base briefly last night. Were you aware of being followed?"

"No, Mr. Zeskie. I ride a motorcycle, and I ride hard. I don't think I can be followed by anyone while I'm on it."

"Unless there is a tracking device on your bike," he hinted. "Mind if we get some of your military people to sweep it before you ride it again?"

"I'll answer that," the Captain said. "Sergeant Jones," he bellowed. The door opened immediately.

"Sir?" the Sergeant said.

"Request a team to sweep Lieutenant Grundy's motorcycle for any electronic devices. Right now. And tell them to report their findings as soon as they are done."

"Yes, sir," the Sergeant snapped.

Mick said, "Mind if I ask a question, Mr. Zeskie?"

"I'll answer any question that I'm authorized to, Lieutenant."

"Has the same probing been directed at Sergeant, I mean, Lieutenant Longren?"

"I am not authorized to answer that question," Zeskie responded, but not meeting his eyes.

Mick looked at the Captain, but his face was impassive. Mick stood there waiting and expecting more discussion, hoping that he could be told if Harvey was even suspected or had been absolutely ruled out. The Captain arose from his chair and said, "Lieutenant, you are to wait in the hall until the sweep is complete. This should alert you to proceed with caution when you are off the base. I want to know immediately if you observe any suspicious activity. Am I clear on that?"

Mick saluted sharply and said, "Sir, yes, sir," and held the salute until it was returned. The door behind him opened, and the Sergeant made it obvious that Mick was dismissed. There was a chair pulled up to the wall, and he walked over and slumped down.

"Could I get you some coffee, sir?" Sergeant Jones asked, and without waiting for an answer, he produced a steaming cup and handed it to Mick. Mick nodded thanks and settled in for a long wait. He was about to call Anna, who was likely up by now, but before he could reach for his phone, the Captain's door opened, and the Captain leaned out and looked at both the Sergeant and at Mick.

"You will surrender your phone to the Sergeant, Lieutenant," the Captain ordered. "Have someone bring him a clean phone, Sergeant. That means right now." And the door closed. As ordered, Mick dug into his pocket and surrendered the phone into the capable Sergeant Jones' hand. Sergeant Jones was just entering the Captain's door when Mick's phone rang. The door closed while it was still ringing, but it stopped at three rings. Someone answered it, Mick thought.

After a few minutes, the Captain's door opened again, and Zeskie came out. "I answered your call from Anna, Lieutenant. I told her that your phone was being serviced and that you would call her on a new phone shortly. She seemed to understand. Do you?"

"Mr. Zeskie, I feel that I am being singled out. Do you people suspect me of being the mole?"

"The case isn't closed yet, Lieutenant. We are being very thorough, as we should be. We are aware of your contacts with Anna Michner and her family, including her grandmother, Triska Michner. They have been checked out by us and by German Intelligence. One thing, however, make no more contact with her brother, Kurt. We know that you only met him once, but you would be wise to avoid any more contact of any kind with him."

Sergeant Jones appeared with a new phone in his hand and silently passed it to Mick. Mick looked it over. It appeared normal enough except it was heavier than he expected. Zeskie saw his careful inspection and clarified, "That phone is clean and cannot be traced. Use only that phone for any conversation."

Mick asked, "Will my conversations be monitored by you?"

"Of course, Lieutenant."

After Zeskie left, Mick called Anna to tell her not to worry, that he was tied up but would call her shortly.

"*Mein Schatz*, is everything all right?" she asked sweetly.

"Just paperwork, Anna. I'll be able to see you soon. Don't worry, please," he said. He knew that someone was listening, but now he also knew that they had always been listening. They knew every move he had made, had been somewhere watching everywhere he had gone with Anna, everything they did, everything they said. It made him feel dirty. He wondered if they really knew about Triska. Was she really with the BND, or was she on the other side?

There was no one to ask. If she was really BND, and they didn't know she was still active, he didn't want to expose her, especially since there was a real spy somewhere. He also didn't really know who on his side to trust any longer. It was just as Triska said. There is no one to trust except yourself.

The phone rang at Sergeant Jones' desk, and he picked it up on the first ring.

"Captain Ritter's office, Sergeant Jones speaking," he said, efficiently, as he had twenty or more times in the last half hour. "Yes, sir. Thank you, sir. I will tell him right away."

Sergeant Jones got up and headed to the Captain's door. Before he opened it, he looked at Mick and whispered, "They found one," and disappeared inside. He was inside only briefly when again the door opened, and Mick was summoned to come in.

The Captain was again behind his desk. "Your motorcycle was being monitored with a tracking device, Lieutenant. The question is, when and where was it placed, and of course, by whom. It could have been there for some time. The device will be sent to a lab in the States to identify its origin, but meanwhile, we have a problem. You may be in danger, and you may put anyone you are with in danger. We don't know if someone wants to kill you, capture you or even entrap you. I advise you to stay on base until this is resolved."

Mick spoke up, "Sir, may I ask you something?"

"You can try. Go ahead."

"If I was monitored by our Intelligence people for some time, as it appears that I was, how come they didn't see someone spying on me and planting bugs and so forth?"

"Good question, Lieutenant. I have no answers for you."

"Another thing, sir, can I trust the CIA to monitor me? After all, our mission was directed by them, and it was a massive failure."

The Captain looked surprised and said, "Of course, you can trust them. They are on our side for heaven's sake. Besides, you have no choice here, Lieutenant."

"Sir, unless you order me not to, I have leave coming, and I want to enjoy it off base. Besides, we might as well let the other side show their hand."

"I don't like it, Lieutenant Grundy, but I won't stop you. Be wary, son," he said with a hint of actual affection.

Mick came to attention and saluted the Captain before leaving. As he went out, he stopped at Sergeant Jones' desk. "Sergeant, I want to talk to the sweep team. Who are they, and where can I find them?"

Without answer, the Sergeant picked up the phone and punched in a number. "This is Captain Ritter's office, Sergeant Jones speaking. Can I send the Lieutenant, whose bike you examined this morning, over to talk with you? Right, thank you, sir." He hung up and quickly wrote the address down and handed it to Mick. "Good luck, sir," he said.

Mick went to the building address given to him. As he approached, a Lieutenant came forward to meet him. "You Grundy?"

"Expecting me?"

"My team swept your motorcycle. It's still where you left it. We found a two centimeter circular device on a magnetic base attached to the underside of the tank. Otherwise, the bike is clean."

"Did that CIA guy in the dark suit show up after you finished?"

"You mean Zeskie? Yes, he came by as we were getting done to be sure the bike was clean," the Lieutenant said.

"Was he alone with the bike after you finished?"

"He was there when we pulled out."

Mick frowned, "Think you could go over it again, Lieutenant?"

"Isn't Zeskie CIA?" the Lieutenant asked.

"That's what he said, but we, Lieutenant, are Army. We watch over our own, don't we?"

The Lieutenant reached into his pocket and dialed a number. "Bradick, get the gear and go over that bike from this morning again. Yes, right now."

When the Corporal came out with a suitcase of gear, the three walked down to the parking area and found Mick's bike. Immediately, the alarm went off on the sweep device, causing the Corporal to dig into the fold of the seat against the tank, pulling out a small device with his finger.

"Gee, Lieutenant, I don't see how I missed this before," the Corporal said.

"That SOB bugged your bike after we left," the Lieutenant said to Mick.

"Thanks, guys. Say, would you mind going over it again?" Mick asked.

The Corporal went over every possible spot on the bike with no more hits.

"Sir, it appears clean, but there are devices which only go off with some sort of trigger, like time. With that type, you usually will miss it unless you are lucky," the Corporal informed him.

"I can't trust it then?"

The Lieutenant and the Corporal both chimed in, "Not completely."

Mick thanked them both and walked toward the barracks. An idea hit him, and he sped up and pushed the doors open with a thud. He looked around from room to room until he found the man he was looking for. "Renolds," he called across the room. A tall fellow with bright red hair straightened up from the pool table. Mick waved him over to a quiet corner.

"Hey, Renolds, you are always admiring my bike, aren't you?"

"You know, I am, Mick. Say, do you mind if I call you Mick, Lieutenant?"

"Hell no, Renolds. We go way back. You can drop the sir stuff when we are alone, you know that," Mick said. "Say, how would you like to trade bikes for a while to see how you like mine?"

"What's the catch, Mick? I know how you feel about that bike. You must have a motive somewhere."

"No catch. I'm thinking of trading it in, and I would like to try some other bike first, that's all," Mick said. "Your bike is a little smaller. Maybe I would like a smaller bike."

"Well, man, you have a deal. We can start today, huh?" Renolds beamed with anticipation.

They traded keys. Just before leaving the grinning Renolds, who was clutching the keys to Mick's powerful motorcycle, Mick turned to face him. "One more thing, Renolds. Would you mind trading cellphones for a couple of days? There is a chick who keeps dialing me. Drives me crazy. If you get a call from her, you should try to hook up. She's pretty cute."

"Man, this deal gets better and better," Renolds chuckled, reaching for his phone. They shook on it, and Mick left to get his coat and helmet and somehow get back together with Anna.

Mick went back to his locker and reached in the back for an old cloth bundle. He carefully unwrapped the Colt 45 caliber automatic and checked the magazine to be sure it was full. He loved this gun because of its legendary hard-hitting bullet, but most of all because it was a very flat and easily hidden weapon. He took out the small leather holster and put it through his belt so that the gun would ride in the small of his back.

As he was sitting on Renolds' motorcycle, he dialed Anna. When she answered, he said "Could you and Triska meet me for lunch somewhere, I'm buying? You pick the place, and I'll meet you there."

He could hear Anna talking away from the phone, and when she came back, she said, "There is a little place that has outdoor dining a few blocks from here. That sound okay?"

Mick agreed that it would be acceptable and wrote down the address she gave him. He wanted to take his time getting there to be sure that there was no tail in case someone was watching or following. Knowing that his enemies would figure it out in time, his training had taught that he would have to adapt and change his strategy often. He started wondering if they had also tapped Anna's phone, and if they were monitoring Anna as closely as he was being watched. No way to know, yet, he realized.

Chapter 19

Chapter 20

First Attempt

Zimt & Zucker
Stuttgart, Germany

Mick rode aggressively on Renolds' bike. It was not as fast as his, but it was still a motorcycle, and it could cut through traffic like a knife. He snaked between cars stopped for a light, jumped stoplights and cut across parking lots. Nothing on the ground could follow him, and he made absolutely sure by making a large circular run across town to the cafe, Zimt & Zucker, that Anna suggested. When he found the intersection, he pulled up on the sidewalk like many bikers do in Germany. He looked through the window and spotted Anna and Triska already inside, and when he came in, exchanged hugs and kisses with them both. There was a little park with benches outside the cafe and after they got their order, they took the food to eat outside, sitting together in a row on a long bench. It was a clear, warm afternoon and after the events of this morning, Mick was happy to be in the company of these two wonderful women.

"Mick, did you get your problems solved this morning?" Triska asked. Mick caught a glimpse of an odd look in her eyes as if she knew something secret.

"Time will tell, Triska. I'm afraid that it is an ongoing problem."

"Anything I can do, Mick?" Triska asked very quietly. She was sitting on the opposite side of Anna, and Anna kept looking back and forth between them as they spoke.

"What happened to your motorcycle, Mick? It seems to have shrunk," Anna asked. She could see the bike parked on the curb on the other side of the little park.

"Mine had a problem, and I have a loaner for now."

"Mick, who answered your phone this morning?" Anna asked.

"That was a technician who is going to repair it. Sorry about that."

Triska was listening intently to Mick's explanations, and at the same time she was discreetly studying their surroundings without calling attention to herself. She detected a car driving by slowly, two men inside looking in their direction. Shortly after, two men who were walking together on the opposite side of the street suddenly separated. One remained standing in a doorway of a small shop across the street. The other crossed to their side, disappearing from view.

Triska leaned forward and smiled broadly. "Listen carefully, you two. You will not look around, and you will not speak." She paused, and neither of them moved, waiting on the rest. "We have surveillance on us right now. There are at least two of them. They are not German or American, because I would have never spotted them so easily. I don't know if we are at risk, but I don't like taking chances with people I care about. In just a moment, I am going to call for extraction for the three of us. I want you two to get up slowly and go into the cafe for something. Stay there and don't look out the window. I am going to remain right here, keeping an eye on what happens while waiting for the team from BND." She gave an almost imperceptible motion of her head for them to begin.

Mick got up slowly and extended his arm to help Anna up. He put his arm around her, and they strolled casually into the cafe. Triska remained in place, fiddling with her clothing, nonchalantly looking around. In her left hand, she thumb dialed a preprogrammed number and followed with three taps on the pound sign. The number dialed was the BND emergency number and computers there quickly located the GPS signal of the phone and checked its ID number. A call was relayed to a waiting team who rapidly assembled, speeding off in two cars. Inside were five heavily armed men who had also had training with the *KSK Kommando Spezialkräfte.* They estimated arrival in under five minutes.

Triska held her position to wait for the team, and when they arrived she would be there to point out targets for them. Inside, Mick and Anna casually moved away from the window near the street. They went to the rear wall, pretending to examine the poster art hanging there, facing each other in conversation, while Mick unobtrusively looked around for threats. Minutes went by agonizingly slowly, with every tick of the second hand a jolt to their nervous systems.

Mick noticed a back door at the end of a long hallway which also led to the toilets. He mentally checked for any obstacles to a quick exit, and as he was considering their options, the rear door opened and a silhouette of a man in a suit appeared, framed by the open door. The door closed behind him, and a dark shape advanced toward them down the hall. Mick slowly moved between Anna and the coming figure and reached toward the small of his back and found the handle of his 45. As the man came closer, Mick could tell that his eyes were searching for something. When the man came fully into the light, Mick could see that his right arm was straight down, his hand gripping a pistol. As they locked eyes, Mick knew that he was the target. He instinctively drew his weapon as he dropped into a semi-crouch, simultaneously firing three rapid shots. The man was propelled into the air for a short distance by the impact of the slugs and hit the wall before sliding to the floor. The gun he had held clattered to the concrete, spinning in slow circles.

As his hearing returned, Mick could hear screams from the customers and staff. He placed one arm around Anna, realizing that she too was near hysteria. He spun around to face the outside door, pointing his handgun in that direction as people fled out the same door. Yelling, loud voices and the screech of tires mixed into a cacophony of noise. A small figure appeared in the doorway waving to them to come. When they got close, Triska grabbed both of their arms and led the way to a waiting car. Mick got a glimpse of a man across the street holding up his hands, while two men in black jumpsuits pointed machine pistols at him. As they entered the car, Mick offered his handgun to the soldier in the passenger seat, but it was refused by a headshake.

As soon as the car door closed, they shot away from the scene. The two large men in the front seat wore black brimmed caps. One held a large automatic rifle, the barrel pointing up at the roof of the car. Anna was trembling and clung to Mick's arm while burying her face in his shoulder. The car slowed to a more sedate pace as they left the area, and they floated along in silence. After several blocks, the car entered an underground garage and stopped near a steel door guarded by two heavily-armed men in German Army uniforms.

"We get out here, kids. Welcome to the BND," Triska said.

Chapter 21

The Proposal

The Bundesnachrichtendienst
Stuttgart, Germany

After traversing endless halls, Triska opened a door to a well-appointed conference room. Mick noticed the thick red carpet and the polished wood paneling.

The ceiling was lit from above, light spilling through etched glass panels making the entire overhead glow. An oblong table of dark wood was in the center of the room, and about a dozen red velvet upholstered chairs were arrayed on each side. There were no outside windows and only a single entry way.

Triska said softly, "Please, Mick, Anna, sit down and be comfortable. I will be right back, I promise." After she left, they were alone in the room, and Anna started crying.

Mick knelt beside her chair and tenderly held her head, pressed her against his neck, and whispered in her ear, "I am so sorry, Anna, that you got involved with this. I put you in danger today, and I'll never forgive myself for it."

She had no words yet for him and continued to sob as he stroked her hair. Behind him, the door opened again, and he could hear footsteps on the soft carpeting. He twisted to see who had entered. Three men, accompanied by Triska, were coming in. Two were dressed in suits, the other covered by a black jumpsuit like the men who came to their rescue. Triska patted Mick on the shoulder in a signal that he could get up.

When he stood, one of the suited men greeted him, "Lieutenant Mick Grundy, I am Gunther Weisman, and I am in command of the Stuttgart BND." He offered his hand, and Mick took it, noticing the swish of his expensive suit fabric. Weisman had a broad practiced smile, but his eyes were penetrating, even threatening. He introduced the other suited man as Herr Shuller, without announcing his official capacity. The muscular man in the back jumpsuit was introduced as *Oberst* Koffman. Neither of the other two offered either a smile or handshake. The three men sat solemnly across from Mick and the two women.

Weisman cleared his throat and offered to pour each of them a glass of ice water. "It would seem that if we had taken a little longer, Lieutenant, you would have dispatched both of them for us!" He gave a little laugh, but Mick was stone-faced and didn't comment. "Really, you have been trained well, Lieutenant. Good work. We have the live one in custody, and we will question him for motive and about who employed him. I suspect that they were only hired thugs, and we will get nowhere with that."

Mick asked, "Sir, how did they know where I was? I was on a clean motorcycle, and I took extensive evasive precautions on my way to the cafe. My phone is even borrowed."

"We may be able to find that out, but my guess is that they were tracking Anna Michner to find you. That might mean a tracking device or perhaps she was simply followed. We will try to get the answers for you," Weisman said.

"Will there be any repercussions for you because of the shooting?" Mick asked.

Herr Shuller spoke to this question, "We are going to list this action on official files as a shootout related to drugs. You have nothing to worry about, Lieutenant."

This time the combat soldier, *Oberst* Koffman, interjected, "These two were thugs only and poorly trained. They were expendable. If the GRU is behind this, next time they will send their best. I'm afraid that you have a serious problem."

The wall phone rang, and Weisman picked it up. He listened for a moment to the caller, and then said, *"senden Sie ihn."* He pivoted back to the table and announced, "We have company."

In a couple of minutes, the door opened, and Zeskie came in. He nodded to everyone and put his briefcase on the polished table and pulled up a chair. He gave Mick a quick but hard look. "Well, Lieutenant, did you enjoy your little adventure this morning?" Zeskie asked.

"You expect me to answer that, Zeskie?"

"Look what happened when you chose to go out on your own. I found out about your little trick too late to do anything about it. By the time the satellite surveillance team located you, the action had started. We got there after the BND had pulled out, and the only thing left was blood on the floor." Mick and everyone else could tell that he was angry.

"Well, since the CIA's brilliant mission to the Crimea, I haven't exactly been given to trust you guys very far. It's hard to tell whose side you are on. For the last time, I am not the mole," Mick said and was equally angry.

Zeskie said, "That, at least, is plainly obvious, Lieutenant. The problem we have now is keeping you alive. Your days as a covert operative are over. They have your number, and they are seeking revenge for the killings in the Crimea, but, more than that, they are getting even with us for their humiliation."

Mick added, "And there is still a mole out there whom you haven't caught, isn't that right?"

"The mole is not CIA. We have a short list which we are still processing, but your name isn't on it," Zeskie said.

"My bike was bugged while it was on the base. It has to be someone who is there now. That means that it wasn't the Turk Captain, and it wasn't Sumker, who is still missing. That makes a very short list, doesn't it, Zeskie?" Zeskie didn't answer.

After being silent during the preceding conversations, Triska finally spoke, "We can only make the hunters stop hunting if the prey is dead. Mick and Anna have to disappear, but Mick has been killed in the shootout. Agreed?"

After some contemplation and discussion, the BND officials and Zeskie agreed that Mick would be listed as killed in action. If there were a mole placed who had access to military records, they agreed that Mick's official military record should also state that he was killed in the cafe shootout. Zeskie would arrange to lose the body and fake the records accordingly, and since there wasn't any next of kin to worry about, that would end it. Zeskie also agreed to provide a safe house in Germany for them and provide the funds for living expenses and allowances.

Anna realized that plans were being made for her, and she grasped the fact that her old life was over. Horrified, she stood up visibly shaking. "I have done nothing wrong. I don't deserve to be taken from my parents and my school, and I absolutely refuse to be hidden away from my life. Do you people hear me? I refuse." She was shouting by the end and sat down with her hands covering her face. Triska put her arm over Anna's shoulder but said nothing to her.

Mick became angry again. "I agree with Anna. I don't want to hide. I want them to come at me so I can kill them." He turned to face Zeskie. "Find the damn mole, Zeskie, and their information will be cut off. I am not ready to quit the Army and hide, and I also absolutely refuse this plan."

Weisman crooked his finger and pointed at his colleagues and Zeskie. They went out the door for a private conference leaving Mick, Anna and Triska. Suddenly, Triska also got up and said, "They are not going to leave me out of this," and left the room.

Mick was aware that Anna had not yet composed herself after her outbreak. He pulled her close and said, "I wish he had killed me back there like he was supposed to. You would be free of it now."

Anna was startled by his statement, and her face drew into a tight grimace. "No, no, no, Mick. I don't want you dead. I love you. Please don't feel that way. I want to be with you always. It's just the frustration I have at other people intruding on our lives."

"What if I resign the service right now, and we get Zeskie to send us back to the U.S. with a new identity? We can get married over there, and in a few years, this will be forgotten, and we can come back and be with your parents again."

Anna started streaming tears down her cheeks. "Mick, are you asking me to marry you?"

"Yes. Dear Anna, will you marry me? I promise to love and care for you forever and forever, and I will never make you unhappy. Please say yes, Anna," he pleaded.

Before she could answer, the door opened, and the five streamed back in, resuming their seats. Weisman looked around and cleared his throat. "Of course, we listen to conversations in this room and know what you discussed. As we heard, you both want to get married and live together so what you have decided isn't very different than what was proposed earlier. The only difference is Germany or America as I see it." He paused to observe for any objections to his summary. "Frankly, we need to have you around, Lieutenant Grundy, because you may still be useful in this spy hunt, either as a hunter or as bait for a hunter. So, get married and congratulations, but you are staying here for now." He gave one of his broad, car salesman, smiles.

This time, Zeskie turned to Weisman, asking, "Have your investigators gotten anything out of the second shooter?"

"Not much yet, but we are threatening to turn him over to the CIA for interrogation. That should produce results," Weisman said with a little chuckle.

Zeskie remarked dryly, "And when you are finished, let me have him, and we will squeeze a little harder."

Weisman stood up, announcing, "I have commitments and have to honor them. Anna and the Lieutenant will stay tonight in our facility, and we can see what happens in the morning." He smiled courteously to the assembly and left.

Zeskie said, "Lieutenant, you will stay alive and in the Army for now until we can figure this out. By the way, are you getting married?"

Anna pulled Mick toward her and grasped his face in her hands, "Yes, Mick Grundy, I will marry you." She flung her arms around his neck, and they had a long lingering kiss. Triska started clapping with merriment and came around the chair to embrace each of them.

Herr Shuller also seemed happy and said, "I am the liaison officer for the BND. With your permission, I would like to help arrange a marriage for you both. We already have your grandmother here, and all we need are the parents, yes?" Anna enthusiastically nodded and looked at Mick for confirmation. He smiled his appreciation at Herr Shuller and put his arm around Anna and drew her in tight. "Triska, can you arrange for your son and his wife to come to the chapel in the BND tomorrow, say about 1600 hours?" Herr Shuller inquired.

"I know that they will be delighted. Yes, that would be nice. Thank you, Herr Shuller."

Oberst Koffman spoke for the first time, "It would be wise to have BND personnel pick them up; also, it may be wise not to tell them anything until they arrive, given the security risks." Everyone appeared to agree that secrecy was important at this moment and that the less information given means the less can be harvested.

"One more thing, Lieutenant Grundy," said Oberst Koffman. "I would be personally honored if you would allow me, as a fellow soldier, to act as your best man tomorrow."

Mick got up to shake Oberst Koffman's hand and said, "It is I who is honored Oberst Koffman. Thanks also for coming to our rescue today."

"Please, Lieutenant, you will please to call me by my first name, Peter," Oberst Koffman said with a smile. "I am happy because this will be the first wedding I have ever attended and to have it here at headquarters...well, it's *wunderbar*!"

Chapter 22

A Gift Of Marriage

BND, Stuttgart, Germany

Sunday morning came streaming into Mick's room through the small translucent glass window high above him. The room was barren except for a small alcove holding a toilet and sink and, of course, the bed that he was in. This was a holding room for some purpose, and the door looked secure as well. A quick glance at his watch showed that it was 0643. He quickly pulled on his clothes and opened the door to scan the hall. There were cameras near the ceiling at both ends but no people. He turned and scanned the ceiling in the room he had slept in, and sure enough, there was a small dot about in the center. They were watching from somewhere.

A heavily accented voice echoed from a hidden speaker, "*Guten Morgen*, Lieutenant. You will please come down the hall, and we will show you where to get your breakfast."

Mick looked longingly at the closed door of Anna's room as he walked past. Anna and Triska had been talking with him in a private lounge until nearly midnight. Among other things, they discussed how and where they were going to live starting Monday.

The more that they discussed the future, the more it was apparent that there were too many unknowns at this time. The more immediate problem of the honeymoon was solved by Triska who suggested that the BND issue some fake papers and arrange transportation to Bad Doberon. She said that she knew some people there who would look after them.

"Triska," Mick had said, "Where is this Bad Doberon, and what would we do there?"

Triska laughed, "What do you think honeymooners do anywhere, Mick?" She continued, "It's a little resort up on the northern coast of Germany. You will find a charmingly restored old town with historic churches and a working steam train. There are occasional concerts given there and some horse racing. Most of all, there is peace and quiet for you both in a place that is safe. I think that it will be a great way to start your lives together and to figure out what comes next."

Walking down the hall, Mick remembered how it all sounded good last night, but this morning he was still worrying about the present. Zeskie would insist on knowing where they were going and that's the least of it. Once his short leave was up, he would be expected to report for active duty, and the U.S. Army made no exceptions.

When he came to a double door, it was opened for him by a guard, carrying a short black machine pistol, who saluted and snapped his heels as he passed. The guard pointed to another long hallway, and Mick continued walking. He turned slightly when he heard rapid footsteps behind him.

"Mick, a moment please," Oberst Koffman said and put his hand on Mick's shoulder.

"Guten Morgen, Peter," Mick said and smiled at his new friend.

Oberst Koffman smiled back and said, *"Kommen Sie mit mir bitte,"* and led Mick into a small side room. He held the door open for Mick and then closed it behind them. The room contained a table and four chairs but was otherwise empty.

"Some news first," Oberst Koffman said. "The man we captured was interrogated until this morning and, as I suspected, is a hired assassin. He is from Bulgaria and has a criminal record there. The man who hired him apparently was nearby when we arrived at the cafe but escaped our notice and got away. The prisoner says that the man was Russian but doesn't know any more about him, not even his name, but gave us a clear description of him. We could press some charges, but instead, we are going to turn him over to Zeskie's men sometime today."

Mick nodded understanding, and Koffman continued, "We are working on various identification for you and Anna and will have it ready by this evening. Your wedding is scheduled for 1700 hours, and Triska is on her way to round up her son and daughter. We posted several men in the area of their home last night to be sure there was no stakeout there, and they are to remain in place until tomorrow." Koffman paused to see if Mick had any questions, then cleared his throat, "Zeskie left word that he was going to contact your superior officer this morning and obtain your temporary assignment to the CIA for the indefinite future. He will be in later to attend the wedding and should be able to tell you more."

Koffman reached into his jacket and slid a small box over to Mick. "This is some more ammo for that excellent handgun that you like. Just in case."

Mick picked up the heavy box and saw that it contained fifty rounds of 45 caliber ammunition. "Thanks, Peter."

"One more thing, Mick," Koffman said. "Give me your right hand." Mick extended his hand as requested, and Koffman proceeded to measure Mick's ring finger for size. "Ah, a large finger you have my friend, but we will manage," he said smiling. "An attendant will also measure for Anna. We have to be prepared!" he laughed.

"Peter, I am overwhelmed by your and your people's generosity and kindness to me. I don't know what to say except thanks, and I hope that I can someday repay you in kind," Mick said with sincerity.

"Mick, my friend, you are marrying a German today, and in our eyes, after today you become German also. We are proud to call you brother. You owe us nothing but to be a good husband to Anna." They embraced with much backslapping and shook hands. "Now for food," Koffman said and led the way.

The cafeteria was bright and cheerful and lit by large skylights. Mick and Peter Koffman stood in line, filled their plates with food, and selected a table in an unoccupied corner. Mick noticed that he was being talked about because of several lingering sidelong glances and huddled conversations. He realized that most of the personnel knew about him and Anna, and when he returned their looks, he usually was rewarded by smiles and waves. Two of the female staff came to their table and asked if it was all right if they came to the wedding. When he said yes, they were delighted and walked away giggling. While Mick and Peter were comparing their respective training and experiences over coffee after the meal, a figure suddenly appeared beside the table.

"Good morning, Zeskie," Mick said after looking up.

Zeskie pulled up a chair and put his ever present briefcase in front of him and snapped the locks open. "*Guten Morgen* to you both," he responded, while digging into the briefcase. After a few moments, he assembled his paperwork and closed the case with a snap. "Lieutenant Grundy, I was able to see Captain Ritter this morning very early." Zeskie shoved some papers over to Mick and said, "Your signature is required for temporary transfer to the CIA. I knew Captain Ritter when I was in Special Forces, and he is a man to be trusted. He insisted on knowing the full story, and I had no choice but to tell him. After all, the U.S. Army owns you, and we have to do their bidding in the end."

"Zeskie, did you tell him where we are going?" Mick asked.

"I assume that he will have to be told, but at this moment, I don't know myself," Zeskie said, continuing, "Once you sign that, you answer to the

CIA for the next six months, but we are required to fully report your activities... in detail... in triplicate. I am authorized to grant you two weeks for your honeymoon, but you have to let me know where and when you are going. We want to protect you and Anna, and I will do everything I can to stay out of your way for two weeks, but after that we need to figure out how to best use you."

Mick studied the documents of transfer as Zeskie spoke. He accepted an offered pen, signed in three places, then pushed the pages back. "I guess I should thank you, Zeskie, but you must admit that my experience so far with the CIA has been a little rough."

Zeskie ignored his comments and then pushed two packets toward him. "This is cash for you both in euros and in dollars, and the other is the usual collection of identities. There are also three different identities for Anna as well and some secure numbers in case you need us."

Mick took the bundles without comment. Zeskie cleared his throat and reached into his pocket and brought out two black cell phones. "This one is for you. It can't be tracked and any attempts to track it will send out alerts from here to Washington. This other one is for Anna. She can use it to call anyone without fear that she can be found. Both are set up with a panic button which will trigger immediate extraction protocols." Mick nodded again and took the phones.

"The last is my gift to you and Anna," Zeskie said and handed Mick a credit card. Mick turned it over and saw that the name Stallman was on it. "You can use it for anything, just as long as it is necessary and in moderation. You understand, of course, that the charges will be closely monitored. The card cannot be traced by any agency, other than the CIA."

Mick found himself overwhelmed. He struggled to find words of appreciation for the two men beside him. They both seemed to understand and patted him on the back at the same time. "No need to feel thanks, Lieutenant," Zeskie said. "We all are proud of you. Guys like you are why the American Army is respected everywhere in the world. People who know what is expected of you are especially grateful that you are serving your country."

Oberst Koffman said, "When you are on your honeymoon with Anna, you are going to be protected by both Zeskie and operatives from the BND. I think that Triska also has some ideas of her own. I hope that you will never see any of us while you are there, but be you can be sure we will be present."

Before Mick could give a response, Koffman's phone rang. The conversation was very brief, and as he put it back in his pocket, he said, "Weisman's office. He wants all of us there right now."

They all got up together, and Koffman led them through the maze of hallways to a private elevator. A passkey and retinal scan of each of them was required for use of the elevator. The door opened to a small elevator, richly appointed with polished wood and thick carpeting. It arrived just outside Director Weisman's private office and seated at the outside desk, a stunningly attractive blonde smiled at them.

"Herren geben Sie bitte." As she got up to open the door, the men silently observed her ample curves. They entered into a sunlit room with sparse furnishings. A desk was stationed with large windows behind it so that the bright light made it hard to clearly see Weisman's face. Weisman waved his arm in the direction of three chairs assembled in front of his desk, and they all sat as directed.

"Gentlemen," Weisman said. "We have early information which requires discussion. "First, I want to hear from Mr. Zeskie what his team has uncovered."

Zeskie snapped open his briefcase and cleared his throat. "The bug found on Lieutenant Grundy's motorcycle was manufactured in Russia. Similar tracking devices have been found worldwide and have also been supplied to Russia's few allies. DNA from the shooting victim, which we collected from the floor of the cafe," he looked up briefly at Weisman to make sure he got the message, then continued, "showed a high probability that the man was Bulgarian or Slovakian, but he wasn't in our database. There have been several unsuccessful hacker-type inquiries about Lieutenant Grundy and the origins are all the same. Moscow." Zeskie closed his briefcase and looked up. "We also track a large percentage of the Internet traffic, and we are currently processing a thread of interest in Lieutenant Grundy."

"Very good, Mr. Zeskie," Weisman said. "By the way, you can have the body any time you want and the captured suspect as well. We aim to cooperate with the CIA." He gave them one of his big fake smiles. "On our side," he began, "we concur that the shooters were from Bulgaria and that the employer is Russian. We have identified him, but it appears that he has temporarily left German soil. There is still a chance that the Poles will retain him, and we are urging them to do so. We believe that the Russians aren't finished with their reprisal games, Lieutenant. They have a source or two somewhere locally, and when they want to be, they can be very inventive. We know that you are willing to kill them, but they also know that, so I doubt that they will make another primitive frontal assault. Be very wary, Lieutenant. We may not be able to fully protect you outside of your military base, no matter how hard we try."

Mick spoke up, "Sir, may I add something to your summary?"

Weisman smiled and said, "Certainly, Lieutenant Grundy. Please."

"To me, sir, this whole episode is really about a spy or spies, not about the Russian need for retaliation, but about a spy among us. I am being sold out by the spy, and I want revenge, as I know the U.S. Army does. There should be a way to feed him false information, if we can narrow it down to one man," Mick said.

Zeskie responded, "Of course, Lieutenant, that is just what we are doing. We can't arrest without hard evidence, or torture without provocation, so we are waiting for a mistake. Have patience, my friend, we will get him."

"If I'm not killed in the process, I would be happier," Mick said.

Zeskie ignored his sarcasm. "The preparations we are making for your safety for the next two weeks are nearly presidential. Go enjoy yourself, and let us worry about the world. You can come back in two weeks and kill someone if it will make you happy."

Weisman stood, as did the three men. "Lieutenant, I am honored to have your wedding here at headquarters, and I would be additionally honored to attend. Unfortunately, I cannot be present today, but I wish you a full and happy life with Anna. I look forward to your continued work with the BND in the future, and I am sure we will meet again." He extended his hand and his smile to Mick which was taken and returned.

The men smiled and nodded agreeably at the attractive secretary on their way to the elevator. Once on their way down, Koffman whispered in Mick's ear, "If I had a chance to spend the afternoon with his secretary, I would not be present for your wedding either." They both laughed.

When the elevator arrived at the lower floor, the door opened, and Triska was waiting in the hall. "Mick, you are to come with me," she said, winking at Koffman and Zeskie, and tugging on Mick's arm.

"Good luck, Mick!" Zeskie called out behind Mick as he was led away.

Triska patted Mick's hand as they walked down endless hallways. "Mick, there are things we need to do and things we have to talk over." She looked up at him in a loving and protective way.

"Dear Triska," Mick said. "You have to be the neatest grandmother any fellow was ever lucky enough to have. I am going to love having you in my life. I never had a grandmother before."

They made a turn through a wooden door and entered a small but plush waiting room appointed with leather couches and armchairs. Along one end wall was a fully equipped beverage and coffee bar, a water closet door at the other end. On the low ornate coffee table were several packages. Triska closed the door and indicated that Mick should sit on one of the couches.

"I went to give the news to Anna's parents this morning. They are so excited about your wedding. So far, they don't know anything about the shooting, and we can tell them after the ceremony all they need to know. They suspect that something unusual has happened and are polite enough to wait for the answers. We went to the clothing store this morning and got some things that they want you to have. My son has a practiced eye for sizes, and I'm sure that you will be fitted correctly. The first package is a tuxedo and fittings. The second, larger package, is clothing for your honeymoon, and the last package is personals we thought you would need. I also brought enough clothes for Anna from home. They are bringing the wedding dress for Anna when they come later today."

Mick felt himself fighting back tears for the first time in his life. He was embarrassed to let Triska see him in a weak moment. Triska sensed this and gave him a big, lingering hug, as she sat down with him on the couch, holding his hand. "Mick, you mean a lot to all of us. We all want to do things for you, and we really want your marriage to Anna to last a lifetime."

"Triska, can you tell me what will happen after the wedding today? I mean, where are we to go tonight?"

"Mick, honey, that is up to you, but I have some strong suggestions. I would like to see you get out of Stuttgart tonight. We can safely put you on a train to Karlsruhe, and you can stay in a really good hotel there for your first night together. Tomorrow, you will board another train to Hamburg, and from there you will rent a car and travel the rest of the way to Bad Doberon on your own. When you get there, I have a contact for you who will guide you for your stay in that area. The entire train trip takes about eight hours."

Mick was silent for a moment and asked, "Are we to travel under one of the identities provided by the CIA?"

"Yes, or one provided by us."

"Are there going to be agents traveling with us?"

Triska laughed, "Of course, Mick, but you'll never see them!"

Mick smiled at her and said, "Your plan appears entirely satisfactory, dear Triska. You spies do all the work, and we play. I like it. Now can you tell me how Anna is and when I can see her?

Triska patted his hand and said, "Long tradition has it that it is bad luck to see the bride before the wedding, and I believe in tradition."

At 1400 hours, Mick was summoned to the small conference room again, and when he opened the door, he was greeted by Anna's parents and Triska who were all smiles. They exchanged hugs and kisses, and both Herr Michner and Frau Michner were wiping their eyes from tears of joy.

"Mick, my boy, I am honored to welcome you to the family. Such plans I have. Excuse me, dear ladies, I mean, we have plans for you. From now on, Mick, you are to call me Alfred, not sir, if you please," Herr Michner said. Triska stood back to enjoy the scene before her.

"Sir, I am honored more than anyone to be wed to Anna and be part of this wonderful family. My promise is that I will do my best for her the rest of my life. I wish I could tell you how much I love her and how much I think about her when we are apart, but I don't have adequate words to express my feelings."

"We know that, Mick. You don't have to say anything." He paused and looked between his wife and Triska for a moment, summoning his thoughts. "We do need to know, Mick, why this is happening here and at this moment." Herr Michner suddenly looked more serious and worried than before.

"Perhaps we should all sit down while I go through this, sir." After they sat, Mick paced the floor in front of them. "As you know, I serve in the U.S. Army Special Forces. We were deployed on a mission recently during which several Russians were killed. There is a spy that our side is searching for, who may be one of our team, or someone who hasn't been identified yet. The Russians are angry and have singled me out and obviously know who and where I am. Their agents tried to kill me yesterday morning when I was with Anna and Triska, and I had to shoot one of them. We were brought here by Triska and the BND for our protection."

Herr Michner looked confused. "What does that have to do with Anna? It would seem to me that you should get away from her to keep her out of harm."

Triska spoke up, "Alfred, the Russians followed Anna, not Mick. They know that the two are involved. They could go after Anna just to get at Mick."

Alfred Michner looked horrified and was speechless. He looked back and forth between those in the room, but his rushing thoughts crowded out his words.

"Please, sir, I would like to add some things," Mick said to him. "I love Anna, and I want to marry her. Since they tell me that I am done with covert operations forever, I plan to resign from the Army as soon as we get this affair settled, but the most important thing right now is to catch the spy. I believe that the intelligence people from the American and German agencies will keep us safe for the present and will give us advice on what to do when we get back in two weeks."

Herr Michner looked a little relieved to know that so many people were there to keep them from harm. "Look, Mick, I have been thinking for some time about your future after the military. The way you look and move, you will be a star of male modeling. I have enough contacts in Italy and here to make it happen. It's a life I know you would enjoy and when you get back, we can talk more about it."

They all had a good laugh at the idea of Mick modeling clothes. He admitted that it was something he had never considered. The stress was broken, and everyone accepted the fact that some events were out of their control, but life must go on. The wedding hour was approaching, and Mick left to get ready.

Chapter 22

Chapter 23

Honeymoon

The Train to Karlsruhe, Germany

Settled in the back seat of the large sedan, Mick and Anna snuggled and touched noses and lips. They were on their way to the train station and the start of a new life together. Their hips and legs touched, sending an electric charge through Mick's entire being. She was actually his, and his forever. He loved her so much that he almost couldn't think about it, the magic of being with this wonderful girl, the love that he never dreamed to achieve, and that they were together because of an accidental meeting. When Mick looked into her blue eyes, he wanted to freeze time for that moment so that nothing could ever take her from him. Annoying pain in the small of his back from the 45 caliber pistol pressing into him was a reminder of the real world waiting for them, but he tuned it out, at least for this moment.

The car came to a stop, smoothly idling, as if waiting for something. Oberst Koffman turned partially around to them from the passenger seat, "We are waiting for a signal that our team is in place. Two agents from the BND will be on the train with you. The CIA are like ghosts, but I assume Zeskie has done what he promised. You will never see them if they are there. Mick, you do have the tickets on you, yes?"

Mick reached into his new leather jacket pocket and displayed the tickets. "Yes, Peter, I have them, and I have the hotel reservation in the name of Stallman. And yes, I have our passports and identity papers with the same name. Quit worrying, my friend."

Koffman smiled briefly and continued to hold his hand to his ear, pressing his earpiece closer. After a few minutes, he nodded back to them that the team was in place and ready for them to come out. Koffman got out first, opening their door and the trunk. "We better say goodbye here, Mick and Anna. You should carry your own luggage and go right into the train. I'll stay here to watch for anything unusual, but I think you are safe enough. My team will be here for you when you return, and we will all work hard, while you are gone, to catch this spy."

They embraced again and Mick gently patted Koffman's face with affection. "Peter, thanks again for coming to the wedding." He spread the fingers of his hand, displaying the new gold band, and said, "And getting these rings for us was a wonderful gesture. I hope we can remain close friends when we get back."

Oberst Koffman drew himself up to his full height and stuck out his chest. His black dress uniform looked magnificent on him, as he would have been first to acknowledge. "Lieutenant Grundy, we shall always be friends. I insist on it." He then relaxed and said, "My first wedding. I have to admit to you how beautiful it was. I cried like a little girl, but don't tell Weisman."

On The Train to Karlsruhe

They were shown to their seats in the first class section by a distinguished conductor, who sported a long grey handlebar mustache and demonstrated a flourish of old-world manners. The seats were very comfortable, and as the train pulled smoothly away, it was hard to tell that they were actually moving. Mick discreetly studied those around him trying to spot allies or enemies without success. Passengers occupying scattered seats appeared entirely ordinary. He settled back and held Anna's hand, and they smiled at each other for the thousandth time. Such joy and contentment came over Mick that he was able to put any sense of danger aside and really relax. The train trip to Karlsruhe was short, and they seemed to arrive quickly. When the train stopped, Mick quickly gathered their luggage, and they stepped off the train. On the platform, he hesitated, nervously looking both ways for danger, but as far as he could tell, they were ignored as people hurried to their destinations. A cab was chosen from a line of cabs waiting curbside, and they were quickly whisked away to the Hotel Blankengurt that Peter Koffman had personally selected earlier. The hotel was constructed in a classic style outside but thoroughly modern inside. Mick presented his credentials at the desk, and they were courteously shown to their room.

Once the bellboy was tipped and the door closed, Mick realized that this was the most important night in his life. Every time he looked at Anna as they unpacked the luggage, his stomach did a flip-flop. He wiped the sweat from his lip several times before Anna noticed. "Mick, are you all right?" she asked sweetly.

"No," he said. "I'm a little scared," he admitted sheepishly.

Anna laughed and came toward him with her arms in an expectant embrace. "Mick, my dear husband. You and I are made for each other. There is nothing ahead but happiness for us. You are my dream come true, and this is the first night of the rest of our lives. Kiss me now and then tell me if you have any doubts or fears." She wrapped herself around him in an embrace and kiss which was nearly ferocious. Mick almost buckled in the knees at first but then returned her embrace with equal passion. He sat her gently on the edge of the bed.

"Know what?" he asked.

"More delay, Mick?"

"We haven't eaten since midday. Don't you think that we should get some food before we lose track of time?"

"No! I have been waiting for months for this moment and food can wait." She started unbuttoning his shirt while smiling at him.

Mick woke up and looked at his watch. 0600 hours. His stomach was telling him strongly that he had to eat soon. Anna was beside him, and he slowly inched toward her face and very softly kissed her cheek. Her eyes flickered, opening to a slit, and focused on him, then a knowing smile appeared on her lips. "What, more! Are you never satiated, Mick?" she said in a slightly horse whisper, then closed her eyes again.

"Oh, Anna, you are a fantasy become real for me. I have been waiting all my life for you but didn't know it until now." Anna's eyes opened again, and she reached for him, pulling him toward her until they were nose to nose.

"I feel the same, Mick. I love you completely and for always, and I am so happy right now," she whispered, and as she let him go, she stretched her arms above her and arched her back. "Say, are you as hungry as I am?"

"I could eat wood right now. When we came in last night I noticed a sign for a small cafe about two blocks away called Hannah's. I'll bet that they open early. Want to give it a try?"

"As soon as I shower." "By the way, who are we again?"

Mick looked serious. "This is very important, Anna. We have to get this right, because we have to look after ourselves and not depend on whoever is looking out for us. If they are out there, I couldn't spot them." He walked across the room and gently grasped her by the shoulders. "You are Frau Patricia Stallman, and I am Herr Rudy Stallman. We are on vacation but work for a travel agency and are scouting locations for our customers. Simple, right?"

"Yes, my master, it is simple. You will remember to speak only German, won't you my Teutonic husband?"

"My dear, as you can tell, my English is spoken only with a distinguished German accent and any English words from me are also distinctly British sounding."

"Mick, you are a true master of language. You could fool me any time. Now, please be a dear and go downstairs and bring me back a coffee for when I get out of the shower," Anna gave a big pucker of her lips as she closed the door to the shower.

Mick pulled on his clothes and found the stairs just off the hall. There was no one in sight, but when he reached the door to the lobby, he suddenly had a flashback to the hotel in Sevastopol and instinctively reached behind him to discover that he had left his pistol in the room upstairs. He opened the door slowly and looked around. There was a normal atmosphere with no obvious threats.

When he arrived at the front desk, the clerk looked up. "*Kaffee*?" Mick asked. The clerk leaned over the counter and pointed with his pen toward the end of the room. Mick noticed that a small food bar was there with pastry and coffee available. A large street level window was just to the right of the food bar, and as he was pouring coffee into a disposable cup, he had a sensation of being watched. He gave a furtive glance out the window and saw a man seated behind the driver's seat of an auto parked at the curb. The man's thin and pock-marked face was partially lit by the diagonal morning rays of light.

When Mick turned to get a better look, the man slowly pulled down the visor to block his view. The man kept one narrowed eye on Mick without any change in expression. Mick asked himself if this was a threat or just his anxiety showing? He finished quickly and took the stairs up two at a time.

When he entered the room, the shower was still running. He went to the window, but the room faced another building, and the street wasn't visible. After Anna came out, Mick had a quick shower, and they changed for breakfast. Mick put the gun on at his back and added his new jacket to hide it.

"Expecting problems, Mick?" Anna asked.

"No, Frau Stallman. Just habit."

They left by the front door. The car that Mick had spotted was gone. False alarm, he thought with relief. The cafe was about two blocks away, and they walked arm in arm, like the newlyweds that they were, and enjoyed the morning. Hannah's was open, and Mick chose a table that gave him a view of the front door. As the customers came and left, Mick surveyed them carefully one by one. Anna was chatty and flirtatious with him to help him relax, because she sensed that he was tense.

"Mick, is this the way it's going to be the entire two weeks? Can't you relax and let the spooks do their jobs?" Anna asked after watching him tense each time someone stood up.

"You are right, Frau Patricia Stallman, my beautiful wife. Frankly, I've never seen the agents protecting us so they must be extremely professional," he answered. He asked himself, what if there are no agents protecting us? The answer was particularly ugly, and he forced himself to not think about it.

As they left the cafe, Mick had the familiar feeling that they were being watched. He turned just in time to see the car from before slowly going by. The pock-marked face was looking their way. Mick stopped and let the car disappear. He looked around but couldn't see any other suspicious activity or people.

"What's wrong, Mick. Do you see something?" She sounded afraid.

Mick patted her hand. "Nothing, dear, I just remembered that I have to make a call when we get back."

They walked a bit more briskly to the hotel. Mick stopped by the desk to remind the manager that they would be checking out and would be down in one hour and to please have a cab at the door. Mick gave him a crisp 10 euro note to be sure it happened. They used the elevator instead of the staircase, and Anna packed while Mick consulted the train schedule. The timing was good, and they would only have a short wait for the train to Hamburg, which would arrive at their destination six hours later. Mick excused himself and went into the staircase to make his call.

He punched the small red button as Zeskie instructed, and in several seconds, a voice came on, "Do you have an emergency, Lieutenant Grundy?"

"No, but I have some questions and concerns. Any way you can put me through to Mr. Zeskie?"

There was no reply, and the phone remained silent. He held on and listened for a response for more than two minutes. "Zeskie here. That you Mick?"

"Zeskie, I have a bad feeling that I have been spotted by the bad guys. Please confirm that you have people around me as you promised."

"I don't know that you have been listening to the news on your honeymoon, Mick, but we have a situation here. Do you know about the bombing in Italy?"

"No, and I don't care about any bombing. Are we protected or not?"

Zeskie cleared his throat, then said, "We had two agents board the train in Stuttgart but had to pull them away last night when you arrived at Karlsruhe because of a threat. There was a terrorist bomb planted on a bus in Italy that was directed at Americans and did kill several. We are spread pretty thin these days, and you still are under the protection of the BND. We spotted two of them on the train with you. Anyway, we had to respond to immediate threats in other areas and needed all the agents. Is there a problem?"

Mick said, "That's just great, Zeskie. At least I'm not disappointed, because that is what I have come to expect. I don't know if I have a problem, but I have a suspicion that I have been spotted. Are you leaving me to fend for myself then?"

"I have noticed that you are beloved by the BND, and we know that they are there with you, and I assure you, they are entirely competent."

"One last question, Zeskie. If I push the panic button on this phone, will you come?"

"We'll try."

Mick hung up and went back to the room. "Anna, do you have Triska's phone number with you?"

Anna widened her eyes and said, "Yes, I know her number. Want me to dial?"

"Yes, and when you get her on the phone, I want to talk to her."

Anna sat down and found her new little black phone and punched in the number. In a moment, she handed Mick the phone.

When Mick identified himself, Triska said, "Trouble, Mick?"

"I think so, Triska. Zeskie said that the CIA was pulled away from watching over us for another mission. I need to know if the BND is there or not. There is someone stalking us and from what I could see, he isn't from our side."

"Hmmm. Mick, I'll try to find out right away. Where are you right now?"

"We are just ready to leave the hotel and head for the train station. The train leaves in about 45 minutes."

"I think that you should go ahead to the train, before they can get organized. If there isn't anyone from the BND covering you, I will personally raise hell about it and get them on at the first stop."

"You'll call us back then?"

"You bet I will, Mick, and please be careful."

Mick hung up, worry on his brow. "There is a possibility that we are unprotected at the moment.

Triska is checking it out. You and I are going to the train as planned. Whatever happens, just trust me and act normally. If there is anyone trying to harm us, we don't want to let them know that we are alone or that we are aware they are watching."

Anna had the fear of another attack overcome her. She couldn't hide her intense fear and started to cry. Mick swept her up in his arms and said, "I won't let anyone harm you, Anna. Don't worry, we will be safe on the train." It was a display of confidence that he didn't actually have at the moment. He remembered that Koffman believed that the Russians would send their best out this time, and they would not be easily spotted. He quickly felt for the gun at his back, and he opened the small box of 45 cartridges and poured a handful into his leather jacket pocket. An extra magazine would be nice, but he didn't have one. He had to remember that this gun only had seven rounds and not fourteen like his Beretta. If it came to shooting, each round would have to count,.

Mick called for a bellboy to carry the bags, which would leave his hands free. The fellow came and happily picked up the bags for the trip to the street. When they arrived, the cab was waiting as expected, and there was no sign of the pock-marked man. The trip to the train station was quick, and during the trip, there was no sign of a trailing car. He began to think that he overreacted and was needlessly worried. The Russians couldn't have known when or from where Mick and Anna were leaving Stuttgart, and besides, there were at least two CIA agents on the train to Karlsruhe. They would have spotted a tail and reacted.

The boarding procedure was effortless, and they were shown to their comfortable seats in the first class section. Mick had a long look in both directions before seating himself. There were six other people in the coach and half were middle-aged women. The three men showed no interest in Mick or Anna and looked like normal German businessmen. The seats behind and in front of them were empty. Mick occupied the aisle seat and as the train slowly pulled away from the platform, he looked out the window. The pock-marked face was there looking back at him from the platform. No doubt now. They had been spotted.

Chapter 24

On Their Own

The Train to Hamburg

One of the older conductors came past collecting tickets. Mick asked, *"Gibt es irgendwelcher Halt zwischen hier und Hamburg?"*

The old man smiled and answered, *"Ja, wir halten kurz in Frankfurt an."*

Only one stop from Karlsruhe to Hamburg and that was about one hour away at Frankfurt. He was betting that the train was free of assassins for the moment, but Pockface would call ahead and have his team board in Frankfurt. If he and Anna got off in Frankfurt, they could be spotted and be in even greater danger while afoot. They badly needed some backup, but Triska had not yet called back.

Mick picked up his black phone and hit the emergency button. A female voice quickly came on, "Lieutenant Grundy, do you need help?"

"My wife and I could be in some danger. We need either extraction or backup right away," Mick said, trying to hide the tension in his voice.

"One moment, sir," the voice crackled then went silent.

About 15 seconds later, a male voice came on. "I see that your signal is moving about 150 Kilometers an hour. You must be on the train. Is your train stopping in Frankfurt?"

Mick answered, "Yes, we are on the train, and there is a stop in Frankfurt."

There was a short pause. "We are thin in agents in Frankfurt at the moment, and we can't get anyone on the scene in the next 45 minutes. If you stay on the train until Hamburg, I can have agents there on the platform when you arrive."

Mick responded angrily, "If we live that long. I need some advice on what to do. Do we stay on the train and take our chances or get off and take our chances?

"Sir, Frankfurt is the capitol of the German Republic. The Russians have an embassy and a large presence there. You will be safer on the train. Do you presently have any threat in view?"

"No," Mick said.

"Good. Are you armed?"

"Yes."

"Our advice is to sit tight and be alert. Once you arrive in Hamburg, we will be there in force. Anything else, Lieutenant?"

"No point in asking anything. I can see that we are on our own," Mick said with disgust.

"Good luck, Lieutenant," The phone went silent.

As he put the phone away, Anna asked, "What's happening, Mick?"

Mick looked lovingly at her and touched her beautiful face. He bent over and gave her a brief kiss on the cheek. "Oh, how I love you! No new news, dear. We must wait for Triska's call and hope that the BND hasn't let us down also."

The train rolled smoothly on toward their destiny with fate. Fifteen minutes later, Anna's phone rang, and she gave it to Mick without answering.

"Hallo."

"Mick, this is Triska. Bad news, I'm afraid. The same emergency that pulled off the CIA also pulled off the BND from you. One of the bombers of the bus in Italy was captured and interrogated, eventually disclosing that bombs were also planted on public busses in Germany, set to explode soon. They are all going a little crazy here. I have a sinking feeling that the Italian bomb was related to you. The Russians predicted how we would react, and this gives them a free hand to get you alone and unprotected. Are you on the train now, and are you having any problems?"

"We are to arrive in Frankfurt within the hour, Triska. Do we get off or do we wait for them on the train?"

"Stay on the train. I have an idea. I'm going to make a call to the Frankfurt Police about a bomb threat for your train. That will insure that the police will stream aboard at the Frankfurt stop. You will be safe at least while they search the train. I am also going to request that they take you both in for protective custody."

The train hurtled toward Frankfurt, rapidly eating up the miles, yet too slowly for comfort. Their salvation was probably waiting on the platform ready to board the train as soon as it stopped. Mick allowed himself to relax and reached out to hold Anna's hand, and they snuggled together with heads touching.

"Is our honeymoon over, Mick?"

"No, Anna, every day with you the rest of my life will be a honeymoon. We'll figure something out. Relax now, we are almost there."

The train slowed a bit, and Mick sat up and looked out the window. The public address system came on with a statement first in German and then in English, "Good day Passengers. An announcement from the Frankfurt Police states that you are to stay in your seats for a brief time after stopping while uniformed officers board to inspect the train. Please have your identification ready for inspection. We will endeavor to keep your safety in mind and the inconvenience small. Thank you."

Mick and Anna could hear the passengers talking. He noticed an older woman get up, holding her purse and a couple of shopping bags, and start wobbling toward them. She looked flustered. When she got just past them, she turned and said in British accented English, "Excuse please, can you point out the toilette door for me?"

Anna turned and pointed toward the end of the train. They both smiled at each other, and the lady turned to leave. Mick watched her silently as she passed. Something was different. He turned and looked down the aisle at her receding back. There was only one shopping bag on her arm. He peered over the seat back in front of him, and a small shopping bag was there. He started to call out to the woman that she had left a parcel, but the woman turned and looked back at him with narrowed eyes as she picked up her pace. Bomb. The thought burst into his mind. He threw himself over Anna, his upper body covering her face and chest just as the explosion occurred.

Mick rolled over and looked at the ceiling of the train trying to understand where he was and what happened. The only sound he could hear was the pounding in his ears. He touched his face and found blood. Suddenly he remembered Anna and tried to look for her. He painfully rolled to his stomach and looked around, blinking hard as blood ran onto his face and into his eyes. She was lying on her back in the aisle four feet from him, and her face was turned, looking at him. He seemed to be unable to use his right arm, and he inched himself toward her by pulling on the seating frames with his left hand. Anna was talking to him, because he could see her lips move, but he could hear nothing but the persistent ringing. As he came closer, he saw blood staining her clothes over her abdomen. He drew forward until his face was a foot from hers, and he struggled to look into her eyes. His vision started fading, and he strained to stay conscious. Just before he passed out, he saw a change in her face. Her lips stopped moving, and her eyes were different.

Chapter 24

Chapter 25

Remembering Anna

Landstuhl Regional Medical Center, Germany
Neuro Intensive Care Unit

"Is he going to recover, Doctor?" Zeskie asked.

Major Andrew Murphy hesitated, fingering the stethoscope dangling from his neck, obviously searching for a clear explanation. "Let me explain this for you one more time, young man. Lieutenant Grundy sustained an open head injury in the right temporal area which required a craniotomy. That's where we take a large piece of the skull off and stop the bleeding. The brain swells after that so we sedate the patient and then repair the bone later. That's where we are right now. He hasn't regained consciousness since the explosion so he can't be fully assessed until then. He is alive right now and that is all we really know. He has other injuries also including a laceration of his neck in the area of the larynx resulting in permanent damage to his vocal chords. There is a fractured humorous bone of his right arm and three or four broken ribs. He has burns and contusions over most of his back. Now I need to ask you a question."

"Shoot, Major."

"What the hell happened to him? We got almost no information from the Germans who brought him in."

"He was targeted by a terrorist who left a small bomb on a train seat. He was with his new wife at the time, and she died at the scene," Zeskie answered grimly.

"According to his military record, there is no next of kin. Is this correct?"

"I'm afraid that his only kin was Anna, and now he has no one. This injury will result in his discharge from the U.S. Army, and he won't even have that any more," Zeskie said.

Major Murphy frowned and stroked his brow, "What about his new in-laws? Do you think that they will help him out?"

Zeskie shook his head, "No, I talked to Anna's parents and told them that it was our fault that Anna was killed, but they are going to blame Lieutenant Grundy anyway. They are very bitter. Anna's grandmother may come around when she overcomes her grief. We'll see."

Major Murphy leaned against the hall corridor outside Mick's room looking through the glass. They could see him on his back, his head thickly wrapped in gauze, his right arm in a cast and a respirator connected to his tracheotomy tube. The Major looked sad. "He could have watched her die, Zeskie. This will leave lasting mental scars long after the body recovers. He will wake up a different man, and he has a lot of reasons to be angry at life. We'll get a psych consult for him as soon as he is able. He is going to need it. What about you, Mr. Zeskie. Are you going to be there for him?"

Zeskie tried to hold back tears as he spoke "Major, I'll let him shoot me if it will help him recover. I hold myself, above all others, to be responsible for this tragedy. The Russians tricked us, and I fell for it. I'll be there for him forever if he lets me, and behind the scenes, I'll work in his behalf for as long as I'm alive." Zeskie turned his head so that the doctor couldn't see him cry. The senior physician patted him on the shoulder before ambling down the long hall.

Two months later
Landstuhl Regional Medical Center
Rehabilitation Unit

"Lieutenant Grundy, you must try. I know that you can do it. From now on, I want you to at least look at me when I talk to you. Do you hear me?" the exasperated therapist said. As usual, there was no response from Mick who just looked straight ahead. The therapist shrugged and left. "What is with this guy?" he muttered to himself as he walked away. He knew that Lieutenant Grundy could move around, because he had watched him move from the wheelchair to the bed unassisted. The occasional direct look that he gave people was intelligent but hostile. Psychiatry occasionally spirited him away for a session but as far as anyone could tell, it wasn't working. As he passed the nurses station, he noticed a short elderly woman and a college-age young man with her discussing something with one of the nurses.

"I'm sorry, *Frau*, his physician has not authorized visits," the nurse said with some firmness.

"Can you call his physician and tell him that his grandmother and his brother are here to visit?" Triska pleaded.

The nurse rolled her eyes but stepped away to call Captain Fisk. As she talked on the phone, she repeatedly said, "Yes, sir. Yes, sir." Afterwards, she walked back to stand in front of Triska and her grandson, apology in her eyes. "He is coming down right away and wants to speak with you. Please be seated in the conference room behind you."

Almost as soon as Triska and Kurt sat, the physician, Captain Fisk, came in. He was a very youthful and energetic military physician assigned to the Rehabilitation Unit. Mick was one of his most problematic cases, and he was delighted to have any possibility of a breakthrough. Triska and Kurt stood to shake his hand.

"Well, this is most welcome. I understand that you both are related to Lieutenant Grundy?" Captain Fisk asked.

"We are related by law. I am the grandmother of his wife, Anna, and this is Kurt, her brother," Triska explained, using flawless English.

Fisk looked pleased and said, "He seems to have physically returned to a functional status but is uncooperative with communication or any physical rehabilitation. He talks to no one, not even the psychiatrists. We have really run out of options, and there is some talk of shipping him home soon."

Triska looked shocked, blurting, "He has no one in the States to return to. He belongs here with us. We would like to try to talk to him if he will let us...please."

Fisk stood up with a smile and offered his arm to Triska. "This way, dear. Let's see what happens when he sees you."

The three moved past rows of beds in the ward until they came to Mick's. He was sitting up and staring straight ahead. There was no indication on his face that he recognized them or even saw them at all. The physician drew the curtain enclosure on both sides of the bed. Triska stood at the end of the bed directly in Mick's view, and Kurt and Captain Fisk each went to a side. She smiled warmly at him and said, "Hello, Mick. We have been waiting to see you for a long time, and we are glad to see you looking so well. It's time for a conversation that I wish could have been sooner. You remember Kurt, don't you, Mick?" As she watched his face, she thought she could see his eyes slowly focus on hers then drift away again. Mick said nothing.

Captain Fisk sighed and patted Mick's hand. "This is the way it's been. We know that he is in there, but so far our best efforts have been useless to get him to return to this life." Fisk shook his head and shrugged his shoulders.

Triska motioned for Fisk to change places with her, and he did. She stood on her toes and tenderly hugged Mick around the neck and kissed his cheek.

"My boy, I love you as much as I love Kurt over there. Listen to me, Mick. Losing Anna was not your fault. No one could have tried harder than you did, and no one could blame you for her death, most of all me. You have to come back to us. There is so much of your life left for you and so much you can do with it. Don't let the Russians win, Mick. We need you. Please come back to us." Triska started to cry, sobbing into Mick's shoulder.

Mick slowly and stiffly lifted his right arm and put his hand on Triska's head. "I wish I had died with her. All I see is her face the moment she died. I sleep with it and wake up to it. I can never figure out what she was saying just before she died. Her lips move over and over, but I can't understand her. Except for the memory of her face floating in front of me or in my head when I close my eyes, there is nothing for me any more." His voice was a shock to those standing beside him. It was raspy and deep and made with effort. It was as though his voice came from another world or from somewhere deep in the earth and had slithered from great fissures of stone.

Triska said, "She was telling you that she loved you, Mick."

Mick responded while he stared into nothingness. "Or she was asking for help from me, and I couldn't help her. All I could do is watch her die." His words were chilling and made the three standing beside the bed feel helpless.

Captain Fisk was intensely interested, and his mind raced to somehow make use of Mick's return to communication. Before he could say anything, Triska summoned him with her finger and led him away for a private conversation. Kurt remained beside the bed.

Kurt placed his hand on Mick's shoulder. "Mick, I know that you remember me. I am Anna's brother. You were led to believe that I was involved with communists and radicals. I am, but not the way Anna and my parents thought. I work for the BND and was recruited by Triska to infiltrate these groups and work from inside. Only a few know my role. I want you to work with me when you are well. We can do a lot of damage to these fanatics from the inside, and they need to pay for Anna's death with their own." He patted Mick as he was talking, but he couldn't tell if Mick heard him or understood him. The curtains parted again, and Triska and Fisk came back to the bed.

Captain Fisk touched Mick's shoulder in an affectionate way. "Mick, thanks for letting us understand what is going on. We can't ease your pain or remove Anna's memories from your mind, but we may be able to help you cope if you will let us try." Mick remained motionless. Triska kissed him on the cheek once more, and Kurt embraced him from the other side before they reluctantly left.

When they returned to the lobby, Triska was still patting away tears with her handkerchief. "Hello, Triska," a voice behind her said. She turned to see Ron Zeskie. "Did you get anything at all out of him?" he asked.

"He talked a little," she said. "He is in deep despair. Perhaps too deep to save. He doesn't want to be helped right now, and he is consumed by guilt. It may not be possible to bring him back."

Zeskie said, "I never even got him to look at me, even though I have talked to him by his bedside for hours. There was never the slightest response. You have accomplished a wonder by getting anything at all out of him. Now we at least know that his brain is working." He turned toward Kurt, asking, "Your name is Kurt, isn't it? My name is Ron Zeskie." He stuck out his hand for Kurt to take, and after an awkward moment, they shook hands.

Kurt looked surprised and said, "You know me?"

"We, Kurt. We know you, and we know what you do. We have always known. We have to know who the good guys are when the shooting starts," Zeskie answered.

Kurt looked perplexed. Triska pulled him down and whispered, "CIA," into his ear. Kurt nodded understanding and smiled at Zeskie.

"I told Mick a minute ago about myself and invited him to come and help me when he is well," Kurt admitted.

Zeskie thought this over and said, "Maybe the thought of vengeance will pull him back to us. What do you think, Doc?" he said to Fisk.

Fisk frowned, "I have no idea what you people are talking about. I do think this has been an exciting morning, and as soon as you leave, I am going to talk to the Psych department about renewing their efforts. You must come back often to see him, and I am going to authorize visits from each of you at any time of the day or night."

Chapter 26

Going Home

Landstuhl Regional Medical Center
Outside Grounds

I thought we would find you out here," Triska said as they walked toward Mick, who was sitting on a park bench enjoying the outside air.

He looked up stiffly at them and gave a small smile. "Hi Triska, hi Kurt."

They sat on each side of him, and Triska kissed him on his cheek. "We thought that we would come by, say hello and see if you would eat lunch with us?" Triska asked.

Mick nodded as if he was thinking it over. He looked at Kurt and said, "I remember that you said you were in an undercover operation with the BND. Is that still true?" he asked.

"Yes, for some time."

"Has it been productive, Kurt? I mean have you found any bad guys for them?"

Kurt looked at Triska for guidance, and she nodded approval to answer the question. "I have uncovered some that later found themselves in prison," he said.

"Ever have some close calls?"

"A couple of times, I was just lucky. They suspected an informer but fortunately chose the wrong one to take out."

"Who, exactly, are these people that you spy on?"

"They usually are recruited from the student population. Typically, they harbor ideals of equality and want to seek out injustice. Innocent enough, but they are quickly brainwashed by the hard core to become Leftist, Progressive, Socialist or Communist or whatever they are calling themselves at the time. Ultimately, they seek to overthrow the government or to destabilize it so that they can get control and impose their system of governance. The ideas, of course, go back to the Marxist revolution in Russia, but what they seem to forget is what happened there. Everybody suffered except those in control. The difference now is the mix of Islam into it. The BND feels that there is an active attempt by forces abroad to cause chaos in Germany, and the same effort is occurring throughout Europe."

"Have you seen any Russians involved with these groups?" Mick asked.

Kurt nodded and said, "We think that the money is coming from the oil rich Islamic areas, but direction and planning are likely done by Russians. I've not actually seen any of the leaders, because they operate at a higher level than I've been able to reach so far, but I have heard rumors about Russians."

Triska interrupted, "The time when Germany was divided was very bad for us. The communist Russians constantly were recruiting and turning our own people against us. For a while, it got better when there was a brief attempt to make Russia a democracy, but lately, it has gone back to the old days."

Mick was silent, staring at his feet. "I am going to be officially discharged from the Army soon, now that I am almost well. Do you think that there is a chance that I would be able to help you infiltrate these radial groups, Kurt?"

Triska leaned around so that she could see his face, and he could see hers. "Wait a minute, Mick. You are not ready to be a spy just yet. I want you to come live with me for a while and protect me as you get better. You need to be really with it both physically and mentally before taking any risks. I know what you are thinking, that you want a chance to kill some Russians. Forget it for now, and just get better. Come live with your Grandmother Triska for now and let me fatten you up and spoil you for a change." She fluffed his hair and gave him a long kiss on his cheek.

Mick leaned into her and let her hug him like a little boy, and they just sat there like that for a long wonderful moment together.

"Greetings, Mick," a familiar voice said.

Mick looked up and frowned. "Zeskie. Don't you ever give up?"

Zeskie smiled and said, "At least you haven't shot me yet, Mick. I have a lot of making up to do with you." Zeskie paused, gathering his thoughts, then added, "I know that I can never make amends, Mick, for what happened. I take full responsibility for it, and the weight of it tears me in half several times a day. It's bad for me, but I can't imagine what you have been through. I keep looking for any way to make things right, but there is no way, so you either have to put up with me popping up like this or shoot me and put me out of my misery."

Mick gave him a hard look and said, "Okay, Zeskie, I'll put up with you. Just don't ask me to ever trust you again." After a moment of reflection, Mick seemed to return to the present. "Did you guys ever catch the spy, Zeskie?"

"No," Zeskie admitted.

"I want to tell you that I always thought it was Harvey Longren," Mick said.

Zeskie said, "I know that's what you thought, and we looked at him carefully, Mick, and never could find a single shred of evidence. Since you were away, Harvey has been on two very dangerous and important missions and conducted himself with distinction. He will be moving up in rank shortly, and everyone but you has a high opinion of him."

Exasperated, Mick exclaimed, "There just isn't anyone else it could be, Zeskie."

"Not true, Mick. In this new age, we have to rule out sophisticated electronic spying or even the old fashioned stuff like a girlfriend who has been told too much. On the other hand, it is likely that we just haven't found an actual human spy who has now gone inactive," Zeskie said.

Mick didn't respond, but anger and frustration radiated from his face.

Zeskie cleared his throat, "I talked to some people, and your discharge papers are on the way. Do you have any place to go, and do you need any help?"

Mick put his arms around Triska and Kurt and said, "I have my family, Zeskie. I will be all right now."

Zeskie smiled, "That's great, just great. I'm happy for you all. Don't worry, though, because I'm still going to visit with you from time to time. I don't want you to miss me. One other thing, Mick..." Zeskie reached behind him and presented Mick with a 45 automatic in a holster. "This is just like your favorite piece, but the difference is that this serial number can't be traced. Please, shoot anyone you like, and I'll cover it up for you. You will notice that it's already loaded. I also have some special ammo to go with it which will trace back to Russia."

Mick accepted the gun and silently put it in his hospital gown pocket.

Triska said, "Enough of serious talk. Time for lunch everyone."

Chapter 26

Chapter 27

The Motorcycle

Triska's Apartment
Stuttgart, Germany

Mick opened the door to Triska's apartment and stood there looking in. Even though she was wonderful to him, he always felt like an intruder. The place was small and only had one bedroom. At his insistence, he was sleeping on the couch. At least he felt welcome and safe here. His clothes were sweat soaked from the long run he had just finished, and he called out to Triska to get her approval to tie up the bathroom. She was gone, and he had the place to himself.

After a long hot shower, he opened the door and sensed someone else in the apartment. He was never without his gun, and he reached under the folded clothes and grasped the handle as he walked into the living room. Mick relaxed when he saw Kurt sitting on the couch reading a magazine.

"Kurt! You are too late to run with me today. I just got back," Mick said.

Kurt put down the magazine and smiled at him. "I have a better idea, Mick. I got a lead on a motorcycle for you, and I came by to pick you up to go have a look."

"Is it legal and is it fast?" Mick asked.

"Neither," Kurt grinned.

"Well, in that case, I am still anxious to see it. I feel sort of helpless without a motorcycle under me, you know."

Kurt nodded and said, "This is special, Mick, and it will take some work to get it on the road, but when we do, Zoom Zoom!"

The house was on the outskirts of Stuttgart, and the bike was in a run-down frame garage in the back. There was a good deal of litter about, and the place was unkempt, perhaps abandoned. Kurt pulled the creaking garage door open, and they peered into the darkness. The contents was a collection of old bicycles, car parts and appliances. Lying on the dirt floor was a black motorcycle, missing its wheels and gas tank. As they came in, Kurt found a pull chain and turned the single light on.

Mick stooped down and examined the bike carefully. There was no indication of brand, and the motor was unfamiliar to him. The shocks were Ohlin's, large and heavy, and the matched brake calipers were Brembo.

"I'd say that this is a custom racing bike, but I've never seen anything like it," Mick said.

Kurt smiled. "This is not a production bike. The large companies only make a few of these at great cost for racing in the Motorcycle Grand Prix. Each one is easily worth over 100,000 euros. The thing to understand is that technology changes so quickly that the bikes are constantly redesigned, and the older ones discarded. They are supposed to be destroyed to keep technical breakthroughs secret, but some are slipped away, and this is one of them. This particular bike was made by Ducati and raced all over Europe by the best of the best. All it needs are wheels and a gas tank. Also, we need to rig up some lights so that it can be on the street."

Mick said, "I'm interested, very interested, Kurt. How much is it going to set me back?"

Kurt said, "That's the best part. I agreed not to call the cops if we got the bike. It's not going to cost us anything! The parts we need might, but I'm still working on it."

"What's next then? How do we go about this?" Mick wondered.

"No problem. I've got a buddy who will come get it, and I have another friend who has some garage space for us. All I needed is for you to want it."

"Okay, Kurt, I'm hooked, and I'm grateful. Come on, and let's get lunch. I'm buying."

It took a month for Mick and Kurt to get the right parts for the bike, and it slowly went together. Kurt wouldn't admit where the new parts came from so Mick assumed the worst. After the fairings were put back on, they stood back and admired their work.

"Black was the right color. The thing looks evil. In fact, it looks fast just sitting there," Kurt observed. "And, I have a surprise for you, Mick," Kurt said and presented Mick with a small package. "This is your license plate. You are officially legal."

They gleefully attached the plate to the rear of the bike, and Mick donned a helmet for the first ride. The big motor started easily and had a vicious snarl when revved. Mick was beaming as he headed out into the traffic. His exuberance faded when he twisted the throttle. Too fast, way too fast. The thing shocked him with its acceleration. He had never before ridden anything so responsive or so powerful. He felt fortunate to return as he idled into the garage with Kurt standing aside, a big grin on his face.

When Mick pulled off his helmet, Kurt asked, "Well, don't keep me waiting. How was it?"

Mick shook his head. "I'm not nearly good enough to ride this thing. It scared me silly, and besides the acceleration, just touching the brakes lifts the bike off of the rear wheel. I need to lie down and recover for a while. We may have overdone it, Kurt."

"Nonsense, Mick. The bike isn't overdone, you are underdone. What we need is to get you back on the racetrack so that you can get used to some speed again."

Mick groaned, "Let me guess, Kurt, you have a buddy for that also?"

"Well, I don't have a world champion to teach you, but I do have in mind a very, very interesting coach," Kurt said, grinning in a devilish way.

Mick was still looking himself over to be sure he was all there. "Let me guess again. This guy is a friend of a friend and a racer of some sort?"

"Not at all close, my friend." "She is a German Superbike racer who is doing pretty well against the otherwise all-male crowd, and she is a former classmate of mine. Can I try to arrange some tutoring for you then?"

"In for a penny, in for a pound. If I'm to survive riding this beast, I need some help. I'm willing!"

Chapter 27

Chapter 28

Glenda Weiss

Sachsenring, Germany

The sound of motorcycles going by was a little terrifying. Their speed was insane, and the shriek of the straight exhaust amplified his fear of getting out there with them. Glenda noticed Mick watching the bikes go by out on the racetrack and correctly gauged his anxiety. "Don't worry, Mick. We are going to start slower than that and work up to it. Didn't Kurt say that you raced bikes before?"

Mick looked at her with a worried face and said, "The track we used is only 2.5 kilometers around. You can't get this kind of speed on it. Besides, I was on a 600cc street bike at the time, and I was a lot dumber than I am now."

Glenda tossed her long blonde hair back, laughing as she stuffed it into her helmet, her head disappearing from view. Dressed in a brightly colored leather racing suit and in her full face helmet, her feminine charm was transformed, and a serious and competent motorcycle racer suddenly emerged. She flipped up the visor and said, "Don't just stand there, Mick, let's get it on."

Somewhat reluctantly, Mick walked to his motorcycle. He realized that he wasn't just afraid of the high speeds or the tight turns of the racetrack. He was afraid of his overpowered motorcycle. Even Glenda raised her eyebrows when she saw it. She knew enough to not ask any questions about where it came from. Mick's bike thundered alive, and they headed down pit lane toward the track with Glenda in the lead. As they approached the raceway, she quickly gathered speed and twisted to look back at him to be sure he was keeping up. She pointed at the tail of her bike to indicate that he was to stay with her. Mick had a sensation of excessive speed as they approached the first corner. He saw Glenda slide off the seat and extend her knee while at the same time twisting to see if he was still there. She was able to lean her motorcycle over at an extreme angle in the corners. Mick thought that they were at their limit of adhesion until a group of three riders passed them on the outside of the turn making at least twice their speed. As they went around the track, Glenda was able to get him up to higher and higher speed. Sometimes she led and sometimes followed to get a look at his technique. They came in after five laps so that she could talk to him about points to work on.

Glenda pulled off her helmet and let her hair spill down her back. "How did you feel about that session, Mick?" she asked.

Mick had a small grin and said, "Well, I am feeling a bit better about it. I still am afraid of this bike, but you are quickly improving me."

Glenda giggled, "Mick, that bike with the right rider would easily best any motorcycle out here. I recognize it now that I have had a chance to watch it in action, but I don't want to know how or where you got it. Now let's sit down and talk about some advanced moves I want out of you on our next session out there."

As the day wore on, Mick's fears dissipated with the concentration needed to keep a powerful motorcycle going fast around a race track. He learned to brake at the last possible second before the corners and to accelerate before the corner ended. He learned to lean off when needed and to lead with his head around the corners. It was obvious as the laps went by that the bike was perfectly suited for a race track and was a brilliant piece of machinery and design. At the end of the day, he was exhausted physically and mentally from the effort, and he was glad to get off the bike.

Mick came up behind Glenda as she was taking off her racing leathers. He lightly put his hand on her shoulder. "Glenda, I can't thank you enough for today. What a great teacher you are. I am almost getting comfortable out there, thanks to you. Is there any way I can pay you for your time or do anything for you?"

Glenda turned around, blushing. She patted him tenderly on his cheek. "It was a pleasure, Mick. You have potential. Probably more than me. We need to keep at it for a few more days and see. You can repay me by being part of my crew when we go racing. The rest of the crew has been complaining to me that we are short-handed and will be only too happy to show you what to do to help. Are you willing?"

"You mean it, Glenda?"

"Of course, I mean it."

"I would be happier than you can imagine to be around this sport and learn. It would also give me a feeling of worth which I need badly right now. Absolutely, Glenda, and thank you."

Glenda looked solemnly at him, her eyes full of feminine expression, "Mind if I ask you a question or two, Mick?"

"There may be some things that I can't tell you, Glenda, but I don't mind if you ask."

Glenda, out of her leathers, was a very attractive young woman and had been around men enough to intuitively know their way of thinking. "I heard from Kurt that you are a dear friend and that you had been through a lot lately. Some of your injuries are obvious and that includes your voice. This woman has to admit that a man like you is very attractive. The manliness that you exude combined with your scars and the mystery of your past...well." She trailed off catching herself before she went too far. "I guess I want to ask if you are married or in a serious relationship, Mick?"

"Kurt and I are brothers-in-law. I was married to his sister," Mick answered slowly.

Glenda looked startled. "I don't understand the was, Mick."

"We were married for one day and then she was killed by a bomb."

"Oh, God, Mick. I'm so sorry that I brought it up. Please forgive me for asking you about it," Glenda said. She had moisture in her eyes as she looked at him.

Mick studied the floor and was silent. He got up and picked up his bag of leathers. "I have to go, Glenda, to meet Kurt. I'll see you tomorrow, and thanks again for today." Mick gave her a little wave and disappeared into the evening light.

Mick walked down the darkening streets. He had no meeting with Kurt, but he couldn't have a relationship with a woman right now. To do so, or even think about it, would dishonor Anna. He didn't want to lay it out for Glenda, but perhaps she would get the idea without being offended. His bike had been modified for the track and had no headlights at the moment, so he was without transportation. He walked toward the little town of Hohenstein and asked a local where a good hotel was. The man suggested Hotel Schweizerhaus over on Weinkellerstrase. He checked in after a good meal at the hotel restaurant and went up to get some sleep.

Mick's cell phone rang, and he reluctantly picked it up. After the click he heard, "*Hallo*, Mick?" It was Kurt, enthusiastic and energetic as usual.

"*Hallo* yourself, Kurt," Mick said. His voice reflected his tiredness, having left his energy somewhere out on the long racetrack.

"Where are you, Mick? I drove all the way over here from Stuttgart to pick you up, and Glenda said that you just walked off."

"I didn't know that you were coming, Kurt. I checked into the hotel Schweizerhaus, and I'm in room 232. Why don't you come over here and get some sleep too," Mick suggested.

Kurt didn't hesitate, "I have some news for you that couldn't wait. Something that I can't say over the phone. I'll be right over." Mick's mind was racing with anticipation of what Kurt was going to say. As much as he tried, he couldn't put the thoughts away. When Kurt softly knocked, Mick snatched open the door. They briefly hugged, and Kurt came rushing in and sat on the bed. He put his finger to his lips and pointed at Mick's black phone. The same phone that he was given by Zeskie prior to the honeymoon. Mick understood immediately, and he accompanied Kurt down to his car and put the phone in the trunk. They walked together down the street toward a small bar before Kurt started to talk.

"One of the radical groups that I meet with are planning something big. I assume that it is some sort of attack on the public. You know, what they call a soft target. It must be a large scale attack, given the secrecy. They have been talking for months about the need to kill German civilians to help destabilize the country. At the last meeting, we were each assigned by the cell leader to obtain specific items, and he told us that we would meet later for more exact instructions. I was ordered to buy twelve small black backpacks from different locations using cash. It sounds like they have bombs or something even more lethal in mind. The news I have for you is that someone they call a guest, from outside our group, will be there to meet with us. To me, this could mean a foreign agent, even one of your Russian friends. Of course, I will report all of this to the BND, but they can't act until the threat is more specific."

Mick didn't have to think about what he wanted. "Kurt, can you get me inside the meeting with you?"

"Mick, this bunch is mostly soft, wild kids like me. They have wild hair and bad teeth and spout radical slogans. You would stand out like a neon sign. Forget it, besides it would blow my cover forever. You have to be outside on this, but I will keep you in the know so that when the time comes you may be able to do things that the Agencies wouldn't do."

"When is this going to happen?" Mick asked, an urgency in his voice.

"I usually get contacted at the last minute, but I would guess at least four or five days from now," Kurt said. "We need to set up a code word that I can say to you over the phone which will mean we should meet in a prearranged spot," Kurt suggested.

"You know that the CIA is likely monitoring my phone, don't you?"

"We have to assume that," Kurt acknowledged. "Zeskie still shows an interest in you, and he is somewhere out there lurking in the shadows at all times. My feeling is that they don't have to know everything we do, and they might not want to anyway, because some of it they might not like."

Mick agreed and allowed himself a small smile. "You bet they won't like it. Zeskie will have to cover for me regardless because of our association. If we don't get caught by the local police, we can do anything we want and get by with it." He pursed his lips in thought and then realized that they could use the old drop site method of communication. "Kurt, we need to set up a drop and pickup spot. Unless our bikes are bugged, no one could follow either one of us. You just let me know by saying, "I still miss Anna, don't you?" and I will go pick up the message. Even if they clue into the method, it will take some effort and time to find the drop site."

They discussed the plans well into the night. As he was leaving, Kurt said, "Glenda says that you are learning quickly. I think you should stay here with her and learn as much as you can for the next three days, because nothing is going to happen during that time. When you are finished, her crew will help you put the bike back together, and you can give me a heads-up call when you are back in Stuttgart."

Mick felt that he was alive again and that his life had meaning once more, even if it was only revenge he was after. After seeing Kurt off, he quickly went back to bed. Tomorrow would prove to be another challenging day. Glenda would make sure that it was.

The motor under Mick purred smoothly through traffic as he rode into Stuttgart toward Triska's apartment. The ride back was nearly 450 kilometers and required two fuel stops. After racing with Glenda for four days, he had become very comfortable at high speed, and on the return trip, he had frequently taken his motorcycle up to 300 kilometers per hour on the Autobahn. He was ready for action now, and he felt more sound of mind and body than anytime since the bombing. He continued to think about Anna constantly. She was never far from his mind, and he still woke up several times at night as the image of her last breath came back again and again. He realized that this would always be so, and the only possible release would be his death, but he wasn't as ready to die now as he had been for so long. He wanted retaliation on anyone who would commit crimes against innocent people, but especially he wanted revenge against the Russians.

The call from Kurt came early one morning as Mick lay looking at the ceiling from the couch in Triska's apartment. He quickly dressed and put on his expensive Italian leather jacket that he had been given by Anna's father. He highly valued it, but at the same time, it was a reminder of his great loss, since it was the only thing he had left to remind him of her, and even though it caused pain, it also brought back the pleasant memory of Anna being there when he put it on for the first time.

The pickup site was simple but would be very hard to find. As he wove his way through traffic, he went between cars, jumped curbs and used alleys frequently. On his motorcycle, especially this one, he simply could not be followed. The pickup was under the frame of an older delivery truck which was always parked curbside in front of a butcher's shop. Mick simply slowed enough to grab the magnetic box from under the left rear of the truck and then sped off. Kurt had placed it by the same method the previous night. Mick turned into a small park and discarded the metal container into a garbage can. He stopped long enough to read the paper before discarding it into another can nearby. Written on the note was an address and a time, nothing else. The meeting was on for late that night. The plan they had discussed was for Mick to be nearby and follow the foreign agent as he left the meeting. Mick had other ideas however, and he headed back to Triska's apartment on the other side of town, making sure no one could follow.

For dinner, Mick took Triska out to eat for a change. They dined at a small place within walking distance and played their usual game of pretending to be foreigners who could not speak German. Since they both could speak several languages fluently, and understood the quirks of people from various countries, it was always fun. As they dined and spoke French to each other, Triska gave Mick a hard look. "You aren't about to do something rash, are you, Mick?"

"Rash? Whatever do you mean, *Grand-mère?*" Mick exclaimed. "Do you mean preventing bad people from killing innocent Germans? Is that really rash?" He always forgot that this old sweet little woman was an accomplished spy and still had access to all the secret information in the world that she wanted.

"I don't care about the bad guys, Mick, all I care about is you and Kurt. I couldn't stand any more loss in my life. I want to keep you both around as long as I am alive. Please don't put either one of you at risk," she pleaded.

Mick had a deadly look about him, and when he answered in his irregular deep voice, it was as though his words came directly from hell. "Never worry about a hunter when he is after prey. The prey is in danger. The hunter isn't."

Chapter 28

Chapter 29

The Big Kill

Stuttgart, Germany

Mick had ridden by the location earlier to scout it. The group was going to meet in an apartment building currently under construction. It was a good choice for a meeting place, because there were several nearby buildings that a spotter could use to detect any threats before they arrived, but it would be a lot harder for them to notice one man alone. He knew that at least one guard would be posted just outside the entrance to the meeting area to screen those arriving. There was no way that he could find and eliminate the other spotters, but they couldn't stop him either, if they even saw him. The meeting was to be at 1700 hours, and Mick assumed that the guest would arrive late to be sure that a raid wasn't in progress, so he planned to approach just after 1900 hours. Kurt was not expecting Mick to come to the meeting, only to follow the guest after the meeting.

Mick wore his black racing leathers and was nearly invisible in the shadows as he moved slowly, confidently, toward the site. It was dark, quiet, and deserted on the street leading toward the construction site, and the only sound was made by his boots against the concrete. As Mick turned into the apartment building entrance, a large man stepped out of the shadows into his path. *"Wo denkst du, du gehst?"* the man asked.

Mick stopped for a brief instance as though he was going to answer. In a blindingly quick move, Mick slashed the throat of the guard and watched him fall, unable to cry out as blood filled his lungs from his severed trachea. Mick continued to walk slowly into the building listening for voices which would guide him to the location of the meeting. He quietly picked his way across building materials, heading relentlessly toward muffled sounds of voices. A closed door had both sound and light seeping from under its bottom edge. He paused and drew out his 45 caliber pistol. The gun was in one hand and an extra magazine in the other with an additional magazine in his pocket. Enough.

When he was ready, he stepped back a bit and, with one hard kick, burst the door wide open. Stepping over the threshold, he methodically surveyed a room filled with stunned, turned faces. Two older men at the front of the room looked equally surprised, their faces grimaced with sudden terror and a realization of what was about to happen. Kurt stared at him in disbelief, also visualizing the horror about to unfold.

Mick opened fire, first at the two men at the front of the room, delivering two head shots in less than one second. Starting with the closest to him, and rapidly and accurately firing on one after another, he dropped seven in place. As he started shooting, there was a rush to get away. They climbed over chairs and each other in a desperate, but futile, effort to escape, but the only place to go was toward the front of the room. Mick ejected the spent first magazine, expertly shoving another one to place and continued firing. There were only two men left after his second magazine fell out of the pistol. He methodically slammed the last magazine in and moved forward over bodies toward the screams of help coming from the remaining two cowering in the corner. There was no help or mercy for them that night, and Mick shot them at point blank range. He found Kurt, who was nearly paralyzed with fear and panic, gripped his wrist, and shouted at him, "Come, Kurt, we have to get away quickly." Before leaving, Mick wiped down the handgun and dropped it on one of the lifeless forms. He bent down and searched the body of the guest for ID but as he expected, there was none. He pulled Kurt's arm forcibly, dragging him toward the door as Kurt looked around at the gore, blood, and twisted bodies whose eyes seemed to look back at him.

"My God, Mick, you just killed sixteen people!" Kurt exclaimed.

"Seventeen. There was one at the door," Mick quietly answered. "Come this way, there is a back door we should use." Kurt was dazed and clumsy but followed where Mick led. "Kurt, listen to me now. Where did you park your car?" Mick asked.

Kurt looked far away but said, "I rode over with someone, I have no car here."

"Good, we'll use my bike. It's just a block from here in an alley," Mick said. As they emerged from the building, two separate gunshots were heard in the distance. Mick looked concerned but didn't say anything, and they continued to make their way toward Mick's bike. "Straighten up, Kurt. Try to act normal, and don't draw attention to yourself," Mick said threateningly as he roughly shook Kurt's shoulder.

"I am going to puke, Mick. Can't we stop?"

"You puke, and I'll make you eat it off the sidewalk. Come on and walk straight, before I slap some sense into you," Mick growled under his breath. The bike at last came into view, and Kurt had only to hang on after they started riding. In the distance they could hear the sounds of sirens getting closer. Before mounting the bike, Mick twisted the metal license plate, bending it up to prevent the number from showing. Kurt was forced to sit on the hard tail section, but they got underway quickly, and after a couple of miles, they headed back to Triska's apartment at normal speed.

With just one look at Kurt's face and clothing, Triska knew that he had suffered some sort of trauma. They had to stop once for Kurt to throw up, and his clothes still reeked of it. Mick was calm and considerate but avoided discussion of what happened. They helped Kurt out of his clothes, and Mick led him into the shower, holding him so that he wouldn't fall.

"Want to talk about it, Mick?" Triska asked.

Mick replied without looking at her, "Nothing to talk about, dear. We both are safe and sound as you wanted." He sat down as if nothing had happened. They sat in silence as Kurt showered.

Just after breakfast, there was a soft knock at the door and Mick got up to answer it, being alone for the moment. Triska wanted to drop Kurt off at his apartment before going in to the BND, and they had left earlier. Mick knew that she was anxious to find out exactly what had happened the previous night, but Kurt had been unable to talk about it or eat anything since they arrived.

Zeskie was standing in the hall. "Morning, Mick. Mind if I come in for a chat?" he said as he pushed past Mick.

"Want some coffee, Zeskie?" Mick offered, while taking a long look at Zeskie who was uncharacteristically rumpled. No sleep, Mick guessed.

"I believe I will, Mick," he answered, sitting down on the couch. He accepted the mug of coffee from Mick and sized him up. "Are you all right this morning, Mick?"

Mick quickly answered as he sipped his coffee, "I feel pretty good this morning, Zeskie. Thank you for asking. You, on the other hand, don't look very rested."

"Very observant," Zeskie said wryly. "I was up most of the night with a big shooting across town. Nineteen people were killed last night and all but one by gunfire. Sixteen of those had a single, but fatal, gunshot wound to the head."

"You don't say. Nineteen?" Mick asked as he peered through the steam from his coffee.

"Yes, nineteen." We shot one, and the BND shot the other. They both were hiding in buildings across from the main action. They were the last link in the chain so nobody got away," Zeskie said in a matter-of-fact way. He continued to watch Mick for any facial activity but only saw a calmness about him. "Well, it was a good thing that the shooting occurred. The room that contained sixteen bodies also had twelve backpacks filled with plastic explosives and the wiring and switches to set them off. It was a good thing that someone stopped them from killing a lot of innocent people. It was a singular act of heroism to take on such a large crowd. Fortunately, we don't know who did it, because we would have to give this person a medal. Of course, we don't know who did it or why. We were as surprised as the ones who got shot, because the BND and our agents have been working together on this case for a couple of months and were ready to pick them all up. Turns out, though, if we had missed one or two, there would have been some deaths we wouldn't want on our hands. This was much better." Zeskie settled back to sip his coffee and continued to study Mick. "The thing is though, solutions like that are going to lead to the killing of innocent people sooner or later. The death penalty without a trial or presentation of evidence reminds me of the Old West. Clearly, it shouldn't happen again."

Mick gave him a hard look and said, "I get the idea, Zeskie. Say no more. I have a question for you now. Did you find any non-Germans in the bunch?"

"Funny that you should ask, Mick," Zeskie said. "We think the two we shot across the street were Russians, and the one killed by a knife in front of the site probably was also. There was one inside that could have been Russian, but we are processing him very carefully because of his likely importance in the case. You can usually tell by the teeth. Russian dentists treat things differently and use different materials for restoration. We are also running DNA on all four of them just to be sure.

Mick nodded approval. "I am feeling even better. Must be your company, Zeskie."

Zeskie opened his ever-present briefcase and handed a wrapped package to Mick. "This is a replacement. I heard that you lost the other one I gave you."

The weight was telling. Another 45 caliber pistol. Mick silently put it away.

"Normally, I would suggest a little target practice just to sight it in, but I don't think you need a lot of practice, Mick," Zeskie said. "By the way, how is your brother. I heard that he was sick last night."

This time Mick briefly looked surprised but recovered quickly. "He'll be okay eventually. I know how he feels, because that happened to me once."

"Mick, please don't do stupid things with your phone again. Just let us keep you safe. We are on your side. Remember that," Zeskie said.

Mick nodded understanding but said nothing. Zeskie got up to leave. "Mick, I care a lot for you. I really could pull rank on you and order you around, because you are still officially in the CIA, but I won't. You work for us, but it feels like we work for you. Stay out of trouble for a while, please, because I have other things to do."

When Mick returned from his run, Triska had returned to the apartment and was there to greet him. Mick studied her face to see if she was angry, but he couldn't tell. She was still too much the old spy to give away anything by her expression.

"Triska. Are you upset with me?" Mick asked bluntly.

"Mick, dear, I understand why you did what you did. I understand that you couldn't tell Kurt what you were going to do without endangering him. The problem for me is that you chose a really radical way to deal with our enemies that is unacceptable, even in a time of war. It just exceeds what we understand as civilized behavior. In this case, you likely saved a lot of lives by getting rid of a bad bunch who were about to create mayhem, but it is not the right way to do it."

Mick was hesitant to bring it up but asked anyway, "How's Kurt?"

Triska rolled her eyes. "He is shaken up. The old first combat syndrome that he'll get past in a couple of days. He sure looks at you differently now, Mick. He had no idea of what you are capable."

"Did you know, Triska?"

"I knew. You radiate it. You look on combat as a soldier, not as a policeman. You don't arrest, you kill. I knew from the first day I met you what you are, what you are capable of. I also know what a fine and dependable man you are and how much capacity for love you had...at one time. Someday, perhaps, the love will come back into your life. You deserve to find and have love and leave the killing to another generation. I hope you can live long enough for it to happen."

Chapter 29

Chapter 30

Meeting Koffman

Stuttgart, Germany

It happened one day while Mick was browsing around in a little corner food market near Triska's apartment. He had a subconscious feeling that he was being watched. He tried to use his peripheral vision at first but felt compelled to look right at the source of his feeling. As he turned, he slid his right hand under his jacket and grasped the 45 he carried in the small of his back. Coming toward him was the smiling face of Oberst Peter Koffman. Koffman put his arms way out for an expected embrace, and Mick did the same. They patted each other's back robustly.

Mick held Koffman at arm's length and looked him over. "What, no black jumpsuit? Have you been discharged?" Mick asked jokingly.

"No, my friend, no! Even an Oberst gets a day off. Say, can you come outside with me so that we can talk a little?"

Mick agreed, and they left the store arm in arm.

"I thought for a moment that you were going to shoot me. I know how good you are at it," Koffman said with a devious smile.

"It's very good to see you again, Peter," Mick said as they walked. "I thought a lot about you in the last several months, but I didn't want to go to the BND headquarters because of, you know, the memories."

Koffman fought back his tears and, after a painful moment, answered, "I have been unable to face you, Mick, until now, because I have been ashamed that we let you down so badly. There isn't any excuse I have except stupidity and incompetence."

They walked a while before Mick could answer. "Peter, I want you to understand that it would have happened sooner or later. The Russians were determined to have their revenge on me, and nothing could stop them."

Koffman cleared his throat. "They took you out and got revenge and thought they were done with you. This new thing, if they figure it out, will start it again. I am afraid for you."

"I have had criticism from several people regarding recent events, Peter. Don't tell me you are another critic."

"Not at all, Mick," Koffman said loudly. Then in a whisper, "I was very proud of you. I wish we could do that frequently. It would save us a lot of trouble. But, Mick, I was a little shocked, also. I don't know if I could do that myself."

Mick stared straight ahead while they were walking. "I guess the reason is that since the day Anna died I only exist as a hollow shell. They can't take anything from me any longer. I don't even care if they kill me. At least dead, I wouldn't have to see Anna's last seconds of life in my mind any longer."

"I would offer some advice, my friend. You need to live as a shadow for a while, away from anyone that they could harm in reprisal if they find out you again are killing Russians."

"Yes, Peter. They could harm Triska or Anna's father and mother. Even Kurt is at risk."

"Kurt is expected to take chances, and he does so all of the time. They think he is one of them, but you are right about the others. Incidentally, I hear that you are riding on racetracks now with a stolen motorcycle. Any truth to the rumor?" he asked with a knowing grin.

"I didn't steal anything, but the source is shadowy, I admit. Blame your agent, Kurt, if you must. As far as racing goes, I am still learning and, as yet, not good enough to be called a racer."

Koffman stopped beside a car and unlocked the trunk. He reached inside and withdrew a small bundle. "We put this together for you, and there may be times it will come in handy. With your training and your gift of language, you are a true chameleon. You can be anybody you choose to be. With a little help and the right ID, you will be very, very hard to find. We still haven't heard that the CIA found your spy, so you would be wise to be cagey and alert with your own people. It is my opinion that Zeskie is a good man, but he reports everything he does, and who knows what happens then."

Mick accepted the bundle from Koffman. They both understood that this could be their last encounter in person, and there was a moment of silence as each gathered their thoughts.

Mick spoke first, "I wish we had spent more time together, Peter. We are much alike. I hope someday that we can still do that."

Koffman had a look of sadness on his face when he responded, "Somehow, Mick, we were born brothers. I feel inexplicably close to you, and even though the future is yet unknown to us, we are destined to share life in some fashion."

On the way back to the apartment, Mick realized that his encounter with Koffman brought him back to reality. As much as he loved Triska, he had to get away from her to keep her from harm. He knew that she would protest any such idea, so he decided to write her a farewell note when he got back instead of facing her, which would be too painful for both of them.

The package from Koffman contained two fresh IDs which would be unknown to Zeskie and the CIA. There was also credit cards, using the same names, which Mick assumed would be likewise protected. A thick roll of cash, in various denominations, half in dollars, half in euros, totaled nearly one hundred thousand and easily enough for a couple of years of high living. A gleaming, unmarked 9mm Beretta handgun was accompanied by extra ammo. Also included was an ordinary looking cell phone with instructions informing him that it could not be traced. The last piece was a new license plate for his motorcycle, the registration papers using the name of one of the new identities.

He could disappear like a morning fog. The BND would know where he was, so in effect he would be trading allegiances, but he realized that he was going to at least tell Zeskie something before he vanished, otherwise he could be classified as rogue and the protection from the CIA, such as it was, would stop. Mick hesitated for a moment while thinking, but eventually picked up the black phone, and without pushing any buttons, just spoke at it, "I need to talk to Zeskie," and then put it down. As he was packing, the black phone rang. It was Zeskie. They had been listening to everything, full time.

"Zeskie," Mick said when he picked it up. "I have to talk to you in person."

"Yes, Mick, you do. Stay there, and I'll be right over."

True to his word, Zeskie appeared shortly. Mick let him in, and they both sat on the couch. "Well, Mick," he said. "Want to tell me about what you want, or should I tell you what you are going to say?"

"What do you think is going on, Zeskie?"

"We know that you just met with Peter Koffman today. We don't know what he gave you, but I would guess it was ID and money and perhaps another weapon. Am I close?"

"For an organization which prides itself on knowing everything, you can't find a spy who is killing Americans. You and I need to be frank, Zeskie. Can we talk without these listening devices?"

Zeskie reached into his pocket and took out his black phone and threw it on the coffee table, and

Mick did the same. Without a word, they left the apartment and walked down the alley together.

"I'm listening, and they aren't. Go for it," Zeskie said.

"I believe that you are looking out for me, Zeskie. Frankly, I trust you. I don't know that we can trust the organizations which are entwined with data until you catch the spy. He has to have been placed in a position of trust and from which he has access to information. I want your permission to go dark to the CIA and the Army. You and I could still connect if you can figure out how, but someone needs to be outside of the information net and out of the reach of the spy."

"I agree with the concept, Mick. By the way, there is some new movement on our hunt that I can't divulge yet. We may be close, but our little spy is smart and shuts down when he feels threatened. It is a confusing picture. I don't know how you could help us right now, but there may be a time when you can. Did the BND provide you with a phone?"

"Yes," Mick acknowledged. "They said it couldn't be traced."

"True enough for regular calls, but don't ever call me on that thing. Tell you what, if we ever need to talk, we can communicate through Oberst Koffman."

They shook hands as Zeskie left, and Mick watched him from the apartment window as he made his way back down the apartment alley.

The door opened unexpectedly, and Triska walked in. From her expression, she looked like she knew everything. "I was waiting for Zeskie to leave, Mick.

Don't worry, I know everything that Peter Koffman told you. I even helped get the papers ready." She embraced him and spoke tenderly, softly, while looking up into his face. "You know that I don't want you to go, don't you?"

"Yes, dearest, I know." He put his hand on her back and patted her softly. "If they start looking for me, Triska, they will find you. I couldn't bear to lose you like I lost Anna." They held the embrace for a long time without words.

Still sobbing and trying to wipe away her tears, Triska said, "I am ready to die, Mick. I have lived a long life of adventure, and it is all behind me now. I cling to you and Kurt, and I am saddened that you both are in harm's way in the same profession I have. It's a bad occupation, Mick. It cost my marriage and all my happiness, and now I live alone except for the short but wonderful time we spent together. The plain truth is that you would be at greater risk here with me, because you would be easier to spot and trap. I hate it, but you have to go for your own sake. I can contact you, and you can contact me at any time without risk, so we will still be close, if only over the phone."

They spent the last hour together holding hands on the couch and looking at each other as if it would be the last time. Mick slowly got up and said, "It's time, Triska. I have to leave, and it might as well be now." He went over and picked up his small bag of belongings and left without another word. Triska folded in grief, her arms clutching her knees, as Mick closed the door behind him.

Mick strapped the bag to the tail of the motorcycle and fastened the new license plate in place. He picked the CIA black phone out of his pocket and crushed it into the asphalt with his boot. Using the new phone, he dialed a number. "*Hallo* Glenda! This is Mick Grundy. I am ready to be your race course servant. Where should I go?"

Chapter 31

Racing

Sachsenring, Germany

Mick held up the sign for Glenda to see as she went by, letting her know her position and lap time. At the speeds the racers were reaching on the straight section, it was hard to understand how they could see the sign at all, much less read it. Glenda was doing very well, running in twelfth position out of a field of nineteen riders. There was excitement among her crew, and they cheered each time she advanced to a new position.

The pit boss was an Italian nicknamed Moto by everyone, because he knew the most about setting up a motorcycle for the race track. The other crewmembers were an odd collection.

Counting Mick, there were a total of eight, and each had a specific task. Mick was assigned to keep the bike fueled and to give Glenda fluids when she stopped. Additionally, he was required to keep her motorcycle clean at all times.

Since Glenda was a rarity in a male dominated sport, she was pursued by the press. Mick, wearing dark wrap around glasses with a brimmed cap to hide his face, stayed in the background and out of any photographs. The team had been at this track for three days, with the two preceding ones taken up with testing and practice. Mick was allowed to go out on the track with his bike early each morning before the racing started and Glenda was always there to help him increase his skills. His lap times were slowly becoming lower than hers, a fact that she dismissed because of his more powerful motorcycle. Glenda rode a slightly modified street motorcycle and had obtained some financial and technical help from Honda but wasn't yet good enough to make the factory team.

Mick had become close friends with Moto, who had become convinced that Mick was a native Italian because of his mastery of the Italian language. In his spare time, Moto worked on Mick's bike and was constantly bringing in another exotic part for them to install on it. Mick grew in confidence and ability once he could focus on the present and force the thoughts of the past out of his head, however briefly. The dreams continued, but at least while he was engaged at tasks during the day, he could forget.

There was a commotion in the pit. Glenda had gone down. Mick rushed out to trackside to try to spot where she had fallen while Moto and two others piled into the truck, fishtailing out across the infield toward a small group of track officials gathered around the wreck. Mick watched helplessly from the pit area as an ambulance raced toward the spot and most of the fans stood, craning their necks for a better view. After fifteen agonizing minutes, Moto came slowly back with her motorcycle in the back of the truck. The race resumed, and bikes streamed past on their way to the first corner.

"What happened, Moto? Is she okay?" Mick asked.

Moto shrugged as only Italians can. "She have pain. Going to get x-ray now." He grabbed his shoulder to indicate the source of Glenda's pain. "Come, Mick, we have work the bike need." Moto clapped his hands and indicated that all of them should start working right away on the fallen motorcycle.

In about two hours, and long after the race was over, a car pulled up, and Glenda slowly got out. Her right arm hung in a splint, and the upper part of her racing leathers dangled behind her. As her team came up to greet her, she raised her left arm to stop them. "I'm all right. I have a cracked collarbone which doesn't need surgery, but I can tell you that it's gruesomely painful."

She motioned to Mick to come toward her. When he did, she said, "The second race is tomorrow. How would you feel if I asked you to take my place out there? I'll be in better shape for the next one in a couple of weeks, but we need to keep our team points up."

Mick said, "Of course, I'll do that for you, Glenda, but I don't think that I'm really ready, and I might disappoint you."

"If you don't get hurt and just not finish last, I'll be proud of you," Glenda smiled. "I have already given your name, at least your assumed name, to the track officials, and we should get some word soon."

Moto raised his eyebrows and his arms to the sky and said, "Much to do, much to do," and headed toward the bike being reassembled.

Mick didn't own a real set of racing leathers, but there was an vendor just outside of the paddock which sold them. Fortunately, they were still open, and Mick left in a hurry to get outfitted in time for the race tomorrow. He came back in a couple of hours fitted with the same colors as Glenda wore. Except for size, they would look the same on the bike. The damaged motorcycle came back together quickly, but Moto insisted that they start testing before darkness to get the adjustments right because of the change in bodyweight.

The morning brought the same sunshine as the previous day, but light shone on Mick differently. This morning he was a real racer. The substitution was announced and several members of the motorcycle racing press showed up to interview him. The team refused all such offers on the grounds that it was a very temporary replacement for Glenda and would only be for one race. When the time came for the race start, Mick was a bundle of nerves. This bike was not nearly as scary as the one he usually rode, but it would still approach speeds of 290 kilometers an hour on the back stretch. He was just getting a feel for it when the allocated time for practice ran out. He kissed Glenda on the cheek and pulled on his helmet.

The bikes started lining up, and because Glenda didn't finish the previous race, Mick was starting from last. The bikes revved up for the start, and at the flag, there was a blinding rush for the first corner. As the race settled into a pattern, the bikes strung out, and Mick felt confident enough to move past the slower ones and gradually come forward. His team waved their arms at him as he went past in a blur. In the final three laps, he felt the fire of adrenaline within him, and he felt invincible. He surged forward and engaged in a back and forth passing and being passed struggle with two bikes in thirteenth and fourteenth place. At the last possible second, Mick accelerated around both of them to finish in thirteenth place. His team was elated, and they rushed out to greet him as he slowly came into his pit. After he took off his helmet, Glenda came out smiling and hugged his neck with her good arm. "I knew you had talent in there, Mick. I am so proud of you!

Mick held her hand and said, "I had the best coach of anybody, and one who gave selflessly of her time to help me out. I am so grateful to you, Glenda, and I am also relieved to turn this bike back over to you. This is your team, and there are reasons that I can't race professionally. This was my one time to enjoy the spectacle of it, but now I have to blend back into the background."

Mick knew that he had to get away before the press found him. He didn't need his face photographed for pubic publication. There could be someone still hunting for him who might see it. He took Glenda aside to explain.

"There is a lot I can't say to you, Glenda. I feel that I will take away more than I leave, but you have to trust my judgment that I should go away now. I'll remember this experience forever, and I'll always remember who made it possible."

Glenda stood, temporarily speechless, while struggling for the right words, "Mick, you have grown on me. Having you here gave me a lot of strength, and I always wished that there could be more between us. I don't know what is behind and chasing you, but I always hoped it would go away. Someday, you will be ready to have another deep relationship with a woman. When that time comes, think of me please."

Mick leaned over and gently touched Glenda's neck with his hand, then picked up his bag and strode toward his waiting motorcycle.

Chapter 32

Contact

Schonach, Germany

The phone was ringing when Mick came out of the shower. Usually it was Triska, but Zeskie did occasionally call when he was visiting BND headquarters. Since Mick moved to Schonach, they kept in closer touch. He was living in the picturesque city under the name of Eric Gasser and taken a six month lease on a furnished apartment.

This morning had been typical of his day which had consisted of a two hour workout at a local health club followed by a leisurely breakfast chatting with retired men who gathered in a nearby chalet-styled restaurant every morning. Mick had not spoken English to anyone in over a week and was beginning to believe his own cover story. When the weather permitted, the afternoons were spent riding his motorcycle around the smaller roads through the scenic Black Forest surrounding Schonach. In his pocket, his phone started to vibrate. Mick knew that he was waiting for something, not hiding, and a sixth sense told him that this was it.

"*Hallo?*"

"Mick? Hi, this is Kurt!" the voice crackled.

"You finally called me."

"You alone, Mick?"

"Of course I am."

"I have something you may be interested in."

"I'm listening, Kurt."

"You once told me that the person you believe spotted you and Anna on the train had something unusual about his face."

Mick instantly remembered the long thin face with the rough skin. From a distance and with the light from above, the face looked like craters on the surface of the moon. "Yeah, Kurt. I called him Pockface. Have you seen him?"

"One of the extreme cells that I have infiltrated is planning something. Talk has been about destroying government buildings, and they seem to be gleeful about the prospect. There's more. I gather that there is to be supervision by someone outside our group, someone who is going to tell us how to do it. I overheard a couple of fellows who had seen him previously, and they referred to a unique skin problem and said that he is tall and thin. The meeting will be soon, but they usually are very secretive about when and where until the last minute."

Mick asked, "Roughly, where is this likely to be?"

"They are all from Karlsruhe, so somewhere near there."

Mick thought over this new information. He was currently just southwest of Stuttgart and not very far from either place. An hour's travel would get him there. He also remembered that Karlsruhe was where he last saw Pockface. "Kurt, if you can give me a one hour notice, I could get there."

"Mick, I couldn't stand the same scene as last time. Some of these guys are mostly talk, although I can't say for sure that they wouldn't do a terrorist act. Please tell me that you will only take out the pock-marked man, and let us arrest the others," Kurt pleaded.

There was a long silence which indicated to Kurt that Mick didn't agree with his plea. Finally, Mick responded, "I can't promise anything, Kurt, but I understand what you want, and I will try hard to do it that way. When the action starts, it usually has a mind of its own, and no amount of planning will make it happen as you expect it to. The main thing is, we don't want terrorists to be able to kill at whim with decent people being helpless to stop them. Finding them after they kill is unacceptable. We need to strike first, before it happens."

Kurt said, "I feel the same way, Mick, but there are laws we must obey if we are to have a civilized society. We have a code of conduct which makes us better than them. Killing indiscriminately should be a thing of the past."

"If you stood there and let a man stab you before you could make up your mind that he was committing a crime against you, you probably deserve to be stabbed," Mick said. "I know that you are part of a group who prides themselves in protecting society the best and most honorable way they know. You will recall that I was part of the same system, and I was trained to think the same way, but

I no longer do. I don't answer to anyone but myself now, and I clearly understand that our enemies give no quarter, respect no laws and are an infection in our society which must be stopped. Stopping someone who is about to kill an innocent person is the only thing that keeps me going. I have no other reason to live, because they have taken everything I ever wanted away from me. At least this way, I may be able to prevent the same thing being done to others."

"Revenge is it, Mick?"

"Yes, revenge."

For the next five days, Mick waited to get the call on the small phone that he had purchased at the direction of Kurt. They both carried similar phones, and even if they could be traced, they would only be used once and discarded. The intent, as before, was to keep knowledge of what they were doing from both the CIA and the BND as well as any foreign spies. Kurt wanted to help Mick get the man responsible for the death of his sister, and for this personal reason, he was willing to disobey rules. He was present when the Director opined that Mick was nothing more than a killer, and even though the slaying of the previous terrorists could be justified, no one wanted a murderer loose to dispense justice as he saw fit. Sooner or later, there would be a mistake which would reflect badly on those in charge.

While Mick was walking down the beautiful old street back to his apartment, he felt a small vibration in his pocket. The little beige cell phone was ringing in silent mode. He picked it up and pressed the button without speaking. Kurt quickly said the address and time and was off. After the disconnect, Mick wiped the phone and discarded it into the next trash can he passed. Kurt would be doing the same thing. Tonight, it was tonight.

Mick quickened his pace toward his apartment. Once there, he looked around for anything he needed to take with him, because he might not be able to return. Other than identification papers, passports and his guns, the only thing he valued was the leather jacket from Anna's father. It had been shipped to Triska the previous day along with the BND phone without using a return address. There was still plenty of cash left, and it would buy anything he needed later. When his watch showed two hours until the meeting, he tossed his apartment keys on the small dining table and headed downstairs to his waiting motorcycle.

Afternoon was illuminated by soft, mauve shades of early fall as Mick approached the meeting site. His bike spun up small waves of colored leaves in the narrow streets as it slowly rolled forward, the echo of the motorcycle's powerful motor reflecting from the nearby brick walls, making a pleasant stereo effect of sound as he passed. He wanted to get a look at the site and the surrounding streets but wanted not to be noticed by anyone watching, so he only allowed himself one pass. His plan was to return after dark on foot as before. The meeting place had an entrance midway off an alley of some length which would probably be guarded from both ends. He realized that he would have to take out both watchers to prevent an alarm, but how to do it at the same time was a problem. Thoughts about it churned in his head as he slowly pulled away from the area. There seemed to be no one around, but an interested party might already be watching from a distance. It crossed his mind that this meeting could be a trap designed solely to catch Mick Grundy. If the terrorists or their puppet masters figured out that he and Kurt were connected, they could have baited Kurt with false information to lure Mick in. If that were true, he and Kurt were both targets. Unfortunately, there was no way to contact Kurt without exposing him.

Mick returned to a busy street about a half mile away, and as he passed the shops, he looked carefully at the signs. When he found what he was looking for, he pulled to the curb and switched off the bike. He entered a little sandwich shop which advertised home delivery of food and patiently waited in line at the cash register. After giving the clerk a list of food and beverages, he got assurance that the food would be delivered within the hour. Mick gave a large tip with a promise of another after delivery, as a small insurance that it would happen on time.

Returning to his motorcycle, he circled the area widely to avoid being spotted. A suitable parking spot was found three blocks from the meeting site. Night had descended, and in darkness, Mick stealthily moved toward a position offering a view of one entrance to the alley from less than two blocks away. He settled into the shadows and waited. After a short time, the headlights of a vehicle slowed and stopped just at the alley entrance. A young man got out, inspecting a paper in his hand. The boy's other hand carried a light colored bag of food, and he briskly started toward the alley entrance. A large man emerged from a nearby car and called out to him. They appeared to argue briefly, and the delivery boy returned to his car. Mick started moving forward as the delivery car pulled away and the other man got back into his car.

The guard was alone in the car and Mick moved silently toward the opposite side. He could hear the man talking on a handheld communication device and overheard what was being said in Russian about the attempted food delivery. The thick-necked man never saw the large arm until it entered the open window on the driver's side and encircled his neck, pulling him gasping and struggling from the window as Mick intentionally broke his neck. He pulled the limp body toward the rear of the car and picked up the dropped communication device. Using car keys from the ignition, the body was placed in the trunk, along with the keys.

Mick started walking around the block toward the other side of the alley. Seventy-five meters from the other entrance, Mick stopped. He couldn't spot his prey, but he knew that the other man was there, likely in a parked car, waiting. Mick took the communication device out and pressed the send key. He could hear some clicks, then an excited voice replied in Russian, *"Mickale, - то, что Вы?"* Mick studied the parked cars as he slowly moved forward, clicked the device again, then turned it off.

A large man emerged from a close-by car and started walking toward the alley entrance. Mick silently followed, closing the distance quickly. Just as Mick arrived behind the man, he snapped his fingers, causing his prey to spin around toward him. Mick's fist struck the man in the neck with enough force to lift him briefly from the sidewalk. He fell backwards into the hard concrete, clutching his throat, as Mick's boot swung toward his temporal area. When the man stopped moving, Mick crouched and listened. After a moment, he stood erect and moved down the alley toward the entrance of the meeting site, while unzipping his black jacket and withdrawing his 45 caliber pistol.

A sign read *Kniel Allee 7* above the dented metal door. This was the place he was looking for. He grasped the metal handle and pulled it hard toward him, then rolled back against the wall when the door swung open, expecting, but grateful for no gunfire. He stopped the door with his hand as it swung closed and entered the blackness. The door clicked closed behind him, enveloping him in a darkness which was nearly complete. He stood still, listening while holding his breath, allowing his eyes to adjust. An odor of mildew and rodents wafted up and crept into his nose, along with a sticky closeness which seemed to blanket him as completely as the darkness. A murmur of voices came from close by, and he turned toward it and moved slowly, being guided by the direction of the sound. Falling water droplets occasionally found exposed skin and trickled down his neck. His eyes gradually revealed more detail, and he could see that he was headed down a corridor with a closed door at the end.

Angry voices became more distinct as he drew closer, and a plaintive moan arose, but muffled, like it was still far away. Mick could hear a man's sharp voice clearly speaking in accented German, *"Wir können mehr für Sie tun. wo ist dein stinkenden Schwager. Wo ist Mick Grundy."*

The voice was asking someone about him. There was the sound of a slap, followed by another moan. Mick reached for the door handle and pushed very slowly inward. The interior of the room became more visible as the dim yellow light from the room spilled into the hallway, casting Mick's shadow behind him. In a chair, a slumping figure's head was lowered, hiding his face. Two men stood close by, their backs to Mick. One was tall and thin.

The door creaked, causing the tall man to turn his head quickly toward Mick, like a startled bird. It was Pockface. Mick instantly raised his pistol and fired three deafening shots at him, all direct hits. The angular shape thrown like a rag doll against the far wall. The room started moving all at once, like roaches on the floor, no longer hidden from the light. Mick fired at a dark, moving shape close to him and pivoted toward the next, when a blinding flash came from a dark corner of the room, and Mick felt himself falling backwards into the hallway. On the floor, Mick felt like things were happening in slow motion, and he struggled to keep his gun pointed into the room. Another shape seemed to float toward him like a silhouette, and Mick fired two shots at it. His ears had been turned off by the gunfire, and for him, there was no sound except ringing. Mick struggled to sit up, his pistol remaining pointed into the room. He caught a flicker of motion in the darkened corner from where the muzzle flash had come, and fired two shots toward whatever had moved. In the brief light made by his gun, he clearly saw a familiar face. But something else was moving toward him around the partially open door, catching his attention and causing him to fire his last round at the object's head. The impact of the slug knocked the man backwards and fully opened the door.

Mick slapped a second magazine into the pistol and searched for another target in the dark corner. A sudden motion caused Mick to fire two more rounds, and in the light made by the gun, he saw another partially opened door across the room, a figure disappearing into the darkness beyond. Mick rolled to a squat and visualized the man on the opposite side of the wall as he fled. He fired a series of shots into the wall hoping to hit the moving man on the other side. The room instantly illuminated by his gunfire, as if the gunshots were flashbulbs.

The man in the chair slowly looked up at him through swollen eyes. Kurt. Mick stood erect and surveyed the room. There were four bodies on the floor lying in spreading pools of blood. The single overhead bulb slowly swung on its long cord, casting harsh shadows, making everything even uglier than it was. Mick moved rapidly across the room to the other door, made a quick look into the hall before withdrawing his head, then moved fully into the hall with his pistol pointing the way. There was no sign of the other man. He had gotten away, but now Mick knew who the spy was.

Mick staggered toward Kurt, catching himself against the wall, and then slowly sagged, sliding down to a sitting position. He put his hand to the side of his head where the pain was intense and felt a warm liquid as the room slowly faded away.

Chapter 33

The Spy Revealed

Private Hospital
Stuttgart, Germany

A hand was shaking him, and he opened his eyes to a blinding light. "Mick, Mick, look at me," the voice called. Mick turned toward the sound and felt pain on the side of his head. Kurt was standing over him, looking into his face. "He's awake," Kurt said to someone as he smiled at Mick.

Mick tried to look around, but things were fuzzy and out of focus. Putting his hand to his face, he noted a stubble of facial hair. "Kurt, is that you," Mick asked weakly.

"I am here, Mick, and so is Triska. We have been here the whole time waiting for you to wake up."

A soft hand came from the other side and felt Mick's forehead. "Hi, grandson. Glad to see you came back to us," a soft female voice said.

Mick turned toward her and smiled "Hi, Triska. Where am I?"

"You are in hospital, Mick, dear. You have been here for three days. You had a close call with a bullet which grazed your head but spared your life."

Mick said, "I must talk to Zeskie right away."

Kurt said, "He has been in and out several times, and I think he will show up soon. Don't worry."

"No, I have to talk to him right now," Mick insisted.

Triska's eyebrows went up, "I'll get him on the phone for you, Mick. Just a moment." She withdrew from the bedside and sat down. Mick could hear her murmured voice, "Yes, he just woke up and is insisting on talking to you right away. He says it can't wait."

She got up and held the phone to Mick's ear, over the head dressing which covered the top of his head. "Zeskie?" Mick said with a raspy voice.

"Yes, Mick. I am so happy to hear your croaky voice again. What is so important?"

"The spy, Zeskie. I saw him, but he got away from me. He was the one who shot me."

"The spy, Mick, you say you saw him in the room with the pock-marked man?" Zeskie said excitedly.

"Sergeant Jones, Captain Ritter's aide. It's him," Mick said breathlessly and then relaxed against the pillow. He could hear the click as the phone went dead and then Triska pulled it away. She reached for Mick's hand and slid hers into it.

By the afternoon, Mick could sit up in bed and eat some food. The neurosurgeon, Dr. M. Bennstein, came to see him and removed the large head dressing but was noncommittal about discharge. Kurt left for a short time but came back before evening. When Mick could finally look at Kurt with some clarity, he could see bruising of his face, especially around his eyes. Kurt had lost a front tooth and kept unsuccessfully trying to hide the gap with his lip.

Mick could hear someone new come into the room. Zeskie put his hand on Mick's shoulder. "You had us worried again, Mick, but you seem to have nine lives after all."

"Good to see you, too, Zeskie," Mick said. "Did you get him?"

"No, Jones has fled. We have spread a big net, but he has a three-day head start. He was never on our list, but now it all fits so well. He was in a position to overhear everything that went on and also had access to a secure computer. Frankly, I was about to suggest the arrest of Captain Ritter, even though I have known him for a long time." Zeskie shook his head in disbelief. "We are looking for his parents back in the U.S. who also have vanished. I'm betting that this was a man raised and trained from birth to be a spy."

"Who were the ones I shot?"

"That was an amazing feat, Mick. If anyone but you had done it, we wouldn't believe it. You are one of a kind, and I am glad you are on our side. The fact that they were looking for you again and now another bunch killed...well, we all think that you have to get out. Way out. You can't always be so lucky." He looked across the bed at Kurt. "You too, Kurt. Your cover is gone. They know exactly who you are, and what you have done. There will be reprisals."

Kurt nodded, "I've already been told."

"Two were Bulgarians. The one you call Pockface was listed as a cultural attache with the Russian Legation in Karlsruhe. We always knew he was left over from the KGB. Nothing changes and good riddance. They have already replaced him."

Mick looked up at Zeskie and said, "What's next, boss?"

"Mick, you have the respect of the German government, the admiration of the CIA, the appreciation of the U.S. Army and the love of some wonderful people, including me, but you have to go back to the States as soon as you are up. There is no choice, " Zeskie said, and let his voice trail off.

Mick looked away, suddenly feeling a mixture of sadness and hopelessness. "I have nothing to go back to and nowhere to go. I would rather die in Germany than leave."

Zeskie said, "Mick, my friend, you would still be working for us there. Keeping you alive here would take too much of our resources, and you would will endanger all those you care about the most. We are going to get you in with the U.S. Marshals Service on the West Coast. Officially, you will be with them, but we have some ideas that you will like. Someone needs to help us track down spies like Jones who are imbedded in our society like germs, waiting for a chance to sell us out."

Triska and Kurt moved to Mick's side and each held a hand. "We love you, Mick," Triska said. "We don't want you to go, but we couldn't stand to see them get you. You must leave for now but know that we will always be here for you whenever you can return. There still is much you can do in the service of free people, whether they live in Germany or the United States."

Kurt was moved to tears and hung his head for a moment to recover. "Mick, my brother. You have saved more German lives than anyone I know, and you have rid our country of some dedicated fanatics. You will never know how good I felt to see you open the door that night with your gun in your hand."

Zeskie snapped open his briefcase and took out a small heavy package and placed it on Mick's bed. "You may be needing this again someday. With my compliments."

Chapter 34

Searching For Sally

San Francisco Hall of Justice

Lieutenant Grover" came over the intercom on Simon's desk.

Simon reached over and pushed the transmit button. "Yes, Sergeant, I'm all ears."

"Detective, there are two calls for you. One is from the Deputy Director of the Human Resources Division, U.S. Marshals Service in Seattle, returning your call. The other is Sergeant Brown who has some information you requested. Shall I put them through?" the Desk Sergeant asked.

"Put the Director on line one, please," Simon said, pulling himself upright and smoothing his hair. When the light turned white, he picked up the phone and said, "Detective Grover," in an official manner.

"Detective Grover, this is Deputy Riggs in Seattle. You inquired about a former marshal, Mick Grundy, is that correct?

"Yes, sir, I did. We are working on a homicide, and I would like to talk with Mr. Grundy, if you have a location for him that you can give me," Simon said.

"No, Detective, I'm afraid not. The man is a ghost. He worked for us for a while, but we could only find him when he wanted to be found. Now, I'm afraid, none of our records would be accurate or of any help to you," the director said with a laugh.

Simon coughed a little before asking the next question. "Sir, one other thing. This homicide of ours I mentioned has a possible connection to the CIA or Military Intel operations. Do you know if Grundy is still connected to those services or is he rogue?"

The Director answered in a stern voice, "Detective Grover, I want to make clear that Deputy Marshal Grundy was a fine member of our service. He could always be counted on and was absolutely fearless while doing his duty. We never felt that there was any hint of corruption about him. His extensive military experience made it hard for him to be in law enforcement, and we felt that he might need more time for adjustment before continuing with us. The other thing that you should know is that he can be very dangerous, and he tends to see things in black and white, never in shades. If you encounter him, you need to make sure he knows whose side you are on."

"Thank you, sir, and I'll keep that in mind." After Simon disconnected the Director's call, he pushed the other button. "Simon here."

"Lieutenant, this is Sergeant Brown. I have a lead for you concerning the blonde female with the arm injury."

"Go ahead, Sergeant," Simon said.

"As you know, Lieutenant, you first requested that the patrols inquire in the grocery and convenience stores about the girl. We didn't get any hits on that one. The second request was about finding witnesses in drug stores. I did find a clerk this morning who remembers a short blonde wearing an arm dressing on her right arm about three days ago. She purchased some feminine products, gauze dressings and paid with cash. They haven't seen her since."

Simon took out his notebook and flipped up a new page "Can you give me the address, Sergeant?"

"Sure, it's the Walgreens near the Golden Gate Heights Park."

Simon walked over to the large city map hanging on the west wall and traced his finger around the park area. Several apartment buildings were near there, but this was a better area than you would expect a street hooker to be able to afford. He shrugged his shoulders. There were probably lots of young women in San Francisco who had blonde hair and an injured arm. Not much to go on. Nevertheless.

He went back to the phone and called the Desk Sergeant. "Sergeant, get hold of Patrolman Jonny Sparks and have him come up here."

Simon thought over the case while he waited. The girl was the only lead. The intelligence services, if they were involved, were not going to give out any information. Still, a homicide was committed in his jurisdiction, and he was obliged to pursue a solution as long as there were any leads, however slender. The other thing about this man, Mick Grundy, was that there seemed to be no way of finding him. He remembered that Mick was supposed to be a PI working around Tacoma. Probably a cover, but there may be a phone number. He searched the Internet, and there it was... "Mick Grundy, Private Investigator," and a phone number. Simon dialed the number and waited.

A recorded female voice answered, "Mick Grundy, Private Investigator's office. Please leave your name, problem, and a contact number at the tone." Simon left a short message to call him at the SFPD but had no hope of actual contact.

Jonny Sparks showed up at Simon's desk a bit breathless. "Out of condition, Sparks?" Simon asked sarcastically.

Jonny ignored the remark and asked, "Something you need help with, Lieutenant?"

"Sparks, you remember the runaway blonde hooker?"

"Sure, she is the lead which may break the case. You find her?"

"No, but perhaps you will," Simon said looking up at him. "Take another patrolman and go from apartment to apartment in the Golden Gate Heights Park area in walking distance from the nearest Walgreens. You are looking for the girl, but also anyone who may have seen her."

Jonny looked tired already. "Lieutenant, there are a lot of apartments in that area. It may take several days to cover them all. Another thing, sir. What if we get no answer to a door knock?"

"What you are asking, son, is the thing that devils us all in police work. You come back again and again, if necessary," Simon said with a little crooked smile. Sparks nodded and gave a little salute before turning on his heels and disappearing down the corridor. Simon kicked his legs up on his desk and settled back with another cup of hot coffee. Serves Jonny Sparks right...no one asked him to buck for detective, he thought as he blew across the hot liquid.

The intercom on his desk came on, "Detective, there is a visitor on the way up. Prepare yourself."

Simon sat up. "What the hell does he mean?" he said to himself. He quickly tidied up the desk, just in time to see a large man in a dark suit headed his way. As the man got closer, Simon could tell that the man was very fit and very alert. He had close cropped hair and a military look about him. Simon could see the narrow dark eyes and the lined face which seem to say, "Don't mess with me."

The man headed straight for Simon's desk and stopped. He looked Simon over, as if sizing him up, before speaking. "Detective Simon Grover?" he asked. There was no offer of a handshake.

"That seems to be me. Who are you, and what do you want?" Simon responded.

The man gave a little grin as if he appreciated a confrontational approach. He pulled out a badge in a black wallet and threw it on the desk. Simon picked it up and read, "Special Investigator, Harvey Longren, Department of State." Simon threw the wallet back to the man.

"I don't recall ever hearing about an investigational unit of the State Department, Mr. Longren. That probably means that you are a spook with a cover, doesn't it?" Simon asked.

Longren ignored the comment. "Look, Detective, it doesn't mean anything to me what you think you have figured out. I'm here looking for information about a case you are working. I can always go over your head." Simon could easily see that Longren was a very tough fellow.

"So, I'm breathless to hear what you want to know and impatient to tell you so that you can get the hell out of here," Simon said.

Longren smiled because he knew that Simon had no ability to refuse cooperation. "Regarding the Lebanese Diplomat who was killed. I understand that there was a female in the car. Do you have her in custody or know where she is?" he asked.

"Just why would a little hooker matter to a big investigator like you? Aren't you more interested in finding the killer?"

"We are interested in the entire case, Lieutenant. Can you just answer my question?"

Simon smiled a little, "Then the answer is no, no. Anything else you need, Longren?"

Longren stood erect with narrowing eyes which stared into Simon's soul. He turned and left without another word. Simon could feel the sweat run down his neck and the moisture on his palms. He swung his legs back up on his desk and resumed his coffee.

Chapter 35

Closing In

Golden Gate Heights Park

Sally was watching apprehensively out her window on the fifth floor, as the two uniformed officers went from building to building on Rockridge. The man had told her to stay in the apartment and not be seen, and she had complied. The boredom was intense. She paced, looked out the window, watched TV but had no communication with the outside world. The man had promised a phone, but so far there had been no sign of him or the phone. She had taken the arm wrap off and was dismayed at her swollen and bruised arm. It was evident that she would have to wear long sleeves the rest of her life to hide the scars.

Although the apartment was well stocked with food, there were no cosmetics, and she felt unclothed without her lipstick and mascara. Once again, she sighed. She could see the two cops headed toward her building, and fear swept over her. Would they just come in? Would they somehow charge her with the death of her pimp? She paced, feeling trapped. Waiting was the worse punishment of all, and waiting in silence was worse than worse. Another problem was her frequent use of cocaine. She didn't feel that she was addicted, but now that she had been without any for several days, she became convinced that she needed some. She counted the money again. There was enough for a quick fix if she could get to a dealer in the area. She continued to watch out the window.

Patrolmen Phillips and Sparks pushed the heavy aluminum and glass door open. This was the fourth large building they had entered this morning. Both of them were in uniform as ordered, but unexplained, by Lieutenant Grover. Their feet hurt, and so far, they had uncovered no new information. No one had seen the injured girl. About a third of the apartments had no answer, and Jonny dutifully wrote the address down for a later visit.

They did the usual, starting at the upper floors and working down. At least that way the stairs were all down, not up. When they eventually got to room 523, Jonny looked at his lists, seeking the name of the renter. This one was occupied by a holding company, and no name was listed. Interesting. They knocked loudly, twice. Jonny kept watching the peephole to see if any shadows floated across the opening, but he could detect no motion. He knocked again, louder, but with the same response and checked the address off for a later visit.

Inside apartment 523, Sally was cowering and shivering in the bathroom, afraid to even breathe. She listened to the voices fade away and relaxed a little. That was it, the last straw. She had to do something soon to get away from here, she thought. She couldn't stand the strain much longer.

From inside the coffee shop about a block away, Mick watched the two policemen leave the building. If they had found Sally, she would be with them. As he watched, they got in the patrol car and left. He knew that they would be back, and he hoped they had not found a witness yet. Mick picked his phone out of his pocket and tapped in a series of numbers.

"Hi, I was expecting you to call," Sara said.

"I figured that you would know who left the phone for you," Mick said. "I am about to get a fresh one to Sally so you two can talk. She is probably stir crazy by now, and I know that she has had some cops banging on her door today. Remember what I said, Sara. Sally is in danger and must stay in that apartment for the present. People are looking for her who may want to silence her. Tell her that she is only to call you on that phone, no one else for any reason. Will you do that?"

Sara said, "Of course, I will do that. Can't you tell me what your role is in this mess and who you are?

"I am trying to catch the bad guy who is after Sally. My name is not important. You must continue to trust me," Mick said.

Chapter 36

Another Hit

El Rancho Drive, Serramonte
1100 Hours

Odd time for the doorbell, Gary thought as he walked toward the front door in his pajamas. Seems like he had been in these pajamas forever, not just three days. He hadn't even bothered to clean up his limo after the cops released it. It was going to cost a lot to fix it, and he didn't have the money right now. He put the nearly empty beer can on the hall table and opened the door.

0130 Hours

The detective pointed his flashlight at the black shiny limo and saw the blown out rear door window. "Hey, I remember that car. It was in the papers a few days ago. There was some foreign diplomat killed in it," he remarked.

The patrolman beside him said, "Do you think that this guy was killed because he was connected somehow, Detective?"

"I don't know, but I do know that the SFPD should have a look at this. See if you can get them to come down here tonight," the detective said.

0245 Hours

Lieutenant Simon Grover got out of the car and slammed the door. There were flashing lights everywhere. It was like these guys have never seen a murder, he thought. He put his badge on his coat so that it could be seen and pushed his way to the front of the little house.

"Who is in charge here?" Simon shouted. A hand went up, and Simon moved toward it. He made his way to the young officer in charge and said, "You called?"

The young detective looked at Simon's badge with his flashlight, then said, "Glad to see you, Detective Grover. This murder may interest you. We haven't seen anything like it before. We found the victim in the doorway of his home, and it is obvious that he was shot. The problem we have is that the wound is so massive and unlike a typical gunshot wound. The victim's head is blown apart, and fragments are scattered all over the place."

Simon could see the familiar limo in the driveway. "Got an ID?" he asked.

The detective nodded and said, "We ran a quick electronic fingerprint and came up with the name Gary Mann. It fits with the ID we found on the premises. He owned a single limo rental unit, and he was also the driver."

Simon nodded his understanding and headed toward the front door. Gary's body was back from the door about eight feet, and most of his head was missing. There was blood coagulating on the ceiling and walls. He studied the angles briefly and turned to the young detective, "This was done by a military issued pistol round which is supposed to be secret. If you look over there in that wall," pointing to the location, "you will find a small hole which will probably continue on through the entire building."

Simon turned to leave, and the young Lieutenant asked, "Is that it? You are leaving?"

Over his shoulder, Simon said, "Don't worry, son. If we find our killer, we find yours, and I'll be the first to tell you." He slowly got into his car and drove away.

One the way home, Simon went over the case again in his head. It was obvious now that the killers were only one killer who was tying up loose ends. Simon regretted that he never followed up his intention to grill the limo driver after Homeland Security got done with him. Now that Mann had been killed, it was likely that there was some information which could have been squeezed out of him after all. His hunt for the blonde hooker, Sally, clearly was for two reasons, and one was to save her life.

The most puzzling question was if the motorcycle killer was the same one that went to her hospital room the first night, why didn't he kill her there? Simon played with his lip as he drove through the night, thinking. What if there are two different motorcycle guys out there, one good and one bad. That would make a lot more sense in some ways, but what are the motives for their actions? He sighed.

Too many possibilities and too few facts to go on to be able to figure it out.

Chapter 37

Gathering Information

San Francisco Hall of Justice
0800 Hours

Patrolman Jonny Sparks was waiting at Simon's desk when he arrived with a smoking cup of fresh coffee. "Sparks?" Simon remarked, lifting his brows.

"Good morning, Lieutenant Grover," Sparks said brightly. He waited to continue until Simon reached a resting position and gave his full attention. "I wanted to update you on our search for Sally, the hooker. Also, I heard about the shooting last night down in Serramonte, and it sounds related to me."

"Of course, it's related, Jonny. It was the limo driver who got it this time. Same weapon, no evidence," Simon grumbled while attempting to sip his coffee. "What do you have on the hooker?"

"Well, nothing really, yet. We went back out last night to get the ones who weren't home in the daytime and got most of them. We found one man who said that his wife had complained about seeing a young attractive blonde in the lobby of the apartment building, but he didn't know if she was injured. He said we had to talk to his wife."

Simon put down his cup, "Well, what did the wife say?"

"She is in the hospital. She had a gall bladder attack two days ago, and he said she should be back tomorrow, so we will talk to her then," Sparks said. "One more thing. There are three apartments in that building that didn't answer our knock. Should we try to enter them and look around?"

Simon rocked to his feet and put down the coffee. "Hell no, you can't enter any apartment. You need probable cause and a court order. We aren't looking for a criminal, just a witness, so we can't ask for one. About the gall bladder lady. Go to the hospital and interview her right now. If there has been a probable sighting of the girl, we might be able to get a stakeout for the building."

After Jonny left, Simon yawned and realized that he had to get a few winks of sleep before any more trips to murder scenes in the middle of the night. He got up and looked around to see if anyone noticed. The Captain's door was closed, so Simon just casually strolled to the elevator. As he was standing there, waiting for the door to open, a female head popped around the corner, and her index finger was wiggling at him. It was the Captain's secretary.

"Before you escape to heaven knows where, Lieutenant Grover, you need to take this call. It came through our desk, and I don't think you want to keep this one waiting," she said.

Simon said nothing but walked toward her with his shoulders sloping and put the offered phone receiver to his ear, "Grover."

"Hello, again, Detective, this is Special Agent April Chauncy. We met previously." Simon instantly had the vision of her divine rear end as it disappeared down the hall.

"You bet I remember. This isn't a social call, is it, Agent Chauncy?" Simon asked hopefully.

"The FBI is just trying to help you with your case, Detective. By the way, I prefer Special Agent Chauncy. It has a nicer sound, don't you think?"

"Yes, it does, Special Agent Chauncy. I stand corrected. What is it that you have for me?" Simon asked.

"The FBI has been left out of the loop with other intelligence agencies in this case, and frankly, Homeland Security appears to be just a pawn. We have some information about the victim, Jamal Mucatric el Camani, that you need to know. He really was a rather important link in passing information from spies to Islamic terrorist groups and other governments, such as the current Russian one. He wasn't trying to buy stolen weapons as you were told. He was paid rather well just to pass along information. We think he was dispatched because of fear that he was about to be arrested, and someone didn't want us to be able to track them down based on what we could discover during questioning. A spy would have to be highly placed to know both where Jamal could be found and that the loop was tightening. We heard rumors about a spy working for the our military in Germany, but he fled before being arrested about two years ago. I don't know if this present case is related to that one, but it is a possible link to this Mick Grundy we spoke of. Have you found him yet?"

"With my resources, he will have to walk into my office for me to find him. I have no idea where he is or if he has any part in this murder. I hesitate to call it a crime, because it would appear that the public was well served to get rid of this Jamal Mucatric el Camani. Too bad about missing the opportunity to expose another spy, however," Simon said.

"Wasn't there another possible witness in the car?" The way she asked, there was no doubt that she already knew the answer.

"You are talking about a little blonde hooker called Sally," Simon said. "She got away from us the night of the shooting, and we are looking hard for her right now. Based on what I have observed, we also have two different motorcyclists involved in this case. One could be protecting Sally, and the other one is likely looking for her. If we find her, it might help solve the case."

"Good hunting, Detective. I'll be in touch if I have any more for you," Special Agent Chauncy said and hung up.

Chapter 38

The Attack

Rockridge Avenue
1900 Hours

Simon decided to go to the apartment building himself and wait there for Patrolman Jonny Sparks when he returned from his interview at the hospital. He parked a couple of blocks from the site and started walking slowly toward it. The light of day was fading fast, and yellow street lights blinked on as he was walking. He became aware that someone was behind him, although he could hear no footsteps. It was one of those moments that you feel that someone is watching you, and you just get a sensation in the back of your neck. He stopped and made a half turn to the rear. A large man wearing a dark jacket was right behind him, but in shadows. Simon couldn't make out his face. There was something about the presence of the man that made Simon feel his gun butt with the side of his arm to be sure it was there.

"Detective Grover," a strange voice said. The voice was deep but throaty and spoken with some effort, and it froze Simon like he was dropped in the Arctic.

"I'm Grover," Simon answered. "Who are you?"

The man moved closer and said, "I am Mick Grundy. You wanted to talk to me."

Simon noticed that the man was within arm's length. Too close. Simon put his back to the brick wall behind him and tried to act casual. "I did want to talk to you, Grundy, about a murder or a couple of murders I am working on. What is your connection in this matter?" It was the best he could do. He sensed that accusing Grundy of being the killer wouldn't be wise given the present circumstances. Simon wished Jonny and his partner would show up right now.

"I know that you have gathered information about me, Grover. There is a lot more to the story, but right now you only need to know that I am not the killer. I am looking for him as you are but using different methods, and when I find him, I am going to kill him," Mick said. His voice was right out of the hell that Simon envisioned as a youth. He wanted badly to arrest Mick for questioning but remembered the FBI agent's and the U.S. Marshall's warning about Mick being dangerous. This close, a false move from Simon would get a response from this man that would not be in Simon's favor.

"Usually, in police work, we arrest and try the subject in court, not shoot him, Grundy," Simon offered.

"Not this time, Grover. I have been hunting this man for years. He was responsible for many American deaths, including my own wife's. One time I got close, but he shot me before I could get him. He is the enemy of all of us, Grover, and he must be killed."

"How do we know that you are not the killer, Grundy? All the facts I have point to you, including the motorcycle that we saw near the crime scene."

"I was the one that you saw near the crime scene. The shooting had already taken place when I got there. Previously I had received a tip that the so-called diplomat was targeted by one of his sources to keep him quiet, but I arrived too late to stop his murder or to pursue the shooter. The shooting south of here yesterday was also his work."

Simon mulled this over. It sounded like the truth, but a lie told by an expert always sounds truthful. He furtively glanced around looking for Jonny, to no avail. Perhaps when this Grundy fellow walked away, Simon could get the drop on him. He had the sensation that this large, ominous man could move quickly and, by training, would kill just as quickly. This was not the time, Simon decided.

"We've talked enough, Grover. Walk away, and I'll stand here to keep you from doing something stupid."

"Wait a minute, Grundy. I have some more questions I want to ask first."

The man in front of him didn't move and was obviously done with talk. Simon realized that there was no other choice except to leave. He turned his back and slowly walked away but also strained his ears trying to hear any sounds coming from behind him. When Simon got to the end of the block, he swiveled his head, quickly looking behind him, but the man was gone. He continued toward the apartment building which was close by and could see two uniformed patrolmen standing there waiting for him.

"Well, Sparks, what did you find out?" Simon asked as he got closer.

Sparks grinned like he had found a golden nugget. "Sir, the lady was certain that the young blonde had something wrong with her arm the way she held it up and covered it with a scarf. The time of the sighting was just after lunch two days ago. She also said that the girl had a cheap look about her which made her stand out as not belonging to this apartment building."

Simon rubbed his chin. "That's pretty thin, Sparks. Nearly worthless."

Simon realized that after all this footwork, he had only this one improbable lead. One factor, though, was the presence of Grundy in the area. If he was the good guy he claimed to be, then he was the one protecting the girl. A eureka moment came to Detective Simon Grover. He realized that the girl was close by, and Grundy was around, expecting the assassin to show up to kill the girl as he had killed the driver. The girl was bait.

How would the assassin know where to look? Another realization hit him. The assassin is following me, he thought. He quickly looked around, narrowing his eyes. Both men were out there right now, watching. Grundy and the assassin, each wanted to kill the other, and Simon and his men were in the middle. Simon patted his chest, and again, despite departmental regulation, he was not wearing his armored vest. The two young officers were waiting patiently for him to give orders.

Simon turned and put his hands on their shoulders. "I know you both have had a long day, but we need stay here for awhile longer. I have the feeling something is about to happen. We are going to split up and wait for this girl to show herself, and we must remain in communication with each other. I want to warn both of you that if she comes out of that building, there is a chance that the killer we seek will appear out of nowhere to take her out. We know that he has been on a motorcycle previously, but I don't know if that will be the same today. There is another party involved who also rides a motorcycle. I'm not sure which is which, that is, good guy bad guy, but both are very dangerous. What we want is to stop another killing and not get killed ourselves. On the other hand, this may be a false sighting of the girl, and then we will just be standing here on tired feet all night."

Inside apartment 523, Sally was watching the street from a crack in the curtains. She had been smoking and pacing all day, and her level of agitation was high. Earlier, she had found the note that magically appeared in the middle of the dining room table. The note provided a phone number for her sister and instructions to call no one else. She had placed the call and on the second ring Sara had picked it up. Sally was so glad to have someone to talk to, they talked and chatted for over an hour.

Sara relayed the same warning about not using the phone except for their personal calls and to not leave the apartment nor answer the door. Sally already had practice with not answering the door, and for the second time in twenty four hours, she had hidden in the bathroom during some furious knocking.

Talking to Sara wasn't enough, she needed a fix. She was looking for someone on the street who appeared likely to either be a seller or a user, and she was prepared to meet any price they required. Enough of this pacing. She had to go out and look for a fix. A last look out the window down at the dark street showed few cars and fewer pedestrians. No one would see her in the dark, and if she went over to the park across the street, she was bound to find someone with drugs, after all, this is San Francisco.

Sally dressed in her one and only outfit and made sure that her purse contained a few hundred, just in case. She used the scarf the man had given her to hide her arm, as she had done previously. After a last big deep breath, she left the room for the elevator. Standing there, she almost changed her mind. The man had told her that some really bad people were after her, and that she was in danger. She resolved to get her mission over quickly and return to her room and its safety. Sally hesitantly, almost reluctantly, pushed the elevator button, sensing the danger awaiting her.

Detective Grover positioned the two uniformed officers across the street in the Golden Gate Heights Park so they would be partially hidden by shrubs. He chose a doorway in a closed shop nearby, which had a good view of the front of the apartment building. Simon wished that he still smoked, because he remembered that was a good way to pass the time on a stakeout. He knew that they would have to stay for at least three hours holding their positions with nothing to do but watch. Each time he heard a motorcycle in the distance, he perked up and observed that across the street so did Sparks and Phillips. At least they were on their toes.

The door to the apartment building swung open and out stepped a short woman. He could see the yellow glint in her hair from the overhead lights in the foyer. She looked around nervously and walked toward Simon's position. This was the girl he was seeking. He knew because of the way she was holding her right arm. As she approached his position, Simon could hear a powerful motorcycle motor start not far away. He scanned up and down the street but couldn't locate where the sound was coming from. Sally was about ten feet from him when the motorcycle's motor suddenly gathered RPM and started rapidly closing the distance. Simon caught a movement against the glare of a distant car. The bike moving toward him and Sally had no headlights. There was no time to think this out as Simon jumped from the doorway and rushed toward the girl, who froze in fear. Behind him was the shriek of the oncoming motorcycle, mixed with some other sound his brain was too busy to process. He pulled the girl into him, twisting toward the plate glass window of a small shop, his body positioned on the street side of hers as the glass all around them exploded with a terrific and deafening sound. They fell locked in an embrace into the shop, glass falling all around and over them. Simon became aware that the motorcycle sound was fading into the distance, and the girl underneath him was screaming at full volume.

Jonny was first to arrive, hysterically shouting instructions at Phillips. Together, they pulled off the glass and helped Simon and Sally to their feet. Sally was still screaming, when Phillips put his hand over her mouth, saying roughly, "Shut up, you stupid broad. The Lieutenant just saved your crummy life. Shut up or I'll tape your mouth closed." Sally resorted to sobbing, her eyes looking wild and hysterical but was quieter.

"What in the hell just happened, Sparks?" Simon asked.

Jonny was excited, answering very rapidly, using a high pitched voice, "That was amazing, Lieutenant, what you did! You would have taken the slug instead of her!"

"Never mind that, Sparks. I couldn't see the motorcycle when he went by. Did you see it?" Simon asked.

Phillips butted in, also excited, "There were two motorcycles, Detective. The first one had a gun in his left hand but was distracted by a second motorcycle which appeared out of nowhere and was overtaking him. I think the shooter lost his focus and missed you when he looked over his shoulder. Lucky for you."

Simon dusted the glass from his clothes and said, "Lucky for us, because that round would have killed us both." The wailing from Sally started again. She tried unsuccessfully to cover her face with her good hand.

Phillips reached out and shook her hard. "Remember what I told you. I meant it."

They noticed that Simon had slumped a bit, and in the light, they could see the sheen of blood on his back soaking through the coat. Simon grimaced and calmly said, "One of you call this in and try to get some help to stop those two before they shoot up the town. You are going to need the helicopter in on this. The other one call an ambulance for me, and someone please take this screamer to headquarters for protective custody until we get this settled." He slid down to a sitting position with his back against the wall.

Chapter 39

The Chase

"Attention all Units. Pursue and apprehend a suspect on a dark colored motorcycle fleeing a shooting at Golden Gate Heights Park, possibly being followed by another dark colored motorcycle. The suspect is to be considered very dangerous and is armed with explosive ordnance."

At the first intersection, the shooter slowed briefly to narrowly miss a car crossing at right angles. Mick was able to gain another twenty feet but also had to slow to allow a second car to pass. Mick could tell that the rider in front of him had spent some time in the saddle and had a fast bike. On a race track, Mick would have caught him very rapidly, but on the streets of San Francisco, things were different. There were cars, trucks and pedestrians to avoid. A race track is a prepared surface, free of loose gravel or potholes and especially trolley tracks. The streets in San Francisco are old and full of the above.

Mick could see that the rider ahead was aware that he was behind him, and Mick fully expected to see the gun at any time. The biggest danger was in the turns, not the straight streets. Mick knew from watching Glenda that a motorcycle in a turn is very stable, and that is when you can safely turn around and look behind you. The shooter was forced to use his left hand to shoot because the right hand twists the throttle. Letting go of the right hand would rapidly slow the bike and allow Mick to overtake him.

They wove through the traffic like it wasn't there. Mick was at an advantage because he could watch the other motorcycle take the obstacles and corners first. He was counting on a mistake, but the other rider was experienced. The rider knew if Mick got close enough, he would open fire with his own weapon. The twisting and turning at high speeds prevented either of them the ability to reach for a gun as they were completely focused on staying upright.

Vince Jones tightened his grip on the handlebars. His hands were going numb, but at these speeds, he dared not relax. He knew that it was Mick Grundy in pursuit, and Grundy had every reason to kill him. If he could catch a break, he might be able to shoot, and at least hit Grundy's bike, then the chase would end. His original plan was to get out of the city after the hit by crossing one of the bridges, but by now the cops would have them sealed off. His only chance was either to lose Mick in the streets, more or less by luck, or, even better, to have Grundy go down. Fat chance, he thought. He remembered that Grundy was trained on a racetrack and had much more skill than he did as well as a faster motorcycle. He accelerated hard on the straight streets but as always, he could see the bright headlights of

Grundy's bike right behind him, gradually closing the distance.

An idea struck him, and he started to watch for trucks. There weren't many out at this hour, but perhaps he would get lucky. He turned up Hyde Street climbing into Nob Hill and then took a hard right onto Broadway, heading toward Chinatown. If there were still large numbers of people there, he might be able to ditch the bike and use the crowds to lose Grundy. He saw flashing blue lights ahead, and staggered across the street were at least four patrol cars. Jones did a hard left on Taylor Street at the last possible second, but Grundy's lights flashed as he followed smoothly around the corner behind him. They were on a course toward the Fisherman's Wharf, a favorite tourist area. The bike screamed under Jones as he alternately went from wide open acceleration to hard breaking.

As he went by Bay Street, he saw what he was looking for and turned hard right on the next block to circle and come back down Bay. There was a fuel truck parked at the 76 gas station. Just what he wanted. He unzipped his jacket to have his pistol ready and just as he came to the station, he veered off and slowed to pass between the pumps and the fuel truck. Mick was very close behind him, and Jones realized that Grundy could open fire at any time. He quickly snatched his pistol and fired two rounds at the fuel truck and opened his throttle to accelerate quickly. The fireball behind him lit up the streets, and he felt the hot wave of expanding gasses push him forward. No way Grundy could have survived the explosion, Jones thought, and he let up on the throttle and twisted around to have a look behind him. The fireball was now a hundred feet in the air and expanding rapidly. On the street behind him was the unmistakable bright headlights of Mick Grundy's motorcycle, and he was headed right toward Jones.

Mick saw the bike ahead of him slow and turn toward the fuel truck. His mind raced and quickly understood what was to come. Mick braked hard and turned away from the gas station entrance and moved to the far right of Bay and accelerated just as the explosion on his left occurred. In the bright light of the flames, he saw the dark motorcycle reappear on Bay Street ahead of him. This time he closed the distance to less than twenty feet as the man ahead twisted to see if he was still there. The two bikes made a hard right back on Taylor and headed north toward the wharf area. At the junction with The Embarcadero, the shooter turned right. Mick knew that Pier 39 was just two blocks ahead and that it would still be heavily populated by tourists. He accelerated hard, hoping to hit the other motorcycle's rear wheel with enough force to upset and possibly crash the bike. Mick knew by watching the racetrack riders that most of the time, both bikes will go down after contact. As he closed the distance, the bike ahead of him moved in front to prevent a pass, and they continued at high speed toward the entrance of Fisherman's Wharf.

Officer Jose Gonzales heard about the suspect riding a dark motorcycle on his intercom, but he never expected to see the bike come into this area. He was standing just outside of the entrance to the Hard Rock Cafe at the right side of Pier 39 Concourse as a bright single headlight rapidly approached his position. A second bike was following closely behind the first, their engines shrieking as the distance quickly closed. He quickly looked around at the scattered groups of people walking up and down the wide concourse. Unsure of what to do, Gonzales reached for his sidearm and started yelling for the crowd to move back. He continued to wave his arms in the air with his gun in his right hand as the bikes came by him and entered the concourse. He watched helplessly while both bike's tail lights came on, and as they started twisting right and left to avoid people and food carts. They disappeared, threading down the walkway toward the bay, narrowly missing people and obstacles. He knew that unless they stopped at the waterfront, they would return down the walkway on the left which was full of outside eating areas, and he started running toward the smaller walkway, pistol in hand.

Mick slowed his bike enough to avoid people in the way and went past, nearly touching them with the handlebar grips. The bike ahead of him was more careless in his panic to flee and knocked two people down, sending them tumbling out of the way. Mick could glimpse boats in the marina to the right of the pier, the black water of the bay dead ahead. He wasn't sure where this was going to end, but the shooter was quickly running out of options. Just before the end of the pier, the lead bike braked hard, and with the rider's foot down, executed a spinning turn to the left. Mick slowed enough to make the turn in a more conventional and controlled manner and lost some distance. After turning, the thundering motorcycles tore through the outside dining area on the return path west of the pier. They went through and over tables, chairs and linen, past scattering diners and waitstaff as they forced their way back out toward The Embarcadero.

Officer Gonzales stationed himself under the overpass, next to the outlet and delivery access on the left of the pier. Across from his location was the old white guard house, flanked by two white concrete posts for protection against vehicles hitting the building. He crouched with his pistol pointing toward the sound of motorcycles getting closer. The bikes would have to pass within ten feet of his location, and he made himself ready.

Mick watched as the rider ahead of him sharply turned around a wooden column, hitting the bike near its rear tire and causing a violent instability. The rider was forced to nearly stop the bike or risk a crash. Mick came to a quick stop and drew out his 45, and with both hands on the pistol, he started firing over the windscreen of his motorcycle toward the shooter and his bike.

Officer Gonzales watched as the pair of lights came toward him, and as the lead motorcycle drew closer, he opened fire on it. He saw flashes of gunfire erupt at the same time from somewhere behind the first rider. The lead motorcycle accelerated toward him, at the last split second veering slightly away, striking the corner of the guard shack with terrific force. When the motorcycle hit the wooden structure, the side of the building ruptured inward, the motorcycle coming to rest inside, disappearing from view. Its rider had been flung off, his body pivoting into the concrete pillar head first, violently splitting his helmet during the impact and tearing his visor off. A fire started inside the small building, and flames started spilling out the broken windows with rapidly increasing fury.

In the ambulance, Simon was lying on his side with medics attending to his lacerations caused by falling sheets of glass. Jonny was riding inside with him and was busy monitoring the action with his scanner. He looked up surprised as the latest information was coming across, and he turned and looked at Simon, not sure that he had heard the broadcast. "Lieutenant Grover, there has been a crash and shooting at Pier 39. Sounds like our boy. An officer on the scene is holding the other rider at gunpoint," Jonny said excitedly.

Simon partially sat up and shouted, "Take me straight to the shooting, boys. I have to be there for this."

One of the medics started to protest but understood the Lieutenant's need to finish what he had started. He picked up the mike and instructed the driver to go to Pier 39. When Simon laid back down, the medic quickly applied pressure dressings to the lacerations and secured them with tape. With the siren wailing, the ambulance made a couple of hard turns and picked up speed toward Fisherman's Wharf.

Officer Gonzales was shaking a bit as he held Mick in his gun sights. After the crash, Gonzales had the presence of mind to grab the nearest fire extinguisher and put out the gasoline fire inside the hut. He didn't need to examine the rider. Because of the amount of blood coming from the split helmet, it was obvious that the man had been killed in the crash. While Gonzales was occupied, he saw the other rider slowly walking toward him holding a large handgun by his side in a ready but non-threatening way. Gonzales had stood up and ordered the man to lay his gun down, but instead the man defiantly tucked the gun away behind his back and then slowly took off his helmet. Seeing the man up close, Gonzales hesitated to go any further than give orders but continued to cover the man with his sidearm. It was the man's eyes, the hard eyes of an experienced killer. Gonzales was not trained well enough to take that kind of risk. Sirens were coming in, seemingly from several sources, converging on the their location. Mick stood there silently and motionlessly without taking his eyes off of Gonzales.

The ambulance arrived shortly after the first two patrol cars. When Simon emerged with help from the back of the ambulance, he saw five uniformed policemen spread out, guns drawn, all aiming at Mick Grundy.

"Put down your weapons, men," Lieutenant Grover shouted. "This is the perp lying on the ground, and he appears finished." With some reluctance, the officers complied but kept some distance, just in case. Simon walked up to Mick slowly and painfully and looked over at the body on the ground. "Got your man, I see, Grundy. Make you happy now?"

Officer Gonzales was standing nearby and offered his opinion, "The suspect crashed and died from his injuries. He wasn't killed by this man, Lieutenant."

As Gonzales was speaking, Jonny Sparks was bending over the body inspecting it carefully. He stood shaking his head, then went into the hut to examine the crashed motorcycle. When he came out, he said, "Not true, Detective Grover. The body has three gunshot wounds, one round went into the back of the helmet and two were placed in the man's back, and both of those bullets exited the chest. There is a single gunshot that hit the motorcycle's gasoline tank on the left side which likely started the fire."

Simon looked at Mick with more appreciation. His first impulse wanted to congratulate him on some good shooting but remembered his position as an officer of the law who should always despise vigilante justice. "You are going to have to surrender your weapon, Grundy, and come in for questioning, you know." Mick remained motionless as if he were waiting for something.

More police cars arrived and the entire section of The Embarcadero in front of Pier 39 was blocked by police cars, all of which had their blue and red flashing lights on. A gathering crowd of curious people crushed their way forward, trying to glimpse the goings on. A tall dark suited man pushed his way through the onlookers, flashing a badge at the police, who let him come forward.

Simon was leaning on Jonny Sparks for support and knew that he couldn't last much longer on the scene when he turned to see the new arrival.

"Well, if it isn't Special Investigator Harvey Longren," Simon sneered. "What are you doing here after the fact, claiming some credit perhaps?"

Harvey smiled his tight smile and looked at the fallen man. "Did this man have anything to say before he died?" he asked. He looked over at Mick without comment, and Mick returned his stare, also without comment.

Simon caught the looks between the two and said, "Do you two know each other, or am I imagining things from loss of blood?"

Harvey looked at Mick as he spoke, "We once worked together in the Army. There was a spy on the base in Germany, at that time, who was passing secrets, and I always thought it was Mick Grundy and so did a lot of other people. Good thing for him that he left the service and Germany before we proved it. Now that he is here, it shows the connection after all. He just managed to kill this man before he could be caught by the police and interrogated. I'm sure that an examination of the facts will prove that Grundy is a spy. You should arrest him now before he gets away from us."

Simon looked back and forth between Grundy and Longren trying to decide what to do. He could arrest Grundy but probably couldn't touch Longren, even if his ID was faked, given his probable connections within some intelligence organization. The group was looking at Simon, waiting on his decision.

Mick had not moved or spoken since he walked to the scene after he fired his weapon, but now started moving toward the body on the ground. At first, Simon was dumbfounded and before he opened his mouth to speak, Grundy reached down to the body and plucked a black cell phone from one of its pockets. As he stood up, he looked first at Simon and then at Longren.

"Lieutenant, you must stop him," Longren shouted with anger. "He is tampering with the very evidence which will convict him." Longren moved toward Mick as if to take the phone from him, but Mick raised his hand in a signal to halt and Longren paused.

"Grundy, what are you doing?" Simon demanded. "Put down that phone right now," he ordered. Several policemen drew their weapons but held them down at their sides.

For the first time, Mick spoke, looking directly at Longren. "Let's find out who was the last person to talk to Jones," he said in a voice that was hollow and distant as if coming from some evil place. Mick pushed the recall button. He held the phone in front of him, showing the face of it to Simon, as the machine dutifully rang the last number in its memory bank. They all waited in silence, and then there was a ring close by. Longren looked around to see if anyone was moving. The ring was persistent and seemed to grow louder as the silence intensified.

Simon was watching intently, and it seemed as though everything was in slow motion. It was as if time itself was slowing down, but at the same time, the event which subsequently occurred was a blur to the eye. As he remembered it later, it started with a sudden movement from Harvey Longren. Something about the quickness of Longren's arm movement startled Simon, and he didn't see Mick until a gunshot cracked the air. Longren fell backward into a motionless lump with a large bullet hole in his forehead. When Simon looked back at Mick, he saw that Mick had already tossed the gun onto Harvey Longren's body and had raised his arms in surrender. The phone in Longren's pocket continued to ring.

Chapter 40

New Beginnings

San Francisco Hall of Justice
1000 Hours

Simon excused himself from the Captain's office and winked at his secretary on the way out. The stuffy room behind him was packed with people. The Captain was in his usual angry state but was restraining himself, because the visitors were too highly placed to be subjected to his usual verbal insults. Not so with underlings like Simon. At least Simon's favorite FBI Special Agent, April Chauncy, was there to look at. The other guy, this Zeskie, was overbearing and demanding. He was the one who insisted that Grundy be immediately released, and of course, the Captain so ordered. Simon thought that he might as well get the hooker, Sally, out at the same time so that they could all party together in there. Simon saw Patrolman Jonny Sparks waiting expectantly in the hall to find out what was happening. They both had spent a fruitless two days and a night attempting to interview Mick Grundy. All they were able to get out of him was a suggestion that they call Ron Zeskie at the CIA. Mr. Zeskie had arrived this morning from who knows where and was graphically blunt about the service Grundy had done for their country on so many occasions.

"Sparks, you go to the women's lock up and check Sally out, and I'll get Grundy and meet you back up here in the hall," Simon ordered.

Jonny nodded that he understood, and they took different elevators down. Simon presented his badge at the lockup desk as a formality and indicated to the jailer to come with him to the holding cell. Mick Grundy was still being held in general lockup, and there were a variety of others with pending charges in there with him. As they turned down the hall to the cell, Simon started to laugh.

Simon punched old Rodger in the ribs, "Do you see that? Have you ever seen anything like it before?" The jailer waggled his head and smiled.

"That's the way it's been since he got in there. I asked a couple of them what was up, but they wouldn't talk about it," Rodger explained.

The cell was twenty feet in length and roughly ten feet wide and was furnished with scattered chairs and beds. In one corner, lying on a cot with his back to the room, was Mick Grundy. The other nine fellows were crowded together against the far wall. They looked at the two policemen like they were coming to the rescue instead of just retrieving a prisoner. When the door was unlocked, Simon came in to the cell and asked, "Did this man threaten you folks, or does he just have rabies?"

One large fellow, his arms covered in tattoos, answered for them all, "No, man, he didn't say a word to us. He didn't have to."

Simon stood by Mick's bed, gently patting his arm, "Rescue is here, Mick. Come on, we are getting you out of here. Your friend came in this morning and is waiting upstairs."

Mick rolled to his feet and stood up effortlessly, like a big jungle cat would do. They left together to the relief of the other prisoners. On the way to the elevator, Simon said, "I have heard an earful from this Zeskie about how you are nearly the second coming of Christ. I had no idea."

He smiled at Mick expecting a response, but Mick was looking intently straight ahead and said nothing. When the elevator door opened on the fifth floor, they could see Patrolman Sparks and Sally Rodgers waiting for them. Sally beamed as they stepped from the elevator and came up and tried to embrace both Simon and Mick at the same time.

"The two men who saved my life! I love you both for what you did for me," Sally said as she looked back and forth between the two. She asked meekly, "Can I at least know your name now?"

Mick bent down and kissed her on her forehead and took her injured arm in his hand and turned it over for inspection. "You are healing nicely, Sally. You are going to be back to normal soon. My name is Mick Grundy. Pleased to meet you," and stuck out his hand to shake hers. She took his hand and then pulled him down to her and kissed him on the cheek.

Sally couldn't stop tearing and wiped her face a couple of times with her good arm. "I know that you are too good for me, Mick Grundy, but I would like to pay you back someday for giving me a life again."

Mick caressed her hair and said, "No thanks or repayment needed, Sally. I would like it if you go stay with your sister for now and get out of this town forever. You have to want to change to change, and if you ever need a job, I really do have one lined up for you. All you have to do is just let me know."

Sally gave Mick a last hug and a wink and then turned to Simon. "You got hurt saving me, didn't you?"

Simon wasn't used to getting thanks from anyone. "Not badly. It's all part of my job, Sally. Mick here shot the guys who were after you, and we have all the information we feel you know about this incident, so we are cutting you loose as of right now."

1300 Hours

As they emerged from the entry of the Hall of Justice into the sunlight, they stopped and looked around. Zeskie glanced down the street and saw what he wanted.

"Want to grab a burger and coffee, Mick? We should have a little talk away from the ears of the cops."

Mick readily agreed, and they walked the couple of blocks in silence. The police had given Mick back his gun and clothing before they left, the case being closed as far as the SFPD was concerned. Even the FBI was satisfied that no more investigation was necessary.

"How did you know about Harvey?" Zeskie asked.

Mick gave him a hard look. "I always told you that he was a spy, didn't I?" He was trying not to get angry at Zeskie now that it was all over. "Look, there was someone with us in the Crimea who sold us out right on the spot. It couldn't ever have been anyone but Harvey. I know that Jones had access to information and passed some along, but he was always controlled by someone else higher up. As much as you, I was surprised to see Jones' face that night in Germany where they were beating Kurt, because I hadn't thought of him before, but I knew that there had to be another one. Thanks again for keeping me informed. I needed to get these two, and you made it happen. Killing them will never erase Anna from my dreams, but at least I can do other things with my life now."

"You did the country a great service, Mick. A trial would not have been in the interest of the country. Too many secret facts would have to be presented in open court, and there is always the risk that a jury will decide to pass secrets to the press. This way it's over."

"One more thing I would like to know, Zeskie," Mick said. "How did Harvey learn to speak Russian so fluently?"

"In some ways, it is similar to your story. He was actually born in Poland, and he and his parents 'escaped' to the West. He spoke Russian, English and Polish from birth. There were two kinds of people in Communist Poland: those who hated the Russians and those who didn't. Both groups pretty much hate the Germans. Unfortunately, we didn't know that he and his family were among the ones who liked the

Russians. He was raised from an infant to think the way that he did, as was Vince Jones," Zeskie said.

They reached the fast food restaurant and after getting some food went back outside to sit on a park bench next to one another. Mick could see that there was something else that Zeskie had to say and was waiting on the right moment.

"A couple of things I need to tell you Mick, and some of it you won't like," Zeskie said. Mick raised his eyebrows but said nothing.

Zeskie cleared his throat and put his food down. "Your adoptive parents' origins were traced carefully since you left Germany. More and more of the vast East German Government records are being examined, even this long after reunification. Your adoptive parents were down on paper as working for the East German Communists. They came to America under false ID and with a cover story of escaping in the night. They intended to have a child bred for espionage like Vince Jones was, but they were barren. They adopted you in the hope of raising you to be a spy but died before they could carry out their plan. The auto accident saved you from being like Jones and Longren."

Mick put down his cup and furrowed his brow. "Some things they said as I was growing up make more sense now. I can see that their views went past the typical liberal college professors that they were supposed to be. At least they gave me language skills and treated me pretty well. There was never any actual love between us, and I guess there was never any way that there could have been."

Zeskie smiled and patted Mick on the back of his hand. "The other thing is interesting... very interesting. When you were hospitalized after Jones took a shot at you, your blood was taken as a routine matter of hospital procedure. You recall that this was a German, not American hospital. A sample of blood for DNA analysis was sent to the BND." Zeskie paused as if hesitant to go farther.

"Out with it, Zeskie!" Mick demanded. "Do I have a disease or infection, or am I just an alien from outer space, like I feel that I am?"

Zeskie couldn't hold it back any longer. "Turns out, Mick Grundy, that Peter Koffman and you are half brothers. His DNA matches yours. You are related! We don't know how this could be true, but it is. I had it double checked in this country to be sure."

Mick could hardly hold back the tears which started forming. He now had another living soul in the world that he could call blood kin. It was too good to be true. He always held Koffman in his mind like a brother, but more like a brother-in-arms. Maybe this explains the natural affinity they seemed to have for each other, Mick thought. He relaxed for the first time in a long time, and he actually gave Zeskie a smile.

They got up to leave and Zeskie said, "Say, Mick, can I give you a ride somewhere?"

"No, I was cooped up in that cell for two days, and I need to walk it out. I have to go find my motorcycle in the police impound lot, but it's not that far."

"We'll keep in touch then, Mick?"

Mick turned toward Zeskie and said, "This isn't goodbye, Zeskie. I think that we will need each other for a long time yet. It's more like the Germans would say to a friend, *auf wiedersehen,* or till we meet again."

The End

A Note of Appreciation

The worst and the best writers seek one thing above all others. A reader who not only reads their book, a work of astounding personal effort, but who shares his/her experiences with the world. We want to know what you think about our work. Truly we do. Of course, we want you to like it, and us, and will be so grateful if you take the time to give us even the smallest amount of praise. I really entreat you to do so.

If you have constructive criticism you want us to hear, please, out with it! Writing is such an isolating experience. I begin to live in my books and come to nearly feel that my characters are real. When someone criticizes one of them, I feel their pain. And some of my own.

But if you enjoyed this novel, I beg you on scuffed knee to give a positive review for me. I assure you that is the best way to see more of my work in the future.

Thanks again for reading this far.

Alexander Francis

Novels by Alexander Francis

Are We A Band Yet?
Mick Grundy...Spy Hunt
Mick Grundy...The Russian Connection
Mick Grundy...Elapid
Beware the Exit
The Green Scarf
Revenge of Jesus
Geminknot
An Anthology of Childhood
Schemers and Dreamers
Memory Gap

Please visit afnovels.com

www.ingramcontent.com/pod-product-compliance
Lightning Source LLC
Chambersburg PA
CBHW061624210726
48287CB00001B/279